Payback in the Guest House

Payback in the Guest House

A Faye Chambers Cosy Crime Mystery

SUSAN WILLIS

Copyright c 2024 by Susan Willis All Rights reserved. No part of this novel may be reproduced in any form by any means, electronic or mechanical (including but not limited to the Internet, photocopying, recording), or stored in a database or retrieval system, without prior written permission from the author. This includes sharing any part of the work online.

Susan Willis assets her moral right as the author of this work in accordance with the Copyright, Designs and Patent Act 1988.
        Susan Willis   www.susanwillis.co.uk

The characters, premises, and events in this book are fictitious. Names, characters, and plots are a product of the author's imagination. Any similarity to real persons, living or dead, is coincidental and not intended by the author.

Also By Susan Willis:

Confession is Good or the Soul
Intriguing Journeys at Christmas
Joseph is Missing
Death at the Caravan Park
The Curious Casefiles
Magazine Stories from the North East
Christmas Shambles in York
Clive's Christmas Crusades
The Christmas Tasters
The Guest for Christmas Lunch
The Man Who Loved Women
Dark Room Secrets
His Wife's Secret
The Bartlett Family Secrets
Northern Bake Off
You've Got Cake
A Business Affair
Is He Having an Affair
NO, CHEF, I Won't!

Chapter One
Faye Chambers

I've always had a good marriage, or so I thought, but lately I've used the word "tricky" to describe us as a couple. I can pinpoint this trickiness to around the time I retired as an author. I'd had a health scare and at the tender age of fifty-five, found I didn't want to write crime novels anymore. A friend had said, 'I didn't know authors could retire?'

I had grinned and replied, 'Well this one has!'

At the time, my husband Allan, had nodded whilst digesting this information and said, 'Look, you don't need to beaver away at that desk writing for months anymore. I can keep us afloat - my salary is more than enough.'

And, I'd been reassured, but now I remember his dark brooding eyes and the tone in his voice. Had it been resentment? Maybe I had missed this back then and he did resent the fact I wasn't working. Although my conscience is clear because in the early days of our marriage, it had been royalties from my crime novels which paid the mortgage and our daughter Olivia's school fees. Maybe, he'd conveniently forgotten this and my retirement had rankled away in his mind.

Of course, nowadays, my small dog sitting and walking business doesn't generate much money, but I do pay the energy bills, which is a contribution to the coffers of running our big house.

I'm sitting in my study in front of his bureau with the polished wood flap down. An old brown A4 envelope is lying flat while I wait for Allan to return home from work. Ordinarily, I would be in the kitchen cooking our meal, but what I've found has wiped out usual daily activities and mundane thoughts.

In the last hour, I've taken out the papers three times, read them, and put them neatly back into place. I think I could recite the words off by heart now and they're burning inside my head like a bonfire.

Smoothing over the envelope with my trembling hand, I know the next few hours are going to be mammoth in my life with Allan. If what the document states is true, and I think of the words "innocent until proven guilty". I've no idea what's going to happen between us in this so-called tricky marriage.

Our Spaniel, Alfie, creeps up to my knees and automatically I bend forwards and play with his silky long ears while staring out of the big bay window into the garden. It's perfectly landscaped by Allan and is his pride and joy. Sitting here in my study, I'll be able to see him pull up on the drive in his new red Audi.

I call it my study because it's a room which Allan has never used. Apart from my big desk in front of the green plush drapes and two filing cabinets, a printer and his bureau, there isn't anything else in the large square room. All his marketing manager paperwork is kept in his office on the high street.

I'd thought his bureau held our family documents, our parents' death certificates, house insurance folder, Olivia's birth certificate and what I'd thought was our marriage certificate. And yes, it does, but there is also Allan's first marriage certificate in an envelope and divorce papers which aren't completed nor signed.

I take a deep breath and repeat the words "innocent until proven guilty", and ask myself, were they just a copy and he'd posted the original?

His car pulls onto the drive and I watch him hurry up to the front door in the rain. It'll spoil his hair, I think sarcastically. At the age of fifty-three, he still has an abundance of peppered grey hair, which he sweeps aside behind his ears.

'Hello!' He calls into the hall but I remain perfectly still in the chair.

I can hear him rushing along the old tiled floor into the kitchen when he calls again, 'Faye!'

'In here,' I shout back.

Allan comes to the doorway and stops dead in his tracks. Obviously by the look on my face, he knows there's something amiss.

'What?' he shouts. 'Is it Olivia? Or the kids?'

His face has paled and I feel bad that he's worried about the family. He worships Olivia and the kids as much as I do and the issue I have with him has nothing to do with them. 'Nooo,' I say. 'They're all fine.'

I see him breathe out heavily in relief. 'Then what? I can see by your face something's happened.!'

He hurries to me and places his arm along my shoulder, but I freeze rigid under his touch. And that, I reckon, is the disadvantage of being married for a long time. As a couple, we know each other inside out and can read our thoughts just in a look. I never have to say how I feel about an issue because he knows, and vice versa. Nice and reassuring in some ways, I've always thought, but I shake this aside now.

His eyes are downcast now on the old envelope I'm still stroking. His cheeks flush and the redness travels to his ears and neck.

'Do you want to tell me about this?'

I feel a run of palpitations start in my heart while waiting for his answer. I breathe in deeply remembering the doctor's words, there's nothing wrong with your heart, it's just stress and nervous agitation. I've been fighting off these palpitations for six months now and they are getting less and less. However, I suppose an explosive row with my husband is bound to be a trigger. I let my breath out slowly and feel my heart rate steady again.

Allan looks down at the green carpet and shuffles his leather brown shoes together. I reckon he looks like a ten year old being caught stealing sweets.

He licks his lips. 'Ah, I see, you've found it,' he whispers.

'Y…you see?' I stutter. 'So, if you wanted to keep this hidden why is it in here?

He lifts his head, pushes his hands deep into his trouser pockets and shrugs.

'Unless of course you wanted me to find it?'

'Well, it's been in there forever, and I'd sort of forgotten about it.'

'You'd forgotten about it!'

I can hear my voice rising although I'm desperately trying to stay calm until I get the truth out of him. "Innocent until proven guilty", I remind myself, and take another deep breath. 'So, is this just a copy and the original was signed and posted to confirm that you were divorced in 1988?'

'Not exactly…'

The words of his answer reverberate through me and I pull out the papers from the envelope with trembling hands. The rain shower has passed and the sun shines through the window onto my engagement and wedding ring. I drop the papers to the carpet, twirl the rings around and then mutter, 'So, on the day you put these rings onto my finger you were still married?'

He bends over to pick up the papers and I fight the urge to hit him hard on the top of his head. 'Well, technically speaking, sort of,' he mumbles, and straightens up again.

I'm stunned and feel quite breathless. Placing my hand across the top of my chest, I shake my head in disbelief. Adrenaline races through me until my fingers tingle. Starting to take slower deep breaths I know I've to steady the palpitations, which I manage to do.

'A…are you alright?' He asks with concern in his eyes, and steps towards me.

I put my hand up in front of him as a warning stop signal. 'Don't come any closer,' I say. 'I can't believe you could do this!'

And now I wait for his usual defensive stance. The one he uses to get out of an argument. Any minute now he'll swing all of this around and make the incident my fault.

He starts to pace around the room and Alfie races back to my side. I stroke his brown furry neck and whisper, 'It's okay, boy, I'm fine.'

Allan shouts on cue. 'Hell's teeth! I was only eighteen and didn't know what to do! I didn't have money for solicitors and just hoped it would be forgotten about.'

I raise an eyebrow at him.

He stands still in front of me and lowers his voice. 'And then when I heard five years later that she'd died, I sort of figured it would be okay.'

I remember the day he told me about her death and how he'd heard from an old college buddy in Cambridge. It had been the day Olivia started school and I'd been distracted. I had banked up the news to talk about on a later date but as our life together was always so busy, I never had done.

'So, you were a bigamist on our wedding day, although it was only for the first five years, and that makes it alright?'

He yells, 'NO! Of course it doesn't.'

Alfie barks now and I put my arm around his neck to comfort him. He hates it when we argue but being only two years old, it hasn't happened very often. Well, not until now.

My mouth is dry and I get up from the chair and hurry along to the kitchen. I pour a big glass of water and gulp at the cold drink. Alfie licks water from his bowl on the kitchen floor and then growls when Allan enters and pours himself a generous measure of whisky.

I watch Allan's movements and think of the dynamics of us as a couple. Being with him should be the safest I feel in my life. And it always has done until now. I look at him stripping off his jacket and hanging it onto the back of a chair. I know I should love and trust him beyond anyone else. But now I know he's not what I've always thought he was, I feel threatened and unsafe. The room seems to tilt ever so slightly and a shiver runs down my back.

Unable to stop myself, I think of my crime novels and how I've often written that everyone has something to hide in life. Now I've found out his secret lie. I look at his broad back in the white ironed shirt. He seems menacing somehow although during all the arguments we've had about commonplace things, Olivia's schooling, paying our mortgage off, and not wanting any more children, he'd never once raised his hand.

'I don't know who you are anymore,' I say quietly.

He swings around and gulps his whisky. 'That's ridiculous! I'm the same guy who went out to work this morning and came home to you as I've always done. You're making a mountain out of a molehill for something that happened thirty years ago.'

I shake my head. 'No, Allan, I'm not. You've made our marriage a sham and I'm not sure if I want to stay here with you.'

He shouts, 'That's not fair! I have been trapped and burdened with this for years - it's been like a sentence hanging over me - so I figure I've served my time!'

Typical, I think. It's never his fault and I always have to feel sorry for him before we make up, but this time is different. It's very different. I reckon our marriage has turned into more than just tricky. And for the first time I see it for what it has become - a toxic relationship.

It had never been the perfect marriage although he wanted us to look like a wonderful celebrity couple in our close happy family. Alongside his perfect career, his perfect house and gardens, and his perfect car. Our holidays have to be in exotic locations so he can brag about them at work to his colleagues. And now, I ask myself, are we damaged beyond repair?

Shrugging my shoulders, I can't answer my own question but know I have to get away from him for a while. I need time to think.

'Come on, Alfie,' I say, and run upstairs.

I begin to throw clothes into a suit case as Allan follows me into the bedroom.

I can see by his crumpled body posture that he's full of remorse. 'Look, I'm sorry,' he says. 'Where are you going and how long will you be away? I mean, what shall I tell everyone?'

I don't answer but shake my head.

He sits on the end of our bed with his hands clasped and looks up at me as I push underwear into my case. 'You're not going to inform the authorities – are you?'

I cackle. 'Oh don't worry, Allan. I'll not be the one to spoil your image and perfect life-style,' I mutter through gritted teeth.

Alfie runs beside me down the stairs as I grab his bowl and food from the cupboard and slam the door shut behind me.

Chapter Two

I stride off down the bank to South Gosforth Metro station with Allan's words ringing in my ears. A mountain out of a molehill indeed, I rage. How dare he? I'm walking fast and Alfie is trotting along beside me as if he too is enjoying the freedom away from Allan.

The sun is still shinning at five and I'm too warm in the tweed jacket which I'd grabbed from the hall stand. It's a man's jacket that I bought in a charity shop but is good quality and I like the long tailored style.

Reaching the open ticket machine area, I stand still and think of who to tell and beg a bed for a while. Of course, I could go to Olivia in Sunderland, but frown, this doesn't seem fair. It will disrupt my granddaughters' routine as I've never stayed over before. Yes, I've visited many times but never slept there. And Olivia has always been a Daddy's girl so it will distress her to hear what Allan has done. In fact, she'll probably make up excuses or search for reasons in disbelief. I shrug, it'll certainly burst her bubble but why should I be the one to upset her? Until I've had time to think, I reckon it's Allan's job to explain his actions.

I hear a metro train thundering through the tunnel, and look up to the board. The train is for South Shields not Sunderland and on impulse I buy a ticket, climb onto the metro and find a single seat, tucking the small case underneath. Alfie settles down lying over my sandals and, for the first time since this morning, I smile. It'll be nice to have a seaside break, I reckon and stare out of the window as we leave South Gosforth station.

Glancing at my reflection in the window, I try to tame down the mass of big curly hair which is cut into a longish bob. I sigh, it needs to be styled properly, but as I wasn't expecting to go out tonight, it'll have to wait until I get to where I'm going. Wherever that may be.

Back in the 80's when big permed hair was all the rage, I'd never had to visit the hairdressers as other women did – mine was natural. Now, I'm using a light blonde colour to hide the smattering of grey and last month, on a whim, had allowed a young stylist to go wild with a few pink and red streaks. Reaching into my handbag, I pull out two small comb slides and push them into the curls. I can't do much about my long dangly fringe but reckon the sea air will make it look windswept anyway.

In my teens, Mam had cruelly said, 'You'll never be pretty or girlish, but you can make the best of what God gave you.'

Which I try to do now by applying a beige lipstick and examining my big teeth for lunchtime remnants of salad. This makes the dimple in right cheek stand out more. I use a dark pencil over my bushy eyebrows and thick black eyeliner to accentuate my oval pale-blue eyes. Which I reckon are my one and only redeeming feature. When grabbing my jacket before I left, I'd draped a long fine scarf around my neck and sigh, my skin is starting to look a little craggy.

Following the upset with Allan, I know I'm not looking my best, in fact, I look wrecked. I feel Alfie's paw on my knee. He knows I'm a little out of kilter and I stroke his long wavy ears in comfort.

The train is speeding down the track and I glance up at the board to see there's only one more stop before South Shields.

Alfie whines and I whisper, 'Not long now and we'll be off the train.'

Not many dogs like the movement of trains and buses, but as ever, Alfie is unfazed by this. In fact, there's not much that does upset him. While other dogs are terrified on Guy Fawkes Night with bangers and noisy fireworks, he often sleeps thought it all without a care.

When we brought him home from the shelter, Allan had said, 'He needs a name.'

I'd nodded and started going through male names in my mind. The TV was on in the background with a quiz show. The question was to name a film in the 1960s staring Michael Caine and I'd called out, 'Alfie!'

The spaniel had lifted his ears and looked straight up at me, and that had been it. Alfie was his chosen name and, like babies, he's grown into his name. So much so, that I couldn't think of him as anything other than Alfie now.

***

We get off the metro which actually runs overhead from the street below, and is the end of the track with yellow and blue boarding. Walking down the pedestrianised shopping centre, I head down Ocean Road to the seafront. It's the only area I know in South Shields and the few times I've been before, it has been in Allan's car. Therefore, this is new territory, but I put a spring in my step trying to see this as a new adventure and not a reaction to the massive upheaval.

I've never left him before, nor him me. And although it feels very strange, I walk fast feeling my big hooped earrings jingle. My battered leather satchel with a long strap bumps off my legs as I stride out, but in a comforting way. I've learnt over the months how walking is a great way to control my palpitations and distract myself with surroundings.

Alfie is loving this and trots alongside me looking up every now and then as if to say, this is better than being squashed up on the metro. I know he'll want to go on the beach but decide this will have to wait until later.

From the Ocean Road Community Association café and hub where people are sitting outside drinking coffee and chatting, I cross over at the traffic lights onto the right side and lose count of the Indian restaurants which, of course, is what South Shields is famous for in the North East. People have always come from surrounding areas to enjoy good Indian food on Ocean Road. And, being partial to curry, I hope it's maintained the great reputation.

I smile at a grey stone statue of a young girl with her outstretched hand pointing the way to the town centre. The inscription on the smooth statue reads, I CAN SEE THE TOWN. That's a great way to replace an ordinary street sign, I think and grin, the council have done an amazing job. Instead of bollards on the side streets, there are smaller grey statues in comic fish designs and three ice cream cornets outside The Clifton Hotel.

On the left is the old entrance to North Marine Park, and of course, opposite is the larger entry to South Marine Park. I bend down to Alfie and say, 'Oooh look, you'll have a choice of parks to stretch your legs and run around later.'

Alfie wags his tail as if knowing there is excitement afoot for him. I've reached the beginning of the seafront in front of the funfair. It's noisy with children running around squealing and booming music coming from the big rides. I turn left and wander along past the bottom of the pier to Littlehaven sandy beach which I know is dog-friendly. Sitting down on a bench, I look out to the calm blue sea and the few trickles of waves on the sand.

I take a deep breath and watch Alfie wandering around the bench as I lengthen his lead. I feel calmer now we've reached our destination. My health scare last year comes into my mind. The palpitations at first had been frightening, but all physical tests and checks at the hospital were normal. I'd had a twenty-four hour tape recording and scan of my heart which had shown no abnormalities which was a blessed relief. The doctors had told me it was nervous anxiety and agitation, which at the time, I had struggled to understand. Basically, at the time, I'd nothing much to fret over. My life had been pretty normal with no major issues, so I had - and still do - struggle to understand why my usual good mental health had slipped down a grade to poor mental health.

I enrolled for cognitive awareness therapy with a counsellor who advised me to adjust my lifestyle to do more peaceful activities that I enjoyed. I agreed and left all the marketing and publicising of my crime novels to an agent which I'd found stressful. Afterwards, day by day and week by week, I lost all interest in the actual writing.

Three years ago both my parents had died within six months of each other and it had been stressful sorting out their house and the post office business, but Allan had been great.

I thought I'd coped through the grieving process rather well at the time, but last year I started dreaming about them in the old post office working behind the counter serving villagers.

However, the counsellor thought I hadn't found full closure. She'd said, 'Stress looks for your weak spots.'

I'd bit my lip and replied, 'But I didn't think I was a weak person?'

She'd continued by saying, 'You're not, but now you've stopped thinking of your parents constantly through the day maybe they are coming back into your mind during the night when you're asleep. But you'll soon find the closure that is right for you.'

The counsellor taught me to use a worry tree which is where I hang up issues that aren't imminent and stop myself worrying about them until necessary. This had worked well, and previously I'd hung our tricky marriage onto a branch.

I shake myself back to the here and now. I have to find somewhere for us to stay for a few days, and from what I can remember, there's a couple of hotels just near the beach. I stand up from the bench and begin to walk along the path. It'll be noisy, I think, but anywhere will do at this stage until I sort myself out.

***

I wander through the doors to the Sea Hotel and approach the reception desk. A young girl in a smart suit looks up at me and smiles. I enquire about a room and she taps on her screen then shakes her head.

'No, sorry, we are fully booked, You'll find all the basic priced hotels are the same – it's the summer season,' she says.

I grimace, why didn't I think of this before? I should have gone to Sunderland and sigh, I might have to if I can't find anywhere to stay.

'Oh, right,' I say, and look around reception.

She nods and smiles. 'You might be able to get into a guest house on Ocean Road, although with the good weather forecast, they might be fully booked too.'

I nod and see a disabled toilet door by the desk. I point to it, and ask, 'Is it okay to use this before I head off?'

She smiles with consent, but I notice the red locked sign on the door handle and slump down onto a chair to wait.

Suddenly, a strange looking guy hurries through the main doors and I stare at him. With long black dreadlocks, he looks like the singer, Prince. He's short and skinny in a navy blue pin-stripe suit. A long wide pink shawl is draped over his right shoulder and I ogle his white leather ankle boots with brown squat heels and zip. I grin, he's certainly not the ordinary type of guy you'd see in South Shields.

Hurrying to the desk, he wails at the receptionist. 'I've lost my ring and I'll just die without it!'

The young receptionist remains calm and I wonder if she knows him as one of their guests. 'No you won't, Sir,' she says. 'We'll find it for you.'

His wail is girl-like which suits his small physique and the flamboyant drape of the shawl over his shoulder. Is it an American accent? He sounds a little like Allan's cousin from New York and I smile. If I'd still been writing, he would have made a great character in one of my books. I had been obsessed with looking at people with their different personalities and this habit still hasn't left me. I wonder if he is from The Customs House because he looks theatrical?

Behind the desk is a small left luggage cupboard which the receptionist opens with a key. 'Now earlier you'd left your holdall in here, so could it be in there?'

The man almost whimpers and hurries through into the cupboard after her. I hear a cheer of success and reckon she's found his ring.

'Oh thank you, honey!' he cries, and ambles back into the reception area. I watch him slip a gold thick-banded sovereign ring onto his little finger as it catches the sunlight from the window. 'I can't thank you enough!'

Mumbling more thanks to her, he heads off towards the exit just as the toilet door opens. An elderly woman hobbles out and makes a fuss of Alfie who croons at her while I slide inside to use the facility.

Chapter Three

I head back up Ocean Road, but on the left hand side of the road this time and stand in awe at the tribute to Grace Darling. There's an old pavilion-like structure with a canopy sheltering the boat with the name, "TYNE" printed on the side. The top sides of the boat are painted in very pale blue and the bottom in white. In the sunshine, it is quite simple but absolutely stunning. The boat is standing on a grey plinth with lengths of knotted thick rope hooped onto its lower sides.

With his big black nose to the ground, Alfie is doing his surveillance around the railings and I smile. It's all new territory for him and I can tell he's enjoying our adventure. When I first got him, I read how a sniffing, slowish walk is often called a "sniffari". Spaniels are trained to find specific scents quicker than humans could and are ideal for detection work with their natural instinct to hunt and retrieve. I smile fondly at him, my Alfie has this in spades.

Next to the boat is a tall light-stone tower and a clock embedded at the top with decorations of circular wreaths and a small balcony of stone railings. The bottom of the tower structure has old shells carved into the four sides, which in its heyday, must have worked as fountains with water and been spectacular.

I wander over to the board with tourist information displayed and learn the lifeboat memorial was built in 1887 to commemorate Queen Victoria's Golden Jubilee. The monument had been strategically placed in between the two new marine parks which were landscaped for the public and residents to use. There are two old postcards and a painting of old lifeboats on treacherous waves at sea heading out to a ship wreck.

Another plaque tells me this is a memorial of the beneficent work of the lifeboat, first built in South Shields in 1750. I whistle between my teeth in awe at the history of this town which, before today, I knew nothing about.

Setting off again, I walk up Ocean Road past the guest houses where most are displaying NO VACANCY signs in their windows. One in particular has a white board outside which promotes QUALITY BED & BREAKFAST GUEST HOUSE. ALL CONTRACTORS WELCOME. This makes me smile wondering if it means you can only sleep and eat on the premises, as opposed to a hotel where you can chill out in your room through the day. And, of course for us, the guest house has to be dog friendly because where I go, Alfie goes too.

I sigh. 'Aww Alfie,' I whisper. 'Maybe we'll have to go on the metro over to Sunderland after all.'

He puts his head to one side and wags his tail. It's as though, he's telling me not to give up. Nearer the top of the road, there's a sign in a window saying, VACANCIES, which is lit up and I wonder if this mean they've got an empty room.

I stand back on the kerb and look at the front double windows and three smaller windows on the first floor with a small attic window on top. It looks well cared for with the outside brick work painted white with a grey trim. There are planters with flowers placed on the five steps up to a newish black door.

I shrug, it doesn't have to be like The Savoy as long as it's clean and safe then it will do to hide away for a few days. I chuckle, if Agatha Christie could do this, then so can I.

***

I press the doorbell and hear an oldish voice shout, 'Come in, why don't you.'

I open the door and pull my case over the door step. I'm greeted by a lady standing at the bottom of the stairs in the hallway with a duster in one hand. I notice her other hand is fixed rigid into a fist and I wonder if she's had a stroke. I reckon she's in her mid-seventies as she ambles towards me smiling.

A red and blue patterned carpet covers the hall floor and extends up an old wide staircase. The ceilings are high with deep white coving which I know are typical of these old terraced houses, but like the outside, it looks well-kept and clean.

'Have you a room for us?' I ask.

For some reason I feel tears prick in the back of my eyes. Maybe it's the words, "for us" I've used that makes me feel lonely. My throat is dry and I try to hold back the tears. Alfie is sitting patiently by my legs as if on guard. He knows something is amiss and as always can tell when I'm upset.

I sweep aside my fringe of curls in an anxious gesture and clear my throat. 'Er, will you take my dog too?' I ask, and stroke his brown silky back. I sigh. 'Isn't it strange? I can bear to leave my husband at home but not him…'

Alfie puts his head on one side and looks up at the old lady as if to say I'll be no bother. It's his begging look which he usually reserves for treats. I put my hand into my jacket pocket and pull out a Waggy chicken nibble. As if on cue, he holds up his paw in thanks. I can see the old lady melt in front of his huge black eyes.

'Is he trained?' She asks.

'To perfection,' I say. 'I run my own dog sitting and walking business.'

She smiles and pats the top of his head. 'Okay, room two is empty which is here on the ground floor.'

She jerks her head as if to say it's along the short corridor behind them next to the breakfast room. Placing the duster onto a small console table, she picks up a pen and hands it to me. An A4 diary is open alongside a bowl of pot pourri.

She says 'It's £80 a night, but I'll just need your name and mobile number for now. I'm, Shirley Jones, the landlady. I live downstairs in the basement but have my own entrance and small garden area, if your pooch needs to go out for a whoopsie.'

I want to giggle at her words but don't. My spirits lift and I shake off the previous feelings. The white door beside the table at the bottom of the stairs has a black number 1 on the front, and the door opposite number 2 which will be for us. I can see how the proximity of the front door will be ideal for Alfie, and we won't need to take advantage of her garden. Taking the pen, I write "Faye Chambers" with the usual flourish I reserve for book signings.

Shirley's bright blue eyes shine as she rolls my name around on her tongue repeating it slowly. 'Now, where do I know that name from?'

I smile. 'Well, I was a local author and have some crime novels which are set in Newcastle. You might have seen them in the shops?'

'Oooh, yes! I have seen them in Smiths. I love to read and thankfully that silly stroke only left me with this useless arm and hand, but didn't affect my eyesight.'

'That's so good,' I say. 'I can't think of anything worse than not being able to read stories.'

She pulls her shoulders back and puffs out her chest in a pink fine-knit sweater. 'Well, fancy that! I have a famous author staying in my guest house, our very own "Catherine Cookson!" Just wait until I tell the ladies at the book club!'

I nod and smile at the commonality. I've been called worse things, I suppose and now to be mentioned in the same sentence as this notorious author is an honour indeed from older readers. While Shirley pulls out a small drawer in the table and lifts out our key, I drop my shoulders knowing Alfie and I have a good start here. Hopefully we'll be quiet and comfortable for a few days.

Shirley hands me a black keyring and starts to amble off across the hall. She taps on the door of room 2 and says, 'This is your room, and further down the hall is the breakfast room. We serve from 7.30am until 9.30am Monday to Friday but from 8am on a weekend.'

She stops outside the breakfast room which conveniently has a small black sign on the door front saying just that. The door is open and I can see five pine wood circular tables with chairs around them. The tables are set with blue and white willow china crockery, and white cloth napkins, as if Shirley has them set in her own home for friends and family to visit. Which I suppose it is, and smile.

Shirley points further down the corridor to another white door with a black sign on the front stating PRIVATE. 'And that is mine. The stairs lead down to my lounge and bedroom, but if you need anything just shout my name at the top of the stairs and I'll hear you.'

'Thanks so much for giving us the room,' I say, and turn to head back to the console table where I left my suitcase. I unlock the door as I hear her wishing us a pleasant stay.

It's a lovely bright square-shaped room with a double bed in the middle. The bed linen is white with a fluffy quilt and four pillows. A door to the side opens into an en suite bathroom. There's a small bath with an equally small shower head over the tub, a toilet and handbasin. 'This is lovely!' I say to Alfie, and he wags his tail in appreciation.

I dispel the long-standing notion of guest houses with pink nylon sheets and army-style rough blankets with shared old bathroom facilities. I look around and open the white wardrobe door and chest of drawers, deciding it's not much different to a hotel room. Which, after all, is what we need at the moment. On the top shelf of the wardrobe is a blue folded throw which I know I can shape into a bed for Alfie on the floor.

Yes, I nod, this will do us just fine. A tray in the corner of the room holds tea, coffee, two mugs and packets of shortbread biscuits. Alfie rears himself to jump up onto the bed and I shake my head. 'Don't even think about it!'

He slopes off with his nose to the carpet sniffing out the room while I make a mug of coffee and fill his bowl with water. I pick up my mobile and text my friend, Penny, who lives in Yarm. We are the oldest of friends and I know she'll worry. I decide to ring her tomorrow and fully explain. I smile. Being the party animal that she is, I know Penny will probably be out tonight anyway.

I type, 'Hi, Penny, just to let you know I've had a huge upset with Allan and have walked away for a few days break. Long story but I'll ring in a few days to explain. Me and Alfie have booked into a guest house in South Shields. XX'

I follow the text with emoji images of a beach, a boat and a big sun so she knows I'm my normal self. Well, I shrug, as normal as I can be in the situation. I can blame Allan for the root cause of this state of affairs and his falsehood, but I can't blame him for my reaction to this.

After unpacking the suitcase, I drain my coffee and flick on the TV set which is attached to the wall. The news is all about the war in the Middle East and I flick over not wanting to see the cruel awful images of humanity at it's worst. Allan often says, 'You're such a softie - you should watch them instead of burying your head in the sand.'

But I simply can't. People have often told me I'm kind, steady and the salt of the earth. Mam had once said, 'You need to toughen up a bit – you take everything to heart.'

I reckon now, she was right. I sigh, maybe it's because of the crime novels I've written that I hate bullies, inequality and injustice which I think sums up any type of war.

My stomach rumbles and I realise it's after seven. Sliding off the bed, I grab my purse and Alfie's blue lead. 'Come on,' I say. 'Let's find some food.'

Locking our room door, I think of the half prepared meal at home which Allan will be eating on his own of poached salmon, new potatoes and salad. I turn with Alfie to head out of the front door when a tall man steps into the hall.

He has a key to room one in his hand and stops as soon as he sees Alfie.

'Now then, who do we have here?' he says bending forwards. 'May I?'

I love it when people have the courtesy to ask first before petting my dog. I smile and nod. 'This is my spaniel, Alfie.'

Alfie practically wraps himself around the man's legs as he ruffles his ears and neck. 'He's absolutely gorgeous!' he says.

I know dogs can sense a welcome like humans do, and when Alfie knows a stranger is happy to see and pet him, he's in his element.

I grin. 'I think so too. We've just arrived and are staying in room two opposite to you so I'm pleased you don't object to dogs.'

He's very thin and well over six foot, I reckon, with a flock of blonde curly hair. He pushes his fringe aside with slim fingers and I smile. Obviously, he has the same problem taming his locks as I do but looks younger – maybe early forties?

'No, that's not a problem,' he says. 'I love dogs. We had a collie dog when I was little at home who followed me around for years. I used to joke and say he was my partner in crime because I was always up to mischief.'

He holds out his hand. 'I'm Lloyd Adams, it's nice to meet you.'

I shake his hand looking into his soft grey eyes and enjoy the lilt to his gentle voice. 'Faye Chambers, and you've already met Alfie. We're just going out to find some food,' I say. 'With arriving late, I'm hungry now.'

Lloyd nods. 'Well, if it's a quick take out you're looking for, the pizza place up the road is very good.'

'Hey thanks,' I say, and gently tug on Alfie's lead. Lloyd opens his room door and we head out the front door.

I smile, skipping down the steps outside. 'We've got a nice neighbour,' I whisper to Alfie as he trots alongside me. A good place to stay and a nice man opposite to us, so things have turned out better than I'd hoped for.

Chapter Four
Lloyd Adams

Lloyd figured Faye was older than his thirty-five years, but she was cute. Hot even, he mused pouring himself a glass of whisky. Some men would be unkind and call her chubby but that suited him fine. He didn't like skinny women. Being thin himself, although he never knew why because he ate like a horse, he liked someone warm and fleshy to cuddle.

He wondered how long she was staying in the guest house and if there would be a chance to get to know each other better. She wore a wedding and engagement ring which made him wonder where her husband was? He liked her big lips and teeth when she smiled – it was friendly and warm. A silly daydream of them walking the beach with Alfie running in and out of the sea filled his mind and he grinned gulping down his first mouthful of whisky.

Although, he sighed heavily, these thoughts wouldn't do him much good now. Faye had been welcoming, which after weeks of being alone and only passing the time of day with strangers, had felt good. He'd shied away from conversation with people, not wanting to draw attention to himself. This had worked well, mainly because as he approached his mid thirties, Lloyd knew his face was growing into what his father's had been – dour and distant.

He wondered now, would a day of harmless flirtation be so wrong and did he have to deny himself everything good in life? Maybe as an icebreaker, he could offer to take her dog for a walk which wouldn't be a chore because Alfie was simply gorgeous.

Childhood memories flood his mind with his sister Estelle and their dog at home. It had been a happy carefree time with loving parents. He struggled to understand how his life could have changed so much in a couple of years.

Lloyd slumped down into the large chair in the bay window at the front of the guest house. Shaking his head, he muttered, 'Who am I kidding!' He knew it was the last thing he needed and the wrong thing to do. He couldn't involve anyone else in his situation – it wouldn't be fair and could be dangerous. In fact, it would be wrong, so very wrong.

The window shutters were still open even though it was dark now. Lloyd opened the old sash window, and could hear a few muffled noises of revellers down on the seafront, but nearby was silent. He listened for footsteps outside on the path and his shoulders shivered. This was his third night here in South Shields and he wondered what night they might come for him. He'd booked and paid for a whole week but at the first sign of them he'd do what older people called "a moonlight flit".

The old guest house felt stuffy and too warm in comparison to his own modern new-build flat which was always cool and airy in the summer. Lloyd took in a deep breath and fancied he could detect the salty smell of the sea.

In his mind, the thought of his escape to the seaside had pleased him and how hiding for a couple of weeks amongst holiday makers was a safe plan. But could they trace him here? Another gulp of whisky warmed him and he shook his head, no, they couldn't because he'd been clever. He had made up the name of Lloyd Adams, thinking it had a nice ring to it.

At the other places where he'd stayed, he had changed his surname, but never using the usual Brown or Smith. Three weeks ago in the first hotel he'd checked into, he had struggled at reception to think of a surname. Quickly, he remembered the list of clients in his dentist surgery and came up with the name "Clarkson".

The scare mongering had started with two missed new patients appointments which were precious in the Leeds surgery and his efficient receptionist had been puzzled. She'd said, 'But they were nearly crying on the phone with toothache.'

The hairs on the back of his neck had stood up. And then, a letter was delivered to the surgery written with red pencil on an A4 sheet of paper, saying, 'We are coming for you.'

This was followed by a wreath of flowers delivered with the words "RIP, Lloyd". He'd known he had to leave. He gave notice to the senior partner and fled. That was three weeks ago and he'd travelled up and down the North East coast, staying in hotels and B&Bs in Seaham, Saltburn and Tynemouth. He'd enjoyed the solitude, especially walking on the beaches and had been surprised at how little he missed his home, community and the job he'd been passionate about since university.

Ironically, a week ago his filling on a molar had dropped out, but wary of making any appointments which would mean using his bank account and old address details, he'd bought a temporary filling kit at a pharmacy and done the job himself.

Lloyd's mind recapped over the big day it had all happened, and how the family had sat next to the mother, a hard-faced woman in her late sixties. He'd found out that the two men behind her were cousins who were orphaned young and raised as her own. One of them had travelled from abroad to be there and stumped up a large amount of money, which to Lloyd's relief had been denied.

Lloyd remembered a phrase he'd read somewhere "the man behind his eyelids" and knew he'd become just that. He'd been brave, oh so brave, but they always seemed to be one step ahead of him.

Chapter Five

I didn't think I would sleep well, but I had. And Alfie had too. When we returned last night with chicken and chips, Shirley had left a big laundry basket outside our room door with a note, hoping it would make a nice bed for Alfie. How kind, I'd thought and padded out the basket with the throw. He'd loved it and hopped straight in snuggling down for the night. We both enjoyed the take out food and Lloyd had been right – it had been good quality at a reasonable price.

When I'd rolled into bed and knew Alfie was asleep, I hadn't thought sleep would come easily because it had been one of the very few nights since we married that Allan wasn't next to me in bed. Other than two nights in hospital when Olivia was born, I'd struggled to remember nights without him. It had felt strange in one way, but in another way it had been relaxing and a relief not to have to think about the divorce revelation which sickened me to my stomach. I'd pushed it out of my mind and once more slotted Allan up onto the worry tree, and then dozed off into a dreamless sleep.

However, the sun is shining now through the white wood shutters at the window and I glance at my mobile. I gasp, it's eight o'clock and Alfie is prowling. Knowing he needs a "whoopsie" as Shirley calls it, I pull on tracksuit bottoms and a sweatshirt, grab my key from the door and head out the front door. He happily does what he needs to do at the nearest lamp post and I scoop up with a little black bag.

'Come on,' I say. 'We need breakfast.'

Back in our room, I clean out the take-away container from last night and fill it with water then pour food mix into his bowl. The smell of bacon sizzling and bread toasting wafts its way along the corridor and I jump into a hot shower. I'd started this year, determined to slim down from my usual size sixteen into a fourteen in jeans, but as ever, this hadn't happened. My love of good food had gotten in the way. I sigh, pulling on a long sleeved T-shirt and my comfortable white linen trousers and then wander along the corridor into the breakfast room with Alfie on his lead by my side.

Radio Two is playing quietly in the background and I hover in the doorway.

'Morning, Faye!' Shirley calls out. 'Come in, I have a table here ready for you.'

I smile and amble between the tables to the back of the room near the kitchen door. 'Thanks, Shirley. Is it okay to bring Alfie in? I don't like leaving him alone in the room and he'll just sit quietly under the table.'

Shirley claps her hands and calls out loudly, 'Listen up everyone, are you all okay with the pooch, Alfie, sitting under the table?'

There's a middle aged couple at a table in the corner, and an oldish couple at the table in front of the window. They all nod and the older lady says, 'Oh yes, that's fine. We have a poodle at home and are very dog friendly.'

I smile and call out my thanks as Alfie heads under the short white tablecloth.

Sitting down facing the room, I've already lost the fight with myself between orange juice and cereal, knowing I'm going to demolish a full English breakfast as a treat. Reasoning with myself, I decide it's a impromptu one-off and a little bit of a holiday, so I'll make up for it afterwards.

Shirley approaches my table and lays a small notepad on the table then picks out a pencil from a pocket in her white apron which is tied over grey slacks and a white blouse. She's overweight like myself but in a homely way.

I say, 'Oh, and thanks for the basket you left last night. Alfie loved it and slept all night.'

She beams with pleasure and I notice how the grey pixie hair cut frames her little face. I order a full English with coffee and she scribbles it down.

A skinny woman wearing a pink tabard over tight jeans and a yellow T-shirt, who I figure to be in her late twenties, hurries into the room carrying two hot plates with a tea-towel.

She hurries over to the corner table where the middle-aged couple are sitting and places the plates down in front of them.

Shirley says, 'This is Luba, my little godsend. After my stroke, I thought I'd have to give up the guest house and move, but she stepped in and does all the things I can't do any more with just one good arm and hand.'

I nod in greeting as Luba hurries past me back into the kitchen. Shirley follows her and then reappears with a little silver toast rack in her good hand placing it down with the plates of breakfast. I reckon Shirley still wants to be involved in the running of the guest house, even though she's limited to her abilities now which is admirable in her seventies. I can only hope I'll want to keep going as she does when I reach old age.

I sit back in the chair, slip off one of my sandals and gently rub the top of Alfie's neck just so he knows I'm still here. There's a nice atmosphere in the breakfast room, which is rather homely instead of a detached ambience in a hotel. The other two couples are chatting about their day ahead and what their holiday plans are.

I'm curious to see who is in which room and if there are other guests upstairs and in the attic room. Allan often calls me nosy, but I dispute this, I'm simply interested in other people's lives. I note there is no sign of Lloyd as yet. Perhaps he's an early riser or late sleeper.

Shirley arrives at my table with a little toast rack now and I butter myself a piece of toast, followed closely by Luba who lays my plate of breakfast in front of me. The smell obviously alerts Alfie, and he raises his head from under the table cloth sniffing the air.

The older lady cries out, 'Oh, just look at him – he's adorable!'

I reach into my bag, pull out his small treat bowl and cut up a sausage into pieces. As I lay it under the table, the middle aged man claps and Alfie, who loves to give a performance, swirls around then dives back under to demolish the sausage. We all watch him wolf this down, licking his big mouth with his long pink tongue.

'He's such a show off,' I tell them all, and can see admiration in their eyes.

My mobile rings and Allan's name is on the screen. The memory of yesterday, how I'd found the papers in the bureau and the row afterwards floods my mind and fills my mouth with a nasty taste. I shiver and swipe off his call. I don't want to even hear his voice, let alone talk to him. Get him back up onto that worry tree I think and finish my coffee whilst looking at the two couples and listening to their dialects. The older couple are definitely

Scottish, whereas the younger couple speak with a faint Yorkshire twang.

If I'd still been writing, I could have made up some great characters from these people I muse. After I stopped, it felt strange at first not to sit at the desk every morning with my coffee, but decided I didn't miss the storytelling as much as I thought I would. My morning rituals were replaced with getting Alfie ready to walk and collecting other dogs to join us, which I love.

When I first got Alfie, I tried a doggie training group in Northumberland. It had been a strange couple of weeks with equally strange people in the group. Someone had a bout of religious fervour, shouting 'Hallelujah!' and 'Praise the Lord!' every few minutes whilst throwing her hands in the air which startled Alfie. A mother who brought her rather large child and laid him on the grass to sleep then hid behind a tree for a cigarette. A partially sighted man with a white stick. I was never exactly sure how much he could see and one of the other dogs - not my Alfie - lifted his leg to pee on the stick. A woman who wore hearing aids which screeched through out the training session. And another lady in a mobility scooter who had to leave early because there was nowhere for her to plug it in, although the trainer kept telling her the scooter was fully charged.

I found out that after the course you can do bronze, silver and gold tests or an agility course, heelwork, freestyle and scent training. It was a six week course to learn the basics but I only did three sessions. Allan reckoned I gave up too easily and should have completed the course, ignoring the other members with their dogs.

Afterwards, I watched dog shows on TV and Crufts once but decided the world of judging looked cut-throat and I would never subject Alfie to this. However, the following week, an elderly neighbour asked if I would walk her dog when I took Alfie out because she'd had an operation and couldn't manage.

And, that's how my own little group of dogs had begun. The neighbour recommended me to her friends and now I often have two to three dogs on a daily basis. I bought a black three-way, no-tangle triple lead which is great to use when taking all the dogs out together. Alfie sometimes gets a little jealous when I'm showing the others attention so I make sure I spoil him afterwards.

As I'm lost in thought, all of a sudden I hear Luba scream and Alfie shoots out from under the table and barks. The old woman's cup rattles in her saucer and the middle-aged man grumps, 'What the hell is that!'

I clip on Alfie's lead and we hurry to the door of the breakfast room. In the corridor outside room one, Shirley is white faced and Luba is holding her up by her arm as she leans against the door architrave. I rush to them, stand next to Luba and peer inside. Lloyd is sitting in a chair with a knife in his chest.

Luba gabbles, 'H…he usually goes out early, so I thought I'd c…clean his room first!'

My heart begins to race and I feel a little breathless. I take a deep breath in and let it out slowly. I grab my mobile and, with trembling fingers, I hit the numbers 999.

Chapter Six

My voice is shaky as I explain the scene in front of me in room one to the operator. She is calm and professional, explaining how she will send the police straight away. She asks if the man is still alive and if his chest is moving. I peer closer into the room. 'Well, he's not moving at all and looks dead to me, but I'm not medically trained.'

She reassures me that help is coming in minutes and she'll send an ambulance too. I click off my mobile and feel struck dumb. I can't believe what I'm seeing in this room. A rush of adrenaline races through my body. How could this happen in a guest house in South Shields? And to Lloyd, who I'd only chatted with last night.

I've never seen a dead body like this and sweat stands on my upper lip. Of course, I saw my parents in the morgue, peaceful and laid out to rest. But there's nothing restful in the sight before me now. The knife and blood dispel this image.

I hear Shirley whimper and snap into action.

I clear the gruff croak from my voice, and say to Luba, 'Why not take Shirley down to her rooms and get her a hot cup of tea.'

Cradling the old lady by her shoulders, Luba walks Shirley slowly back along the corridor. I hover in the doorway and hear Alfie shuffle next to my ankles. Ruffling the top of his head, I whisper, 'It's okay boy.'

I sigh, but it's not okay and know there'll be no need for an ambulance because Lloyd is well and truly dead. My body feels suddenly chilled with a feeling of utter sadness for what's happened to this seemingly pleasant man. I remember the few minutes with him at the door and his welcoming smile. His quietly spoken voice and how he'd fussed over Alfie. Obviously a dog lover, I think and my chin trembles with pity.

Of course, we don't know the circumstances of what's happened, but to die like this in a traumatic incident is awful for anybody. Alfie whines as if in agreement because it seems much worse in a guest house surrounded by strangers. I'm not thinking it would have been kinder to happen in a person's home, but if so, Lloyd might not have been alone. I can hear Luba telling everyone to stay in the breakfast room as there's been an incident and the police are coming.

I remember writing in my crime novels how it's imperative not to touch anything. The research I'd used of psychology in a crime scene comes into my mind, and I repeat to myself, 'Use the same footsteps as the person in front of you as if you're walking in deep snow. Keep to the edges of the room away from the affray. Initially, no one should speak a word at a crime scene and should use the process of one in – one out.'

I decide to keep guard outside the room until the police arrive just in case any of the other guests come along to spy at what's happening. I commit to memory everything I can see in his room, which is the same size as ours, but the bathroom door and window are on the opposite side. Lloyd is sitting in the big black armchair near the window. The shutters are closed as is the window and it feels stifling hot. The old radiator is piping out heat and I presume it's been left on all night. Three flies are buzzing on the old windowsill.

I stare at Lloyd dressed in the same clothes as I'd seen him wear last night by the front door. Without stepping inside any further, I crane my neck to look at him. The blade of the knife is fully inside his shirt with only the handle visible. There's a patch of blood stained on the light grey shirt around the entry site, but no more blood anywhere else. The only disturbance in the room is a glass tumbler tipped on its side with brown liquid half spilled out onto the cream carpet. I take this to be whisky as there's a bottle of Johnny Walker on the TV stand.

His hand is hanging limply over the arm of the chair. It is immaculately clean with soft looking skin and clipped fingernails. A medical professional, I wonder? Certainly not an engineer or gardener. There again, any office worker would have clean fingernails but not necessarily well manicured. Somehow I can see him in blue operating garb and wonder if he's a doctor? If so, who would want to kill a doctor, and I shake my head knowing this didn't make sense.

The wardrobe door is ajar and I can see his few clothes on hangers which appear to suit his age of mid-thirties. Modern polo shirts, chinos, and two pairs of knee length shorts. Definitely not an older man's collection of clothes, however, his suitcase on the top of the wardrobe is not the modern wheelie variety, but an old battered leather-look suitcase with a carry handle and straps. This doesn't fit the image of Lloyd, somehow?

Alfie raises his big nose and sniffs the air.

'Yeah, Alfie, there's definitely a strong smell of cloying perfume hanging around,' I whisper.

He gives a bark in response. Since I got Alfie, I've started talking to him rather than to myself as I had done previously. It's as if he knows what I'm thinking and feeling. A little voice in the back of my mind says this was something you used to do with Allan, but haven't for a while because he distanced himself. And, I now ask the sad question, has Alfie taken over where Allan left off?

I feel, rather than see Luba behind me again as she breathes down my neck. I turn to her but know she's not wearing perfume and I'm not either.

Her voice quivers in a thick Eastern European dialect. 'This man is dead!'

A part of me wants to laugh and cynically comment, "you're not kidding, he's bound to be with a knife in his chest", but I don't. It's not the right response to her dictionary-learnt English and may embarrass her.

She's wearing a baseball cap with her fine black hair in a pony tail pulled through the gap at the back. On the floor, at the side of the doorway is a grey compartment tray with a sturdy handle. Inside are two spray cleaners, a duster and a packet of blue J-cloths. She purses her big plush lips and whispers reverently, 'It's a shame because he was a nice man.'

Just as I'm wondering if she's had Botox and, staring at her striking brown eyes, I hear the sirens outside on Ocean Road. I know they're coming to us and hurry to the main front door of the guest house. With the sleeve of my T-shirt pulled over my hand, I open it wide. Of course, one of the other couples may have touched the handle after the killer did, but all the same, I figure it's best to be sure.

Two young police constables run up the steps from the pavement and I stand back with Alfie outside our room door. The tallest PC glances inside Lloyd's room and puts his arm across the chest of the shorter PC.

'Good God! Don't go in there until the DS arrives!'

The shorter PC shouts, 'I'll get the tape!'

He shoots back outside to their car and on his return, stretches blue and white tape saying POLICE DO NOT CROSS across the bottom of the steps. He hurries back to us all and repeats the same process across Lloyd's doorway. The taller PC swings around to me and asks, 'Did you find him and call this in?'

Luba answers straight away, 'No, I found him. I was going in to clean the room.'

He nods, 'And have either of you been inside?'

I shake my head. 'I rang 999, but I've kept watch to stop that happening until you got here.'

He nods again and I see another car tearing up outside. 'Here's the DS,' he mutters.

Chapter Seven

A very tall blonde woman runs up the steps. I reckon she's got to be at least six foot dressed in black trousers and wearing a body tactical vest which shows off her taut biceps. This woman, who looks to be late twenties, works out and self consciously I think of my own flabby arms. The DS takes out blue covers and gloves from her pockets and pulls them on over grubby white trainers.

On her shoulder is a strap holding an iPad and immediately as she steps into Lloyd's room, she begins to tap on the screen. This, I reckon is modern policing whereas years ago, she would have had a small notepad.

She barks out orders to the PCs. 'One of you get outside and look around the back and front pavements, and the other one get these people out of the corridor!'

I look behind to see the oldish and middle-aged couples standing down the corridor outside the breakfast room peering along to see what was happening. The short PC opens his arms wide guiding everyone, including me and Luba, back down the corridor.

We all backtrack and into the breakfast room once more. Luba hurries into the kitchen area stating she'll make everyone fresh tea. Shirley is sitting on a chair with her head in her hands at the end table.

I rush to her and stroke her arm. 'Shirley are you okay?'

She pulls her hands away from her face and I'm glad to see she has more colour than previously when they'd found Lloyd. I suppose she might be susceptible to having another stroke and bite my lip with concern for her. Alfie rushes to her side and places his paw onto her knee as if to say "it's okay, we're here". Shirley ruffles his head comfortingly and I smile at my beloved dog.

'Yes I'm okay Faye, thank you,' she croaks, and pulls out a white handkerchief from her sleeve. 'Never, in over thirty years, have I had anything like this happen. It's shaken me to the core, I can tell you. I can't get over the shock of seeing him sitting there like that!'

I pat her arm. 'It's horrible, but we don't want you making yourself ill again. The police are here now so we might get to find out exactly what's happened.'

Shirley nods. 'I thought when I first met him and gave him his room key that I knew his face from somewhere, but if so, after the stroke many of my memories are now diminished or have disappeared altogether,' she says. 'Or I could be getting him mixed up with some other local man.'

'Don't fret yourself over that now, Shirley. It may come back to you at a later date.'

She smiles. 'I suppose you've written about awful things like this in your books, have you?'

I smile at the old lady. 'Well, I have, but my stories are all make believe and I like to study characters. Or some people might just call me downright nosy.'

Shirley smiles for the first time and I can tell she's feeling more settled.

I say, 'I try to make the reader into the detective who solves puzzles and mysteries throughout my novels.'

Luba arrives carrying a tray with cups, saucers, a milk jug and a sugar bowl. She places it down on their table with a plate of biscuits.

Shirley rambles, 'God, she's a blessing all right. Luba has been here for five years now and I don't know what I'd do without her. Her hubby went back to Poland because he was too homesick but she's making a new life here for herself and her little boy.'

I watch Luba return with a large teapot and begin to pour out cups of tea for everyone while taking a sideways glance at Shirley. Her brown eyes are full of concern.

'Yes, I can tell she's worried about you.'

Shirley nods. 'She works like a dog and organises me some days. Before the stroke, I never had a plan when I did my own cleaning, and now, even stripping and making the beds is a challenge with this stupid useless hand,' she says, and clutches it with her other hand.

I pass Shirley her cup of tea and gulp at mine. My throat is dry and when I look under the table, I notice Luba has cleaned out Alfie's bowl and filled it with fresh water. He greedily laps at his water while I spy the plate which holds custard creams. They're my favourites, and Alfie sniffs looking hopefully at them, but I shake my head and dejectedly he goes back to Shirley's knee. I'm tempted to take a biscuit but after the huge breakfast I've eaten, I manage to restrict myself.

Sipping her hot tea, Shirley continues. 'Luba made her own timetable and the whole guest house is spotless now. She dusts and hoovers after stripping the beds when every guest leaves. She deep cleans the kitchen every weekend and mops all the floors, cleans the windows inside once a month, and even weeds the front area and pot plants.'

I smile. 'I wish she'd come and do mine - I hate housework,' I joke.

A text pings onto my mobile from Penny and I read her message.

'Sorry, I was out last night – what the hell is going on? I'm coming up – what's the name of the guest house?'

I smile and know it'll be good to have Penny here. It'll be nice to see a familiar face in the guest house where I'm a stranger surrounded by other strangers. However, I knew if Allan came, he would make this happening all about him in some way. And I don't want to know anything about him at the moment. He'd only complicate matters whereas Penny will support me. I give her the name of the guest house and turn to Shirley.

Holding the mobile in my hand, I ask 'This is from my friend Penny who wants to come and join me. Have you any more rooms which are empty, or do you know another guest house she can stay in?'

Shirley nods. 'She can go in the attic room upstairs. Luba will clean it later as the family who were in there left very early this morning.'

I smile and thank her.

The oldish lady with her broad Scottish accent shouts over to us, 'Hey, Faye, do we know what's happened yet? Shirley reckons the man called Lloyd was dead in his room?'

I notice Shirley and Luba haven't mentioned the knife in poor Lloyd's chest, so I decide to measure my response. I get up and walk over to her and her husband, who is now sporting black sunglasses. 'Nothing as yet, the police have just arrived but I'm sure they'll want to speak to us all later.'

He grunts. 'Us? Why would they want to speak to us?'

'Well, I think it's just procedure,' I say. 'Sorry, I don't know your names?'

His wife intervenes. 'I'm Lily and this is Ken. We are down from Glasgow for the week - we come to South Shields every year.'

Lily has what older ladies used to call a "shampoo and set", achieved by using slim rollers with white plastic tags to clip them to the hair. I remember doing my grannie's hair with them when she was in the hospice and brushing her hair into a bouffant style. Lily pats the back of her hair now as if in reassurance.

Lily turns to her husband and says, 'Take those bloody sunglasses off when you're inside – you look ridiculous and you're showing us up!'

I smile at the "Darby and Joan" relationship. 'Aww, it's nice to meet you both,' I say. 'With just arriving late yesterday, I don't know anyone here.'

Out of the corner of my eye, I can see the middle-aged couple leaning across their table to catch what we are saying. I reckon I should say hello to them too as we are going to be here for a while. I walk over to their table.

'Hello, I'm Faye Chambers,' I say. 'This is a dreadful thing to happen on my first morning here.'

Whereas Lily and Ken were keen to chat to me, I get the feeling this couple are not as forthcoming. Maybe they like to keep themselves to themselves, I think and stretch out my hand to the man. But the man stands up, shakes my hand firmly and the woman gives me a big smile.

He says, 'Yes, it is. This is our third day because there was a mix-up at The Clifton Hotel where we thought we were booked into for the week but their computer said otherwise, so we are in here as everywhere else was fully booked. By the way, I'm Mark Reynolds and this is my wife, Brigit.'

There's a certain snootiness in his voice and manner as though the guest house is a big step down for them. I want them to know that I'm grateful to be here and it's a good place to stay, other than a guest having a knife plunged into his chest, of course.

I nod. 'Me too, it was a quick decision to come to the coast for a few days but I didn't factor in the school and summer holidays. However, Shirley has been so kind and given us a lovely room which I think is just as good as any hotel.'

Mark is a good looking man but with a poor skin. I wonder if he had acne when he was younger? I notice, even though Brigit is still smiling, she doesn't speak a word but stares at Mark with a reverential look as though he's some type of demigod. Did I look like that with Allan? I shrug, perhaps in the early days of our marriage, but no longer. I pull my shoulders back knowing this feels good.

Mark shrugs. 'Shirley tells us you're an author and have crime novels set in the area?'

'Yeah,' I say. 'But I'm retired and don't write now.'

With the breakfast room door open, I can hear different footsteps in the corridor which make a clanky sound like tap shoes on the wood floor inside the front door. And now an older male voice. It's certainly not the sound of the young PCs voices.

'Where is she?' I hear this voice boom.

There's more scurrying about and the tall PC appears in the door of the breakfast room.

'Our Inspector has arrived and he'd like to talk to you – follow me, please?'

Alfie, who still has his chin on Shirley's knee, lifts his head. Realising I won't be in his eyesight, he is up straight away and at my side in a jiffy. I clip on his lead and we follow the PC back along to Lloyd's room.

Chapter Eight.

The booming voice seems to get louder the nearer I get to Lloyd's room. It sounds like a headmaster at assembly getting children to pay attention. I'm expecting to see a big man to go with the voice, but stop still in my tracks outside room one in the doorway.

I'm face to face with a short medium built man with what I can only describe as a nondescript face. He's wearing a light coloured suit and a white shirt which would look better if the collar was open, but I can tell at a glance he's not the type of man to dress without a tie.

'Wait there,' he barks.

The hairs on the back of my neck stand up to attention as if I'm one of the children in assembly. The DS is standing to the side of the room in front of the wardrobe and is still tapping on her iPad. I look at her face now. She has heavy shaped brown eyebrows and a long nose. I think Allan would unkindly say that she's just missed being pretty, but I think she looks focused and strong. She's obviously fought hard to prove herself in a male dominated profession.

She turns to me now. 'This is Inspector Jackson and he'd like a word with you shortly.'

I nod and Alfie looks up at me. I ruffle the top of his head knowing we have to wait quietly.

There's a thoughtful expression on the Inspector's face and he seems to have an air of calm around him. Much more so than the others. He pulls out a small black notebook from his trouser pocket and twangs the elastic strap on the front between his fingers repeatedly.

Looking at the DS, he asks, 'How did the person or persons gain access to the guest house? I suppose all the guests will have keys as well as the landlady?'

I nod to myself knowing this is a good question. On the key ring Shirley gave me is a key for the front door and a different key for the Yale lock on my room door. His question makes me wonder, if you're a couple do you both get a key like you would do in a hotel with room cards. However, maybe in a guest house there's only one key per room. Of course, with being alone, Shirley only gave me one, but do Mark and Brigit have a key each?

He spins around towards the two PCs. 'I know these old terraced houses have thick walls, but go to the houses on either side and talk to the neighbours to see if they heard anything, and check for broken windows or locks!'

The PCs jump to attention at the Inspector's authoritative voice and hurry out through the open front door.

Another good call, I think, knowing this whole street is lined with guest houses. When I walked up the road yesterday, I'd counted seventeen of them and one hotel. Therefore, I figure, if they're all full there must be at least a hundred people milling in and out of these properties on a daily and nightly basis.

The Inspector ducks underneath the taped door and strides over to me and Alfie who raises his head sniffing the air, as if to ask "who's this?"

'Okay,' he says. 'So, you are the landlady?'

I shake my head and point to our room door. 'No, I'm a guest staying in the room opposite.'

He spins around to the DS. 'I thought you said this woman called it in?'

She looks down at her iPad and clicks her tongue. Her cheeks flush and I can see she thinks she's made a mistake, so I decide to step in and help.

'The landlady is an old lady who got an awful shock. I heard the scream and came to help. I rang 999 and told the operator what we'd found.'

He looks me up and down. 'Ah right, and your name?'

'Faye Chambers,' I say. I want to be cheeky and ask him to introduce himself because I don't appreciate the sarcasm in his tone. However, I know he has a job to do and finding a dead body in a guest house in South Shields has to be a rarity. I take a deep breath and tell him how Shirley and Luba had discovered Lloyd.

'Yes, yes,' he mutters, and heads back under the tape where he strides over to the window and where Lloyd is sitting dead in his chair. I remember more of the research I often used and repeat to myself "nothing is unimportant in a crime scene". Every murder has its own characteristics and the one thing in common is consistency. Don't be distracted by the obvious – look for the unremarkable. And, in my humble opinion, it sure looks like Lloyd has been murdered.

Taking out a small pencil from the pocket in his jacket, the Inspector begins to scribble and I can tell he is looking for commonalities. Ah I think, old-school for this man, no tapping on an iPad for him, unless he's left it in his office and prefers to record in writing.

He chunters more to himself than anyone else as he scribbles. 'There's no signs of a struggle. No thrashing about with arms or hands. No clawing fingernails. No furniture turned over. No frenzied attack. All he seems to have suffered is one big stab with a knife into his chest.

It seems as if this man was accepting of his fate and didn't protest.'

I can't help but smile because he's noting everything I had done earlier. There's more kerfuffle at the front door as a small white van pulls up outside. A bald-headed man climbs out of the front while a younger guy opens the back and lifts out a grey metal case.

The DS says, 'Here's the crime scene manager now.'

'Who is it?'

'It looks like old Ted.'

The Inspector groans and then grunts. 'It takes him twice as long as anyone else, but I suppose he is thorough.'

I stand back against the door of my room with Alfie while, dressed in white paper body suits, they stride past me, under the tape, and into the room.

The bald-headed man called Ted shouts, 'Out now! Both of you get out of the room!'

The DS and the Inspector walk towards the open doorway, duck underneath the tape and hover outside. He grumbles to Ted. 'But we've got blue covers on our shoes!'

Ted retorts and shakes his head. 'I don't want anyone walking where the killer might have done.'

Ted places his hand on the younger guy's arm as he starts taking one photo after another and whispers, 'Step carefully, lad.'

There appears to be tension between Ted and the Inspector. I shrug, past history I wonder? Ted crouches down in front of Lloyd in the chair and seems to stare at him for a long time. I watch the Inspector shuffle his feet with impatience.

He mellows his voice a little. 'So Ted, was the killer on his own or did he have an accomplice to hold Lloyd down in the chair? What type of knife was it? Kitchen or a street knife?'

Ted grunts but there's a smile playing around his lips. He looks up at them, 'Oh, what a shame I left my crystal ball at home! You'll have to wait for details until I've finished.'

The DS sighs heavily at the banter which is obviously irritating her. They both turn around to face me and Alfie now.

The Inspector looks at us with piercing hazel-brown eyes in what I'd call a small face and neck for a man, or maybe it's the baggy shirt collar which gives this appearance. I reckon he's younger than me - around late forties or early fifties.

'So, how long have you been here, and do you know this man?' He asks with a jerk of his head towards the room.

The DS reminds him. 'He's called Lloyd Adams.'

I shrug. 'Well, I just arrived yesterday at six o'clock, so no I don't know him,' I say. 'But I did chat to him last night.'

'Okay,' he says. 'So maybe you were the last person to see him alive when you spoke to him.'

I nod. 'Could be, it was around 7pm when I took Alfie out.'

The Inspector looks around and over my shoulder. 'Alfie? Who's he?'

I smile and glance down to Alfie. 'My spaniel.'

He clicks his tongue and I bristle. This man is beginning to irritate me with his supercilious manner and attitude.

He asks, 'And did Lloyd behave any differently last night - was he on edge?'

'How do I know?' I say and hold up my open hands. 'I've never met him before, so I wouldn't know if he was different or not.'

He actually turns his back on me and Alfie as though we're irrelevant in all of this. Alfie looks up at me and I nod my head as if to keep him quiet.

'Yes, well, I'll be interviewing everyone later,' he snaps. 'Including you!'

The DS smiles at me as if in apology and I feel sorry for her having to put up with his rudeness. My heckles are definitely rising at this man.

He looks at Ted now, but yells at the DS. 'This is a crime scene and no one is going anywhere until I'm finished, and satisfied with my enquiries, and SOCO are done. I want all the guests kept here in their rooms or the dining room. They are all my suspects and are locked-in until I say otherwise. We need to find out at interviews what date and time they arrived, and how long they are staying in the guest house. And, at what stage each of them saw Lloyd Adams yesterday. I'll want to know what time exactly everyone retired to bed in their rooms, at 11pm, 12am, or later, and if they heard anything during the night like a broken window, or maybe if anyone has lost their keys!'

'Yes, Sir,' the DS mutters whist tapping furiously on her iPad.

Ted calls, 'You can come in now, but keep to the edges of the room. His pockets are empty, so I can't find any ID on him.'

The Inspector ducks under the tape, strides back inside followed closely by the DS, and I step further towards the door again to watch what they are doing.

DS begins to gabble out her theories. 'Why hasn't he got any bank cards, passport, or driving licence – everyone has some of these about their person – don't they?'

I remember checking-in with Shirley and how she'd asked for my name and mobile number. Shall I say this to them or keep quiet? He hasn't asked for my input and the few words he has said have been in an unpleasant manner, so I decide to keep shtum and tell them later when he interviews us all.

However, as they're searching, I do wonder about Lloyd's mobile. Of course, he would be in the minority if he didn't have a mobile because I can't think of anyone I know that doesn't have one. Even older people, like Ken and Lily seem to have joined the social media brigade. But it's definitely a consideration.

They begin to look through the set of drawers and with his blue gloves on the Inspector rummages amongst underwear and socks that she had previously checked. He scrunches a pair of black socks in his hands and pulls out a roll of bank notes.

Grinning, he flicks through the notes, and says, 'This is where I keep my cash at home. There's about £300 in here, so that's why he's got no cards – he's using cash.'

With flushed red cheeks, the DS holds out a sample bag and I notice her hands in blue gloves are trembling.

Is she scared of him or annoyed with herself that she missed this and should have found it first?

The Inspector points to a open lidded pizza box lying on the TV table. I can see there's one dried-up, sorry-looking piece of pizza left. 'Was this delivered? Find out,' he snaps.

The tall PC has come back inside and is standing behind me. DS shouts orders to him, flaying her arm about, in a motion of agitation about the pizza take-out. I feel sorry for her, but note the name on the box is from the same place where we got our food last night.

Lloyd must have gone there later in the night or maybe as the Inspector suggested, had it delivered. The shop should have a time on the till roll, and I smile as the DS tells this to the tall PC. Listening to the Inspector's comments and orders makes me wonder, is this gained from age and experience in CID?

Between his small gritted teeth, the Inspector mutters to himself. 'I like to cover all bases and follow protocol to the letter.'

The DS has followed both the PCs to the front door and they huddle together in the doorway. I watch them whispering between each other. The tall PC's head jerks over his shoulders and I can tell they're whingeing about the Inspector. And then I hear one of them call him JJ.

I step a little closer, and hear DS say, 'He's the best we've got in CID and he always has my back.'

That's good to hear, I think, at least he has some moral attributes. I smile at this nickname because he looks nothing like a young guy with a laid-back preference to JJ.

I wonder what his first names are, and if he knows they call him this behind his back. They all separate as the Inspector comes back out of the room and stands in front of me again.

Once more, he stares into my eyes and I feel the back of my neck twitch. He's making me feel guilty for some reason as if I had something to do with Lloyd's death. My impression is that nothing will get past this man, which I suppose is as it should be.

I clasp my sweaty palms together and say, 'I…I only spoke to Lloyd briefly because he was petting and fussing over my dog outside our room.'

'Then tell me what he said!'

He snaps again, almost shouting this time and Alfie gives a low groan, not his growl as such, but I can tell he feels threatened at this man's attitude. I bend over and ruffle his ears in comfort.

Now that he's rattled Alfie, I'm annoyed and pull back my shoulders. He's arrogant and looking down on everyone, including me. I decide to speak to him in the same manner he is using to us.

I repeat the few words I'd exchanged with Lloyd the night before, and tell him my observations of the guest house and how we found Lloyd in the room.

'Enough!' he says. 'God help me from amateur sleuths! I can't have you interfering, but I bet you've been watching or reading Vera novels – have you?'

I look at him with incredulity. His sardonic attitude tells me that he has no idea of the genius imagination that is the author Ann Cleeves who creates outstanding storylines in whodunits with amazing threads of mysterious characters. In my opinion, she is up there with the greatest female crime writers.

'Well really!' I retort, planting my feet into a stance ready for battle. 'Not only do I read crime novels, I actually write them and have undertaken copious amounts of research! Have you any idea of the commitment, hard work and dedication it takes to do this?'

'Hmmph,' he mutters under his breath. 'Well, I'll take your statement later when I've got time to listen to your jabbering.'

I click my tongue at his rudeness and at the word "jabbering". Is it because I'm a woman, or is he this rude to everyone he meets? Misogynistic? I stand still with my arms folded across my chest and glare at him. He's not going to get the better of me, I rage.

He has the good grace to look down and shuffle his feet in shiny brown shoes which I remember had made the clanking noise when he first arrived. His feet are little for a man which I suppose fits in with his small physique. I know my mam would call him neat and tidy. His cheeks flush a little which, in a strange way, looks quite cute with his small button nose.

He wipes his forehead with the back of his hand. 'God, it's not every day we discover a dead man in a guest house!'

My shoulders droop with compassion at his predicament and for what's happened to poor Lloyd. I shrug. 'Well at least I used to write crime novels…'

He smiles for the first time which lights up his face into a much pleasanter image. 'And now you look after your dog instead?'

I remember that he hasn't actually introduced himself and I'm determined he isn't going to have the last word between us. I ask, 'And you are?'

'I'm John Jackson, Detective Inspector.'

The DS calls out, 'Sir, the Coroner has been notified and is on route to take charge of Lloyd being taken away.'

I nod, and head off back down the corridor.

Chapter Nine

When I reach the breakfast room, I can tell by the conversation between the two couples and Shirley that she's told them Lloyd has been stabbed. Understandably, there's an atmosphere of apprehension between everyone. They all look up when I sit with Shirley and decide to update them. I know the drill and procedures from writing my crime novels, which is a few years ago now, but it can't have changed that much.

I call out, 'So, the Inspector wants everyone to remain here in the guest house until he's had time to interview us all.'

Luba is tracing a pattern on the tea-towel with her finger and looks up at me.

She stutters, 'A...an interview?'

I smile hoping to reassure her. 'Yes, it's just a few questions to see if anyone saw Lloyd last night, and what time everyone retired to bed, and if you heard any noises during the night,' I say. 'Think of it as another lockdown in here until further notice.'

Luba begins to pick the skin on her thumb nail, and I see Shirley place her good hand over Luba's in a comforting gesture. 'It'll be fine – you weren't even here last night, so you're okay.'

Lily huffs. 'Well, we all know lockdown drill after the pandemic we've been through. I hated not being able to go out and Ken was just about demented being caged inside.'

I look up to see the DS hovering in the doorway.

Shirley smiles at her. 'Come in, would you all like a tray of coffee or tea?'

The DS smiles back. 'Thanks, but I think we're all okay,' she says. 'I just wanted to ask everyone to stay either in their rooms or in here until we've had time to talk to you all.'

Mark's eyebrows furrow together, and he asks, 'And how long is this going to take?'

'It'll take as long as it does until the Inspector has the information he needs,' she answers curtly. Obviously, the DS doesn't like being quizzed about the information she's given and isn't going to put up with backchat.

His face reddens now. 'Look, this is ridiculous!' he states. 'I can tell you now that neither me nor my wife saw anything of this man yesterday and we can't stay inside past 5pm. We have tickets for the Customs House which I'm not prepared to miss!'

'All the same, theatre or not, you will remain here until we say otherwise,' she snaps, and begins tapping on her iPad once more.

He folds his arms across his chest and huffs. 'This is an absolute disgrace, and if I miss this play, you'll be paying for the tickets which weren't cheap!'

The DS stomps back out of the room. If Mark had said this to the Inspector, he would have got a mouthful back from him, of this I'm sure.

With her good hand, Shirley pours coffee and I nod, hoping the hit of caffeine will give me a much needed boost. I notice she is wearing her wedding and pearl engagement rings on the fourth finger of her good hand. I reckon she had to remove these after the stroke and sigh in empathy.

Sipping my coffee, I look at Luba with her eyes downcast and wonder why, out of us all, she seems the most anxious. Does she know Lloyd and is he an old friend? Or has she made friends with him since he arrived in the guest house? I suppose it could be an entirely different reason if she doesn't know him. She seemed to take fright at the word, "interview." I wonder if her paperwork was in order to work here when she came from Poland? I shrug, but there again, Shirley told me Luba had been here for five years so that doesn't ring true. Maybe something horrible happened to her in Poland and she has a natural fear of the police in her own country.

Alfie dives under the table for a drink out of his bowl, and I give him a couple of treats while I munch into a custard cream biscuit. Mark seems the only guest who is annoyed at being locked-down. Is this suspicious? Does he know Lloyd and his reaction is to make himself as scarce as possible. I sigh, my imagination is running riot again as it used to when I wrote mysteries. Mark is probably just irritated because he's paid a lot of money for his tickets at the Customs House.

And although Ken had commented before about talking to the police, this time he didn't retaliate to the DS. He and Lily seem to have accepted the lockdown as something which has happened and there's nothing to be done about it, which I think older people do.

I can hear the Inspector's voice in the corridor again and smile. I think of his comical nickname, JJ, and his off-putting manner. If I'd been writing about him, I would say he had a charismatic bypass and definitely has no pleasant bedside manner. He reminds me of the actor, Ben Miller who starred in the TV drama series Professor T.

Allan and I had loved every episode. Me, because it wasn't the ordinary bad cop/good cop storyline, and Allan because it was set in Cambridge and he loved seeing familiar scenery, especially King's College. I liked the way the professor sat up on the roof top alone, thinking through his case and staring out across the city skyline with his quirky OCD mannerisms. So far, JJ doesn't seem to have these, but his personality does remind me of the Professor.

Spookily, my mobile tinkles with a message and Allan's name is on the screen. I delete it straight away. Any other time, I would be thinking about how he was feeling and worrying about him. But now I'm not. At the moment, I feel so hurt at what he did, I don't care about his feelings. Which, as my mam would have told me, will pass, but I don't want him in my mind at all. I seethe, and slot him back up onto that worry tree.

My mobile lights up with a call and I see Olivia's name. I can't, and don't want to ignore this call, and answer. My daughter is in tears because I've left her dad and she is worried.

'Look, I'm at the coast having some peace and quiet for a few days, but I'm absolutely fine,' I say.

She whimpers, 'Okay, Mam, but you'll ring me if you need me?'

'Of course I will, darling, and Penny is on her way up to join me.'

I can tell this has settled her mind, but I haven't mentioned South Shields because I know they'll be in the car scouring hotels in the town looking for me. And I still want some more time away from Allan - well, as much peace and quiet as one can get in the middle of a murder scene.

Although I haven't exactly lied, my cheeks flush. However, the coast could be Tynemouth, Whitley Bay or any of the Northumberland beaches, so I know they won't find me. I've managed to reassure and calm her down and I sigh with relief. I can't bear to think of my daughter being upset and know Olivia's next phone call will be to her dad to tell him the update.

Finishing my coffee, I watch Shirley and Luba disappear into the kitchen area where I see a shelf full of cookery books. I smile at my early memories of looking at books on shelves.

Writing was something I'd done since leaving university whilst working in a bookstore which was long before I had become a published author. My obsession had been with crime novels mainly by Agatha Christie, and how she included children's rhymes - five little pigs, and four and twenty blackbirds - into her stories. I'd copied this theme into my short stories, the first being about a weird doll in a toy hospital alongside a strange clowns face, which are scary to small children. All the while, I'd held tight onto my dream of becoming an author.

In fact, thinking back now, Waterstone's was where I met Allan. He'd literally charmed the pants off me. Within two weeks we were living together in a crummy little flat in Jesmond, which thirty-four years ago, was still seen as shocking.

However, we'd thought we were New Wave and fearless. My father was from Amble, a small mining village, and was disgusted with me and Allan because we weren't married. I smile remembering the conversation six months later when I'd asked him, 'If we get married, would you pay for a church wedding with all the trimmings?'

Gruffly, he'd stated, 'I'd pay for bloody Durham Cathedral if only you'd get a ring on your finger!'

So, we married in Gosforth Parish Church. I had pushed for the wedding more than Allan because I'd missed a period and knew Olivia was inside, although I didn't tell him straight away.

A few months before the wedding, he noticed the small mound in my belly, and said, 'It's just as well we're getting married because I want our child to have my name.'

Looking back now, I remember all the conversations we'd had and how it was the hip thing to say, we didn't need a piece of paper to vow our love for each other and stay together forever.

Allan had told me about his first marriage which only lasted two months and how his ex-wife had run off with another man. He'd known it had been a mistake on the day of the wedding at the Registry Office. Afterwards, he moved up North to get away from the small village near Cambridge and the humiliating scandal and gossips. His parents had been mortified.

Now, I tut loudly, no wonder he hadn't been keen on marriage because he hadn't divorced his first wife. God, I rage, at myself, how naïve and gullible I'd been to believe his every word.

Alfie whines, which brings me back to the here and now, and I know we both need to visit the toilet. We head to our room where I can see they are getting ready to take Lloyd to the mortuary. Shirley had seen the town's undertaker van parked further up the road earlier. However, the tape is still across his room with the door firmly shut.

The Inspector spins around at the front door where he is talking to another man and I wonder if he is the coroner alongside Ted.

'Can I take Alfie out on the roadside for a toilet break?'

I refrain from using the word "whoopsie" and grin. The Inspector nods and Ted leans down to ruffle Alfie's head as we pass by, which I appreciate. I hear their conversation about the Spaniel breed of dog which makes me smile. As I head out of the door, I think it's true, as is often said, we are a nation of dog lovers.

Chapter Ten

After Alfie has relieved himself, I hop back up the steps and into my room. I stand in the bathroom washing my hands and stare into the mirror. Jeez, what a morning, I think. So much for a quiet few days to take stock of my situation at home. The back of my neck is hot and sticky, so I pull up my curls and secure them with a big clasp on top of my head. A few whisps escape, but it feels cooler. I look further into the mirror and apply lip gloss and then smile.

I open the window as the sun is out already and the room is stuffy. I'd planned to take Alfie down to the beach for a run around, but now of course this will have to wait. I'd seen my poor dog look longingly at the park gates when he'd been doing a whoopsie earlier and bend down to him. 'You'll have to wait, Alfie,' I whisper.

Taking a deep breath, I step back outside into the hall where the Inspector is hovering. I stand by the hall table remembering the guest book.

I say, 'I'm sure you'll have noticed but all the guests have to sign in here when they arrive.' I point to the large diary opened at yesterdays page.

'Really?' he mutters. 'No, I hadn't actually.'

Still wearing his blue gloves, he flicks the pages back, obviously scouring the details for Lloyd's entry.

I continue, 'When I arrived, Shirley asked for my name and mobile number, so maybe Lloyd did the same and left his?'

'It's here,' he says. 'Three days ago but just his name – there's no mobile number?'

I smile. 'Ah well, Shirley might remember what he said about his mobile?'

He nods. 'Good shout,' he says. 'I'll get the DS to talk to her straightaway.'

His tone is much nicer now. There's no more shouting and sarcasm when he bends forwards and pats Alfie on the head. My loyal dog stands still with his paws set rigid, looking up at me, and I can tell he's still on guard and not sure about this man.

I smile down at Alfie and whisper, 'It's okay, Boy, he's one of the good guys.'

The Inspector beams at us. 'Look, I'm sorry but I think we got off on the wrong foot earlier which was all my fault and well, I'd like your help.'

I'm surprised at this apology and for a few moments it takes my breath away. However, I'm keen to take hold of the olive branch and smile. 'Of course, anything I can do to help, just shout up.'

Alfie obviously knows now that relations between us are better and he creeps closer to the Inspector for more petting.

'So, it's Faye, isn't it?'

I smile and nod. 'Yes, Inspector.'

'Please, call me John,' he says. 'Now, we have a time of death from SOCO, who are getting ready to leave. They reckon he met his fate probably between midnight and 2 a.m. this morning. And, they tell me the initial cause of death was by a knife plunged straight through Lloyd's heart. He wouldn't have stood a chance, but instant death will be confirmed at autopsy.'

I gasp, and put my hand over my mouth. 'Oooh, the poor man!' I say, in a quieter voice. 'But, I suppose at least he didn't suffer.'

John sneezes loudly, pulls out a large cotton handkerchief from his jacket pocket and blows his nose hard. 'Sorry, it's hay fever – I hate this summer heat!'

I pat his arm. 'Oh, my father used to suffer terribly with that.'

John looks down at my hand on his arm and a softness floods his eyes. Was that too much, I ask myself? I know we are getting along better and he's being nicer now, but maybe he doesn't like the human touch. I withdraw my hand immediately, and I swear I see a look of disappointment in his expression. Move on, I think and change the subject. My curiosity is piqued, wondering what he's going to ask of me. 'So, how can I help?'

'Well, I'm not sure if you noticed it when you found Lloyd this morning, but there was a definite smell of heavy perfume in his room?'

My mind whirls. 'Oh, yes, I did. In fact, at first I thought it was from the cleaning lady Luba, who was standing next to me, but later discovered she wasn't wearing perfume, and I wasn't either. But it did seem cloying as though it was hanging around in the air.'

He nods. 'Hmm, interesting, it was the first thing I smelt when I entered the room.'

Drawing my eyebrows together, I ask, 'But if it's a female perfume, which I think it was, would a woman have the strength to drive that knife deep into his chest?'

'I wouldn't have thought so,' he says. 'But maybe if it was someone like my DS, who is very strong and works out in the gym every night, then maybe.'

I smile, and decide however much he was shouting at her earlier, it's obvious he holds her in high regard.

'So, that counts me out. And poor Luba who works around the clock, wouldn't have time for the gym. Old Lilly and Shirley wouldn't have this strength, but I don't know anything about Brigit as yet.'

He shrugs. 'Yeah, so I'm wondering if your dog could sniff out anything in the room because Ted reckons that Spaniels have a natural instinct.'

I grin and my chest swells with pride that we've been asked to take part in his investigation. 'Yes, they do. When I first got him, I learnt that Spaniels are trained to find specific scents quicker than humans because they have a sniffing, slowish walk which is often called a "sniffari".'

John repeats the word "sniffari" and grins. 'Sounds good to me – so could he try?'

I nod and John opens Lloyd's room door. Wearing his blue gloves, he holds up the police tape for me and Alfi to duck under.

I let Alfie off his lead and he looks at me as if to say "really?"

I nod and whisper, 'Go for it!'

And off he goes padding around the room with his big nose down on the cream carpet.

John murmurs, 'Of course SOCO have been in here since and the air could be mixed with chemicals they have used and will disguise the cloying perfume, but it's worth a shot.'

I nod. 'It certainly is and you never know, Alfie might sniff something out, although he's often more interested in chicken treats.'

We both smile at each other, and I know the icy atmosphere is long gone. It has been replaced with a relaxed understanding and a mutual effort to find clues as to what's happened.

He brings out his little notebook and scribbles something down. 'I've written down the word "sniffari". It'll impress everyone when I get back to the office.'

'It will that,' I say. 'I see you don't have an iPad like your DS?'

He gives a little shudder. 'Nope, I'm blessed with a great memory but I must admit, at my desk, I do love my spreadsheets and a critical path to keep me on track throughout the cases.'

I remember my days of writing and how I had character cards of murder victim, killers and witnesses pinned to my desk. However, I always wrote from the seat of my pants and often didn't know where my story would eventually end up.

I take a sideways glance at John, and know an outcome - good or bad - on his spreadsheet would suit him well. I can tell this man needs to record a satisfactory ending to his cases and won't accept defeat in closing his spreadsheet without an arrest. For some reason, now I've got to talk with him, I'm filled with confidence. And perhaps he instils this in all his team, which is deserving of the DS's comment about him being the best in CID.

'You see, I look for traces that people leave behind,' he says, and lowers his head down to whisper in my ear. 'And don't tell anyone but I have a parrot at home who repeats all my sentences!'

I giggle, and Alfie lifts up his head as if to say "I'm done". We all duck back down under the tape again and John wanders off to talk with Ted, while I turn towards the breakfast room.

As we head along the corridor, Mark and Brigit walk towards me. I'm surprised to hear Brigit speak as it's usually Mark who is forthcoming.

She says, 'We're are going back up to our room to watch TV to fill in the time until the interviews begin, but I've told Shirley where to find us.'

She has a quiet, mouse-like manner and lilt to her voice, as if she doesn't use it much. I nod and, leaving Alfie off his lead we head back into the breakfast room.

Chapter Eleven

When we enter the room there is only Lily and Ken sitting alone. Apparently, Luba and Shirley are downstairs in her private rooms.

I smile at them in greeting. 'I've just seen Mark and Brigit going upstairs to watch TV.'

Lily chortles. 'Oh yeah, they're probably scrolling through all the channels looking for episodes of the soaps where he had a minor walk-on acting part twenty years ago!'

'Really? I didn't know that?'

With his head down and still wearing the sun glasses, Ken mutters, 'He's nought but an old has been!'

As I'm puzzling over this comment, Alfie leaves me and races back out into the corridor and along to the door with, PRIVATE on the name plate. I hurry after him and can tell by the way he's scratching at the white door, he is desperate to go downstairs into Shirley's quarters. This makes me wonder, has he smelt something?

Taking hold of the collar around his neck, I try to keep him back from scratching, but hear Shirley call upstairs to us. 'It's okay,' she says. 'Let him come down.'

I open the door and Alfie automatically races down the stairs. I hurry after him, apologising when I see Shirley sitting in an old fireside chair in a small lounge area. Luba has a duster in her hand and is running it along the long windowsill. There's an old sideboard in the corner with an equally old electric fire and the TV set on a stand. The walls are covered with framed photographs making it feel cosy, with a slight smell of cigarette smoke hanging in the air.

They turn to greet him, but Alfie ignores both of them as I quickly explain about the Inspector and the perfume smell in Lloyd's room. His big nose is on her green carpet and he's sniffing on a track following something along to the opposite door.

'What's through there?' I ask Shirley.

'Oh, it's just my small kitchenette.'

I nod. Pulling my sleeve down over my hand, I open the door and Alfie flies through it and into a smaller galley-shaped room. I hurry after him as he is standing at an old brown door. And then he starts to bark loudly and scratch again at the bottom of the door. Immediately, I know he's found something. There's a small window above the little sink which looks out into a garden area mainly flagged with paving stones but full of planters and flowers.

I call through to Shirley, 'Does this door lead out into a back lane of some kind?'

Shirley nods. 'Yes, the lock on the gate broke a few years ago but we just keep it on the latch for the bin men coming.'

I shout at Luba, 'Go and get the inspector, please and don't touch another thing!'

Luba rushes out of the room and I stand next to Alfie, talking to him all the while. My mouth dries and my heart begins to race, but it's not the worrying palpitations, it's a good excited feeling. Alfie and I are doing something worthwhile, we are on the trail to discover and help in the case. Hopefully, we can find out, how and what happened to Lloyd. I smile, it feels like I'm living through one of my storylines but in real life.

Shirley rubs her good hand along the back of her neck. 'Oh dear, so does this mean they got in through the back garden and door?'

I snap back to what she is saying and know everyone isn't feeling as excited as we are. This is causing upset and fear to the old woman. I can see she is shivering and I wrap my arm along her shoulders. 'It might do, but we'll wait until the Inspector comes down.'

Shirley has had an awful jolt. It would be upsetting enough if it was a simple burglary but the shock of Lloyd being killed in one of her rooms as a guest is even worse. I can tell by meeting her that she feels responsible for her guests and their safety.

Hoping to lighten the atmosphere a little and reassure her, I whisper, 'Or perhaps Alfie is just desperate for a whoopsie.'

She smiles at last. 'He's such a lovely little dog – we've all taken kindly to him in just one day.'

My heart lifts at her praise while I hear the tapping of John's shiny shoes on the corridor upstairs and I know he is running to join us. John and Luba sound like a herd of elephants charging down the stairs and running into the small lounge.

I lead him through into the kitchenette and cry, 'I…I could be wrong but I think Alfie has found something to do with this door. He's very excited and never usually barks like this!'

He whips out his mobile and shouts out, 'Ted! Don't leave, we might have found something around at the back door!'

John clicks off his mobile and breathes out a sigh of relief. 'I've just caught him pulling away in the van.'

I gabble, 'M...maybe someone got in through the back lane and not from the front street as we all previously thought?'

He slaps his forehead. 'I know! I've slipped up here right enough. Just because we all came through the front door to the guest house, I never thought about the back!'

So, I reckon, he is human after all and watch his neck flush. Admitting to one's mistakes isn't easy and sometimes people look for excuses or other reasons rather than blame themselves. But John has the good grace to acknowledge his mistake.

Alfie is barking wildly now and we hear the van pull up in the back lane.

Shirley asks, 'Shall I get the key?'

No,' John says. 'Leave it to them, please.'

Out of the small window, I see the young lad from SOCO race through the old rickety brown gate into the garden area and begin to start dusting with a brush.

Ted arrives down the stairs, huffing and puffing with more kit in a bag. He approaches the inside of the door, and shoos us all into Shirley's lounge.

John, myself, Luba, Alfie and Shirley all look at each other in the small room. I stand with my hands behind my back and cross my fingers. I stare at Luba's chunky earrings in the shape of an ingot and decide they look heavy enough to pull at one's earlobes.

There's a clock on the mantle ticking loudly in the silence and I take in a deep breath. I look at John and see his Adam's apple wobble. He must be swallowing hard, I think and obviously he is as anxious as we all are. I cuddle Alfie into my side and his bark descends to a gruff groan now.

John turns to Shirley and asks, 'So, I noticed on your guest book in the hall when Lloyd checked-in that he didn't leave a mobile number as the others have done?'

Shirley nods. 'That's right, he told me he had lost his mobile down on the seafront.'

John nods in understanding.

And then suddenly the young lad outside shouts, 'I've got a print!'

I clap my hands together loudly. John grins and, with a gleam in his eyes, he bends down to fuss over Alfie. 'Good boy!' he says, ruffling his ears.

I feel ten feet tall and thrust out my chest. 'Who's my clever, Alfie, then,' I almost squeal.

Alfie looks up at me, puts his head onto one side, and has almost a nonchalant look on his face, as if to say "well you only had to ask".

Ted puts his head around the door. 'Has anyone been out of this back door this morning?'

I look to Shirley and she shakes her head. 'Nooo, not with what's happened – we've both been upstairs all morning.'

Ted smiles. 'That's good, now all of you need to get out of here, please. Go upstairs until we've done a proper assessment.'

John opens his mouth to retort, but Ted raises his eyebrow. 'If you want your documented evidence, Inspector, then I suggest you do as I say!'

Shirley eases up out of her chair. I clip the lead back onto Alfie's collar, and Luba walks slowly to the staircase. We all follow her sedately up the stairs and along the corridor into the breakfast room once again.

The Inspector turns to Shirley and smiles. 'We might as well take your statement first, Mrs Jones,' he says, and I hear her sigh.

Chapter Twelve

The DS appears in the breakfast room and asks everyone, except Shirly, to go to their rooms for fifteen minutes while they interview her. We all plod out onto the corridor and Allfie runs along to sit outside our room. I'm amazed that, within just one day and night, he has his bearings in the guest house and knows exactly where our room is situated.

Without touching the open guest book on the table, I glance at the open pages while putting the key in the lock. Once inside, Alfie promptly hops into his make shift basket-bed. Perhaps he's tired after his successful "sniffari" I muse, and make myself a mug of coffee from the tray.

Sitting up on the bed with the cushions behind me, I think about the layout of the guest house, knowing John will have the plan of the rooms on his spreadsheet. The guest book is set out in room numbers, so I've found out what rooms we are all staying in.

In the side of my case, is a block of post-it notes and I write everyone's names on a separate one. I arrange them in order of position in the guest house and their room numbers.

I know Shirley lives in the basement flat with a secluded garden outside and I add Luba to her post-it. I write, Shirley may have known Lloyd in the past but her memory is shot after the stroke. Luba seems to have a fear of the police.

Lloyd was in room one with a single bed. I write, He is the victim but where has he come from?

Me and Alfie are in room two, a double room which is also on the ground floor in front of the breakfast room.

I write, Of course, I've never seen Lloyd before in my life, nor any of the other guests.

Ken and Lilly, are on the first floor in room three, a twin room above mine. I write, Don't know anything about this couple other than they are Scottish and a little bizarre. Need to find out more.

Across from theirs is room four, a double room where Brigit and Mark are staying, and above Lloyd's single room. I write, Don't know much about this couple other than he's a has been actor and she's mouse-like. Need to find out more.

Plus there is room five up in the attic, which is empty now, but where Penny will stay when she gets here. I write, Penny hasn't arrived so she can't know anything about Lloyd.

I scramble up from the bed and stick the post-it notes in order of position on the inside of the wardrobe door.

I've already thought long and hard about last night, but after crawling under the white soft duvet, I'd heard nothing whatsoever. I had been in a deep sleep so didn't hear any noises of doors opening and closing or raised voices. And if Alfie had woken up, I know I would have too. I seem to have the same inbuilt alarm which I had when Olivia was a baby and asleep in her cot.

With the layout of rooms, I reckon if anyone was going to hear anything it would be Mark and Brigit who are above Lloyd's room. Of course, this is the first thing John will ask everyone in their interviews, but I would like to know too.

When I hear the DS and John back out in the corridor, and see the men from the funeral parlour coming up the front steps, I sigh knowing they must be taking poor

Lloyd away now. After a few minutes, Alfie jumps up out of the basket and looks imploringly at me as if to ask for a walk.

'We can't as yet, Alfie, but the minute we are released we'll head outside,' I promise him and he whines.

When all is quiet once more, I open the room door and poke my head out to make sure nobody is about. I listen for my neighbours on the stairs or the landing above and hear nothing – there is utter silence. The corridor is empty and I figure because it's well over fifteen minutes, we can head back along to the breakfast room.

Ken and Lily are there sitting at their usual table and Luba is wiping over the corner table where Mark and Brigit had sat earlier.

Luba tells me, 'Shirley is downstairs because everyone has gone now, but Mark and Brigit are being interviewed by the police in their room.'

I nod and plonk myself down at the table for two where we'd sat for breakfast. I think this seems a long time ago now. Being restricted in my movements is an isolated situation had never entered my head before the misery of the pandemic. I wonder if everyone is thinking the same and if they dislike being behind locked doors as much as I do?

During the pandemic restrictions, we all had to find new activities to entertain ourselves inside our homes behind locked doors. Some people did podcasts, used a PlayStation and gambled online, in fact, the internet came into it's own, especially for children's school work.

Older pursuits like knitting, reading, baking and craft works were also popular. And fortunately, we have a big garden which Allan and I walked around like a race track trying to keep our limbs moving. I'd been terrified one of the family would catch Covid and I admitted to Allan one night how scared I was.

He'd grasped my hands and agreed. 'Me too, and it's because we don't know what is going to happen,' he'd said. 'I mean, what if no cure is found and we all perish?'

At first, I'd been glad he was as scared as I was, but then his words had spun around in my mind and I never slept for two full nights. I felt as though it was all spiralling out of control, especially when I saw doctors on TV not knowing how to treat patients and make them better.

In my novels, even amidst murders, weird characters and deathly plots there is always a level of control. However, as the Covid daily death totals soared and the doctors looked helpless fighting against the spread of the virus, I'd been scared silly. And when Boris Johnson caught Covid, it proved more than anything that no one was safe and anybody could end up in hospital fighting for their lives.

It wasn't until our wonderful scientists in Oxford developed the first vaccine that my shoulders dropped a few inches and I could see light at the end of the tunnel, although there were still very dark shadows. Thankfully, none of us contracted Covid in the early days, and I know we had been the lucky people, where many hadn't and suffered dreadfully.

I look at the other guests now and wonder if they are thinking about Lloyd? Are they too scared to say? I know there's always a certain amount of attraction to the macabre and Lloyd's death had certainly been that. In worst case scenarios the common thought is often "Oh, God, I'm glad that didn't happen to me", but all the same people are fascinated by the event.

I'm looking for sinister traits amongst everyone here as John will be doing, and my train of thought conjures up whispered conversations between us guests in the corridor or on the stairs. I sigh. I'm letting my imagination run riot, and know I should resist making up stories about this group of people. At the end of the day, they are all probably as innocent as me and Alfie.

Luba's mobile is bleeping constantly in the pocket of her tabard. She pulls it out and looks at the screen.

She breathes out loudly. 'Social media is going crazy with posts on Instagram and X about the guest house!'

I meander over to her, and she shows me her screen. #murderinguesthouse #manisdead #SouthShields #police

I sigh, and shrug my shoulders. I don't do much on Facebook or X nowadays since I've retired. When I wrote everyday, I was fairly active promoting my books but now I've handed all of that over to my agent. I'd far rather talk to everyone which I decide to do now.

There's a jigsaw spread out on the table where Lilly is sitting filling in pieces. I wander over to them and Alfie follows. He crawls under their table and promptly falls asleep lying over Lily's open toed brown sandals. She is wearing pink ankle socks, which don't really suit her white pleated skirt, but the outfit makes me smile. Anyone can see they're not affluent and this couple have never been jetsetters to Spain or Greece for their holidays. An annual beach holiday to South Shields, is probably all they've ever been able to afford.

'Sorry, just move Alfie if he's bothering you,' I say. 'He needs a good walk but until this is all sorted, he'll just have to wait.'

Lily smiles. 'Nah, it's lovely to have him because I miss my little pooch when we are away. My neighbour loves him though and she's looking after him.'

'It's nice to have good neighbours, isn't it?'

She smiles, clutching her woven orange bag with white pearly handles further onto her knee. There appears to be copious amounts of crochet wool inside, although since we met this morning, I've never seen her work anything with it. Lily seems too busy nosing at everyone coming and going in the breakfast room. She has a big necklace around her thin neckline which is made of green plastic discs matching her blouse. She fiddles with one of the discs.

'That's a jolly-looking necklace,' I say.

She preens herself. 'Thanks, I got it in a charity shop for a fiver.'

I notice the picture on the jigsaw box is of Marsden Rock and, as I collect blue sky pieces to fill into the jigsaw, I say, 'Now that's somewhere I'd like to visit while we are here.'

She smiles, 'Well, Ken will tell you all about it because he spends at least two days there every year when we come down.'

I look at his small weasel like face. Ken is wearing an old grey rain coat with the belt tied tightly around his waist, even though it's warm and stuffy in the breakfast room. He's very tall and skinny and has a brown scruffy rucksack hanging over the side of his chair. I can't see fully what is inside but it seems to be a collection of different sized notebooks. He seemed lost in concentration but with Lily's voice, and at the sound of his name, he looks up from a notebook he's reading.

'Yes, it's a marvellous place to see. It's a good twenty minute walk or you can take a bus along the seafront,' he says. 'And when you reach the tall tower of the restaurant, just go down in the lift and walk out through the patio doors. The whole of the beach and three rocks are right in front of you.'

I smile. 'Hey, thanks, Ken, and is the restaurant dog-friendly?'

He nods, and I watch him pull out a short pencil - the type you get in Ikea - and begin to scribble in the notebook, stopping every now and then to lick at the end. I wonder what he's writing? Is he making comments about what's happened to Lloyd and his observations about us all in the guest house? I shake the ridiculous notions from my mind, knowing he could be a bird watcher or train spotter - not that we are surrounded by birds and trains in here, I think but smile at him.

As many elderly couples do, she begins to talk about him as if he wasn't here. 'Ken hates being locked inside and was a nightmare to be around during the pandemic.'

I nod. 'We were the same and especially as we weren't allowed to travel. I craved escape to the places we loved; big skies, the beaches and desolate countryside or the Yorkshire Moors,' I say. 'Although, on a monthly basis before the pandemic, we rarely went there.'

Lilly smiles. 'Same as us,' she says, and sneers at her husband. 'I wish he'd take those dark sunglasses off inside, they make him look creepy, although…' she ponders. 'He does have an eye condition and they're recommended by the optician.'

I fit three pieces of the blue sky into the jigsaw. 'Ah, I did wonder,' I say. 'But if they help his eyes then maybe it's worth wearing the glasses?'

'I know,' she says, and frowns. 'But he stares relentlessly at people and I can tell it unnerves them. I'm sick of telling him to stop doing it because it's not nice to unsettle people.'

I shrug but don't want to get involved in their bickering, so I don't comment. Although I must admit, when I first saw him wearing the glasses, it felt a little strange.

Lily continues, 'I mean, there's a difference between staring and observing, isn't there? And to complete his idiotic image, he has a van at home filled with heirlooms because he reckons as pensioners we should try to get things cheaper and then sell them on, but he never does this. So our house is just full of junk!'

Lily slots in two pieces of the seagull flying above the rock in the jigsaw and smiles in satisfaction.

'And how long have you been married,' I ask, looking for more sky pieces.

'Nearly fifty years,' she muses. 'And although I love him dearly, I can't bear him snoring in my ear all night, so we've got a twin bedded room and I wear ear plugs. We get the same room every year when we come down. Shirley is such a poppet.'

This information proves to me that Lily wouldn't have heard anything last night from Lloyd's room if she was wearing ear plugs. I cross her off my list of suspects probably as John will do when he interviews them.

I see Lily shiver. 'Are you cold?'

She shakes her head and rubs both her arms. 'No, but there's an atmosphere in this guest house. I felt it even before that man was killed, and I'm wondering if it's haunted?'

I lick my top lip, and raise my eyebrow. Lilly clasps my hand in her old wrinkly-skinned hand, and says, 'Look, don't worry about the dead because they won't do you any harm, it's the buggers walking around you need to watch out for!'

Alfie stirs under the table. Knowing he's as restless as I am being couped up, I fish out a little chicken treat from my pocket and give it to him.

She asks, 'Are you interested in the spirit world?'

I shake my head and ruffle Alfie's head for comfort. 'Not really,' I say warily.

'Well, to take part you have to be open minded and interested in the spirits which I am,' she says. 'At home I've got a white lace cap to welcome them into our house. I did have a tape with whale music and an incense stick but I had to bin it because it made one of my friends feel seasick.'

I want to giggle but can tell she's serious so I stifle it down.

'I often do seances at home to see if there's anybody around us,' she says. 'So, Faye, shall I see if the poor man's soul is still floating around the guest house looking for a way out, like we all are?'

Ken grumbles. 'If you're going to start this crap, I'm going upstairs to read.'

He scrapes back his chair and stands up. I decide this isn't something I want to get involved with either, and make my excuses to go and find Shirley.

Chapter Thirteen
Lily Campbell

Lily had seen the look of scepticism on Faye's face and in her manner while she'd explained the spirit world. As well as Ken, they both thought she was potty to believe in the spirits but she knew how important they were in finding the truth.

Her oldest daughter had said last year, 'Mum, I think you've got that Alzheimer's Disease – you're going dotty in your old age!'

She'd taken a deep breath and retorted, 'Alzheimer's is memory loss, not madness! And, I'm certainly not mad.'

'You're like an old witch sitting there with a white cap on,' she'd said. 'You need to be careful or they'll burn you at a stake!'

Not wanting to fall out with her daughter, she'd swallowed down her resentment and annoyance, loosened her shoulders and tried to make light of the comments. 'No, I'd need a wart on my chin and pointy hat before they do that.' And they'd both laughed.

People, especially her family, think when you get old that you haven't anything to say anymore, and what you do say is meaningless. Lily agreed with the Salvation Army TV adverts who said that old people became invisible. She gritted her back teeth and seethed, but that wasn't going to happen to her. She cursed under her breath, people would listen to what she had to say, even if it was through the spirit world.

The breakfast room was deadly quiet now, and she filled with melancholy to be back home with all the family around. This was unusual because she always loved her summer holidays away from the bedlam in their small bungalow. With three daughters and sons-in-law, and nine grandchildren between them, there weren't many days when it was just herself and Ken at home.

'We like to keep ourselves to ourselves,' she often told people in the small estate where they lived on the outskirts of Glasgow. However, her favourite place was in her big chair in front of the bay window where she could watch all the comings and goings from the other bungalows. Ken often said, 'You blame me for staring at people, but you do exactly the same from that window!'

But Lily never thought she was spying on her neighbours. She was simply taking an interest in her surroundings. So, she mused, what was the difference in doing this here with the people in the guest house? None, she comforted herself, and looked over her shoulder to make sure she was still alone. She knew when people were missing, it was often said that he or she wasn't here on earth, but here with you in spirit.

Lily nodded, and decided to try and get in touch with Lloyd. With closed eyes and her hands flat out on the table, palms uppermost to show the spirits she was open to talk, she went into a trance whispering, 'Is there anybody there?'

She waited a few minutes and, after nothing happened, Lily repeated the sentence with a louder voice. Still nothing happened, and was about to give up when she heard an old man's voice which said, 'It's Charles here.'

Her heart leapt and she smiled in pleasure. 'Hello,' she whispered. 'It's good to talk – who are you looking for?'

He didn't answer her question but said, 'I hadn't seen the car coming when I crossed the road. Before I knew what happened I'd heard the metal of the car hit my legs and down I went.'

Lily repeated her question but he simply recapped over the same incident and then left her.

She shrugged, this wasn't from the dead man in room one because she'd passed the time of day with Lloyd yesterday morning and he was a man in his thirties. So, who was this spirit called Charles? Maybe it was a relative of Shirley's who was trying to connect with her?

Lily shook her head, tutted, and left the spirits to themselves. She'd known there were lost souls in this guest house. She had felt them around her during their last visit, and more so this year when she'd walked through the front door with Ken dragging their suitcase.

She thought back to this morning and all the commotion when Lloyd had been found. And, especially what Ken had said, 'I'm going to tell the Inspector that I never stirred all night and didn't hear any noises.' And then he'd followed this with a warning to her, 'And don't you go contradicting me!'

She'd felt a cold sensation run up her back. Although Ken was much milder in temperament nowadays, he'd been very handy with his fists when they were younger. And the old fear of him had never really left her. Now, he was thin and frail in his seventies, but when she'd met him, he'd been a big menacing man working in the shipyards. It had been after their third daughter was born and he'd been made redundant, that he got involved with antiques and art works as a step up to something more lucrative, or, at least that's what he told everyone. This, of course, never happened and they were still as poor as they'd always been.

Lily sighed, and brought herself back to the here-and-now. She knew different about the statement Ken intended giving the police Inspector because she'd heard him get up in the night at least twice for the loo. He was waiting for an appointment about his enlarged prostate so this wasn't unusual for him.

She tutted, if he told the Inspector he'd not woken, it would be a down and out lie. Deep in thought, she raised her eyebrow, but why would he want to lie to them? Did he know Lloyd? And had Ken been involved with whatever had happened to the dead man? Doubt and suspicion filled her mind when it came to her husband. If Ken did know him - had he arranged to meet Lloyd down here in South Shields?

Years ago, Ken had been involved with some dodgy art dealers and Lily had questioned his financial arrangements with these underhand men from Glasgow. However, this didn't hold true because she knew Lloyd was definitely not from their area in Glasgow. Their broad Glaswegian accent wasn't something you could loose in a few years - it stayed with a person for a lifetime. And if this was true, and Ken did know Lloyd, she knew her husband would deny all knowledge of doing so.

She pushed aside the jigsaw puzzle on the table in an effort to get ready to be interviewed by the inspector. Rummaging in her bag, she pulled out old-fashioned white lace gloves and slotted her fingers into them. Not only did Lily want to look her best, but she was ready to do battle if needed.

Chapter Fourteen

When I leave Lily to her spirit world, and Ken hurries upstairs to their room, I hear loud sobbing and look along the corridor to see Luba holding Shirley's arm to escort her downstairs. My mind whirls trying to think if there's been more revelations.

I hurry along and ask, 'What's happened now?'

Luba answers, 'Oh, nothing more, it was just talking with the Inspector has upset her.'

Shirley beckons me with her head and I follow them both down the staircase with Alfie padding along behind us.

Luba comments, 'The Inspector is writing up his notes and then will question Lily and Ken in the breakfast room.

I look at Shirley's pale face and see her shoulders shake as tears spill from her eyes. She's obviously distressed. 'How about a nice cup of tea,' I offer.

Shirley staggers over to the sideboard and, with a trembling hand picks up a bottle of gin and pours a good measure into an empty glass. Topping it up with tonic from a small can on the tray, she says, 'I need something stronger – does anyone else want one?'

Luba shakes her head and I refuse.

Slumping into her chair, Shirley takes a large gulp and then fishes out a packet of cigarettes from the side pocket of her chair cover.

'If this offends anyone then so be it, ' she says.

Luba hurries over to the small window and opens it. I can tell Luba is used to Shirley doing this and I smile at her consideration. Shirley lights a cigarette with her trembling good hand and takes a long drag, blowing smoke towards the window.

Alfie ambles over to Shirley and lays his head on her knee. My heart melts at him and his empathy for the old lady which she obviously finds a comfort.

She ruffles his ears as she talks. 'A…apparently he'd got in through the back gate after tinkering with the old lock, which broke a few years ago and I always meant to get it fixed. We always leave it on the latch for the bin men to collect the rubbish,' she says. 'The Inspector said they don't need keys nowadays and can open locks with bits of wire. I…I can't show you because they were dusting for fingerprints and said not to go near until it's finished.'

I say quietly, 'I think they've gone now, Shirley, but just sit calmly for the rest of the day and try to relax.'

Shirley nods and stubs out her cigarette in a tall ashtray with a twirly top next to her chair. It's something from the 60s and, as I look around her lounge, I see many more pieces from that era. The old chintz covered sofa is lumpy and I plump up a cushion to fit over the worn spring.

She whimpers, 'To think he'd crept past my bedroom door before mounting the steps up into the front lobby and room one is really scary!'

I remind myself that although the house feels an intermediary place to us as guests, where people come and go to stay for a short while, this is her home. Therefore, she looks upon every room in the house as her own and not just her private quarters.

'A…and I never heard a thing!' She sobs quietly.

I try to soothe her. 'But they're very clever nowadays and can muffle sounds, Shirley.'

Luba interjects by saying, 'Faye is right, none of this is our fault.'

I look up at Luba and smile as she heads through to the kitchenette and switches on the kettle.

Shirley begins to ramble the thoughts in her mind. 'I've always felt safe here because it's home,' she says, looking around the room. 'But not now that peace has been shattered.'

I know after a burglary this is the most common feeling for people. A feeling of a stranger going through your personal things is very upsetting. And the situation of a dead body is even worse than a burglary.

'No, Faye, I'll never get over this and what's happened to one of my guests! But why him, and why here? I mean, what is everyone going to think of me – my reputation around here will be shattered!'

I shake my head slowly, knowing these questions are spinning around in my mind too and have been since I saw Lloyd in that chair. I swallow hard, determined to find out, but mumble, 'Aww, Shirley, you'll soon feel settled again.'

I don't have much confidence in my own words and worry this might be the end of the guest house for the old lady. In her seventies, this may well be too much to put behind her and move forwards, which would be an awful shame. Luba will also have this in the back of her mind. The insecurity of getting another job will weigh heavily, especially as she has her little boy to raise.

Shirley nods. 'The Inspector asked me if I knew anyone who would want to do us harm, but of course we said no, because there isn't anybody.'

I console her. 'They'll ask everyone this, Shirley, it's a standard question.'

She shakes her head. 'I've lived here all my life and we started this place in our twenties. Of course, it was different back then, but I've known all the other landlords for years. We always said if we look after our guests well they will come back again, and they do. I've quite a few families that return every year– they love my guest house. Some of the old landlords are still on Ocean Road but mainly they're younger people now with families making a honest living. We've always had a good community spirit in South Shields.'

I nod creating a mental image of these landlords and their properties - which is different to singular hotel chains. 'Well, Shirley, once everyone knows this incident with Lloyd is nothing to do with you and the guest house then your reputation won't be affected and I'm sure the Inspector will find the culprit.'

Shirley smiles. 'You're such a comfort to me, Faye.'

I pull my shoulders back determined not to let what's happened effect this lady anymore than necessary. How I'm going to do this with or without the Inspector, I don't know, but I'll give it my best shot. I ask, 'So, are you friendly with your neighbours on either side?'

'Yes, of course. The woman on the right hand side does childminding as well as running their guest house and Luba's son goes to her after school if she is still busy in here.'

Luba pops her head around the door with a milk carton in her hand. 'Yes, Rose is a very good woman,' she says. 'Do you want coffee?'

I smile and thank her.

Shirley is still rambling. 'If we are fully booked, we send holidaymakers to the other guest houses and vice versa. We've helped each other build up our businesses and there's never been any rivalry or competitiveness – we've always worked together,' she says. 'I've already had three of my friends further down the road ring to ask if I'm okay, but the Inspector has told us not to talk about it yet.'

She drains the gin from her glass and I see more colour in her face now. Her hand is steadier and her tears have dried. I'm getting a better idea of the area and Shirley's standing in the community. I ask, 'So, is there not much trouble around here?'

Shirley smiles now. 'Well, in the past we've had a little episode of petty thieving and a couple of drunken punch ups outside on Ocean Road, but nothing serious, well not like this!'

I nod and wonder what family she has. 'And, have you no family that could come and stay with you for a few days until things settle down a little?'

She shakes her head, 'No, we never had children,' she says, looking up at her wedding photograph on the wall. 'The doctor told us there was no reason why we couldn't, but it just never happened. I have a sister but she's down in Exeter and we're not that close.'

'Ah, that's a shame.'

Shirley smiles. 'But, I have Luba, who is like family to me now,' she says. 'And you, Faye, do you have you any children as well as this gorgeous little dog?'

I grin. 'Yes, as well as Alfie, I have a daughter, Olivia and two granddaughters who are twins.'

I begin to tell her about my family in Sunderland, carefully avoiding the topic which is my husband and the reason I'm here alone. Luba brings in two plates of sandwiches and crisps. She places the small plate on the coffee table and Alfie lifts his head to sniff at the food. Never one to miss out on any type of food, he pads over to my side and I pull him in close to me.

'I've made these to keep us going while we are locked-up,' she says, and turns to head for the stairs. 'I'll take the bigger plate upstairs for the police, and fill up the kettle in the breakfast room.'

I think about the difference the small word makes. Locked-up here has a totally different meaning to being locked-in, as if we were in a cell in a police station accused of wrongdoings. My stomach rumbles and I'm amazed to see the mantel clock at 1.30pm. Gosh, where has the morning gone, I think and no wonder I'm hungry again.

Shirley rubs her neck and thanks Luba. 'She's a little gem, and I know I've said this before, but I really don't know what I'd do without her!'

Luba returns with coffee and a treat for Alfie in a small bowl. I take it from her and see small cut pieces of cooked chicken. 'Aww, thank you, you're spoiling him and he'll expect this when we go home!'

We all laugh and Alfie demolishes the chicken in seconds, licking his big mouth as if to say "that was scrummy".

I take a sandwich and sip my coffee as do Luba and Shirley. It's cosy sitting here with Luba on the other corner of the sofa and Alfie between us. He puts his head down to snooze.

Luba says, 'And this has messed up my morning plans because I was going to clean out the attic room for your friend coming this afternoon.'

'Oh, don't worry about that. Penny can always bunk in with me if the room is not sorted. You've had more than enough to cope with today as it is,' I say. 'Do you always clean the rooms in the morning?'

'Yes,' she nods. 'Check out is by 10 a.m. and I get the rooms cleaned and made ready for the next guests even if nobody has booked into them. And then I wash the dishes and clean the breakfast room setting out the crockery for the next morning.'

'Well, it's a good job you didn't start upstairs first or poor Lloyd wouldn't have been found until much later.'

I remember how anxious the Polish woman had been when interviews were mentioned earlier, and decide to try and find out more about her. 'So, do you live near here, Luba?'

'Oh, yes, just three streets away in an upstairs flat. It's close to the school for my son, Borys,' she says. 'So, we are on hand, as you say here.'

I want to explain the word "handy" but bite my tongue. I'll not get anywhere by being pedantic with corrections and we all know what she means, so I smile. 'What a lovely name and how old is he?'

Her face floods with softness and her striking brown eyes gleam with pride. 'He's just five and is obsessed with aeroplanes.'

I grin. 'I would have loved a boy but we decided after Olivia was born that one child was enough.'

I cringe a little knowing that it had been Allan who didn't want another child and not me. So why do I use this as my stock answer to people as if it was a joint decision because it wasn't. Probably, I think, to complete his image of the perfect couple.

I'm wondering how I can get the conversation around to what else John had asked them without further upsetting Shirley, but Luba answers this for me in her next sentence.

'The Inspector asked us if anyone has been following or watching us suspiciously,' she says, and pats the back of Shirley's hand.

I can tell she is more relaxed about the questioning now that it is over. I lean forwards to her, knowing this answer could be important. 'Oh, and what did you tell him?'

'I told him no, there wasn't anyone interested in us because this is something I'm very careful about. My ex-husband wants Borys and me to go back to Poland to live, but I've refused. Borys loves his school and I know he'll have far more opportunities later in life here than in Poland.'

I nod in understanding and drink more of my coffee. And, there's the answer to my earlier suspicions. I'm glad there's a valid reason for her nervousness over questioning. As I was when Olivia was small, Luba only wants what is best for her boy and her motherly urge to protect him will always be paramount in her mind.

She continues, 'If I can't make the timing fit, I only trust one person to collect him from school which is Rose next door, but Shirley is very good and relaxed with timings.'

Shirley nods. 'He's a lovely little lad and I enjoy having him here – he's not a minute's bother.'

Luba drains the coffee from her mug. 'There's only one man I think is a bit weird - the old man with the dark sunglasses. As you say here, he's creepy, so I stay well clear of him!'

This is an understandable response because I felt the same at first. 'Me too, he's definitely not run of the mill and I've wondered what he writes in his notebooks? Do you know him well, Shirley?'

Shirley laughs. 'I've told her before and I'll tell you now, he's just an eccentric old man with strange mannerisms. They've been coming to me every summer holiday for quite a few years now and although he's perfectly harmless, he does seem to get stranger every time they come down. And, I think Lily is going a little potty too!'

We all smile. This is interesting and it's good to have another opinion about Ken and Lily from someone who knows the couple better than my two conversations with them.

I nod. 'And what about Mark and Brigit?'

'Ah, my guests in room four, well it's the first time they've stayed here and all I know is the tittle-tattle I've heard about him being an actor.'

Luba raises an eyebrow, 'What is this "tittle-tattle"?'

'Shirley means gossip,' I say, filling in for her.

Luba whispers, 'Well, apparently he's been in one soap opera on TV but that was over ten years ago, and now does adverts for washing up liquid which he thinks are beneath him and is hoping to get into a new play.'

I smile, but tiredness sweeps through me and I think Alfie has the right idea snoozing on the sofa. I decide to take a lie on my bed before it's my turn for interviewing by the police.

I stand up to leave and Alfie jerks awake. 'I reckon Mark is going to be furious if he misses the play at the Custom's House tonight,' I say, and head across the room towards the stairs.

Shirley eases up out of her chair and thanks me for the talk. As we head through the lounge she looks up at a photograph of a good looking old man and traces her finger along his jaw line. 'This was Charles, my husband who died five years ago in a road traffic accident,' she says. 'One minute he was here – the next minute he was gone.'

Chapter Fifteen

When I head into my room, I open the wardrobe door and, with my pen, I mark the suspect post-it note for Luba with a big X, it's not her!

I lie on the bed and, with my mind thinking through all I've learnt, I doze off to sleep. I'm woken from my snooze on the bed by loud knocking on the room door. Alfie barks and is up at the door with his tail wagging furiously. 'What the…' I grumble and slide off the bed. Opening the door, I'm enveloped in Penny Forsythe's arms.

'Ooooh, darling!' she wails dramatically. 'What on earth has happened?'

Untangling my body from her arms and my face from her long hair, I hold her at arms length. When we were young she'd had bright red hair but now it's a lighter shade as she tones it down with a blonde colour.

A lump of tears comes into the back of my throat at her familiar and warm embrace. I swallow hard while Alfie practically throws himself at her. She bends down to gather him up in her arms and plops herself down into the chair next to the wardrobe. With the blue throw around him, she cuddles Alfie into her chest like a babe-in-arms and he croons in appreciation and love for her.

'Be a sweetie and bring in my case, Faye,' she says, snuffling her face into his fur.

I look out into the corridor and see a huge - and I mean huge - red suitcase with another jazzy carpet bag balanced on top. And here we are again, I think. It's like being back in schooldays as she plays the celebrity glamour puss, and me, the sedate assistant.

We always called each other besties and she has remained my closest friend ever since.

Puffing, I drag the case into the corner of my room and close the door. 'Who let you in the front door?'

'A police woman - tall, blonde and full of herself!'

'That's the Detective Sergent,' I say. 'I feel a bit sorry for her really because she's overpowered by an Inspector who is more full of himself than she could ever hope to be.'

Penny grins, crosses her long legs clad in cream silky slacks and raises an eyebrow. 'Ooooh, tell me more,' she says.

Stripping off the brown flowery tailored jacket and flinging it onto my bed, I look at her perfectly matched outfit and make-up. Since our schooldays, my friend has always been very tall and skinny with extremely long legs and boy-oh-boy does she know how to make the most of these at every opportunity.

Penny left Newcastle after we finished college and moved to Middlesborough and, although I haven't seen her for a while, we talk at least twice a week and text each other practically every day. She's always been the closest thing I have to a sister and I love her dearly.

'I'll tell you later about Allan, but for now, you might have to bunk in here with me until the attic room is ready. The guest house is in a bit of an upheaval today.'

She nods and pushes her new big black glasses up onto her nose. She'd sent a photograph last week from the opticians and I think they're too big for her face but she loves them, so that's the main thing.

'Look, Faye, I can always pay for us to stay in a posh hotel nearby if you need rest and some pampering?'

I smile at this offer. Penny had married a lawyer two years after I'd married Allan and, although they had not been blessed with children, they'd bumbled along together until four years ago when she left him. The day after her divorce papers arrived, she had a windfall win on the lottery. She skipped out of her job in HR for a big company in a less salubrious area of Middlesborough and bought a detached house in upmarket Yarm village. She began to enjoy life, or so she tells everyone, except for me. I know her better.

'No way,' I say. 'I'm happy hiding away in this guest house, especially now there's been a murder!'

Penny scrunches up her fine eyebrows. 'Ah, I thought you'd given up all of that with your book writing?'

I shrug. 'I have, but as you know, old habits are hard to break.'

Alfie cuddles further into her chest and Penny rubs under his chin. I can tell he's loving the attention and I smile, hoping this will make up for missing his long walk this morning.

'Make us a cuppa, Faye,' she says. 'I'm parched with leaving Darlington so early on the train.'

I squeeze past them in the chair and switch on the kettle. When talking about Penny, Allan had often quoted 'You can take the girl out of the party, but you'll never take the party out of the girl!'

And I'd always agreed with him, but now I reckon, this party life is beginning to show on her. Some might say she's flighty and believes in having a good time at all costs, which is true but as we've got older, she reminds me more of Joanna Lumley in Absolutely Fabulous, still up for the party but looking a little tired around her eyes.

I remember talking to her ex-husband after they'd first married and he'd said, 'Penny had a smile for every man who passed her by but I always thought it was me who had her heart. She was the star of the show but this was fine because I'd been content waiting in the wings for her,' he'd said. 'Taking selfies was her passion, but I hadn't minded because she was a beautiful woman and I loved seeing them on Instagram and Facebook, especially when we were out together. I'd tried my hardest to keep her happy and content at home.'

I sigh, knowing both men have missed the other side to Penny. They don't know her vulnerable side and the upsetting childhood she'd had. Which, even now, she has nightmares about. But I do and her inner fear of not being loved, or being loved by the wrong relative. My mam had once said of her, 'Underneath the fun and gaiety lies a troubled soul.'

Penny looks around the room. 'I must say, it's not bad for a guest house and is certainly better inside than the old outside appearance,' she says. 'I got a taxi from Sunderland station and when I saw Ocean Road, my heart sank because it looks so old and run down.'

I open the little milk jiggers on the tray and spin around. Grinning, I pout, 'Stop being such a snob! There's nothing wrong with the place. It's clean and as comfortable as any hotel.'

'Hmm, well the last time I was in South Shields was years ago to see Sarah Millican at the Custom House because she's from here.'

I nod and fill the mugs with hot water. 'Oh, really? I didn't know that.'

Penny grins. 'I love her shows. She's funny and a bit near the knuckle sometimes, but she's brave enough to say what we are all thinking and haven't the guts to bring out in the open!'

Handing her the mug of tea, I tell her how we'd arrived yesterday, how I'd chatted briefly with Lloyd at the doorway and then the lengthy story of what has happened this morning.

'Oh my God!' She cries. 'I bet you got a shock when you saw the dead body?'

She places her hand on my arm and I notice she's bought herself another big ring with sparkly bling stones. I nod. 'Yeah, I did. I've written about them often enough but to see one in real life was awful!'

Penny sips her tea listening carefully to the events following this and l know she's rapt. There's nothing she loves more than a juicy tale.

She asks, 'So, are you all locked-in here until this Inspector says otherwise?'

I nod. 'His name is John Jackson. He was foul at first and I had him down as a misogynist but afterwards he redeemed himself with a nicer attitude towards us both.'

'What did he say?'

As if we were still teenagers, I stand with my hands on my hips and with a mannish gruff tone to my voice, I say, 'Heaven help me from amateur sleuths who have watched Vera!'

'Noooo,!' Penny wails.

'Oh, yes! So I gave him a gob full back and stormed off.'

I know Penny will be appalled at this manner because she had a high standing in the company when she worked in HR and her boss was devasted when she left. He'd once told me how Penny had a voice like soft treacle and that he'd never heard anyone communicate with his staff in such a way. She welcomed people to the company but at the same time didn't stand for any nonsense.

With her usual dry humour, she says, 'Maybe the Me Too movement hasn't reached the police force yet?'

I feel awful for badmouthing him now because John and I have made friends and I've seen a different side to him. 'Oooh no, I couldn't see John abusing women in an intimate or crude way,' I say. 'He's too reserved, and actually quite shy in his interactions, or at least he has been with me since then.'

'Well, just remember Faye, two people can assess or interpret a situation in totally different ways.' She drains the tea from her mug and asks, ' So, how old is he?'

'Younger than us, I'd guess. Maybe late forties or early fifties, unless, as we say, he had a hard paper-round.'

She giggles. 'And a wedding ring?'

I tut, does she ever think about anything else other than men, but I smile knowing this is just Penny and her outlook on life with all its possibilities. I change the conversation away form John, and say, 'But our Alfi has been the star of the show so far!'

I tell her about him tracing the scent to the back door and, at the sound of his name, his ears prick up above the edging of the blue throw. Penny lifts him up and away from her looking into his face. 'Oh, what a clever boy!' she exclaims. He licks the side of her cheek with his long pink tongue in gratitude and she laughs.

Seeing her like this with Alfie tears at my insides because I know what a great mother she would have been. One day at school when we were thirteen springs into my mind. We'd been lying on the side of the playing field after a game of netball. Her red hair had been in long pigtails and she'd chewed the end of one of them declaring how she wanted at least three children when she got married. I'd giggled and we'd talked about the process of actually conceiving the babies to which Penny had known way more than I had.

She'd always been the leader who I followed around like a lap dog. I'd been brighter at academic classes whereas she'd excelled in all sport events and of course gained an A* in boys and relationships without commitment. Even now she is still sporty, running every morning and playing tennis and golf at home.

Penny asks, 'Was that your suggestion?'

'Nooo, there was a nice crime scene officer who made a fuss of Alfie and I think he told John how great spaniels were at sniffing out scents.'

She smiles. 'Ah, I thought it was from you because you see things other people miss.'

I think about this and know it's a complement. 'Really?' I say, and shrug. 'I reckon I'm just myself, but suppose I do have a certain way of looking at things which is different to other people.'

'Yeah, you could say that,' she says and laughs. 'Well, I've more faith in you than your randy Inspector has!'

Now, I laugh at the word we would have used at school. 'Emm, did you actually say, "randy"?'

We collapse into giggles as though we are back behind the bike shed in school uniforms with our skirts hitched up above our knees.

I hear Lily's voice outside in the corridor and figure John has finished interviewing them as they go upstairs to their room. There's a gentle tap on my door and I hurry past Penny as Alfie jumps down from her knee to the carpet and barks hello.

I open the door wide and the DS is standing there with the never-ending iPad dangling from her shoulder. John is standing behind her. 'We just wondered who your new guest is, and if we could talk to her?'

Penny stands up and, pouting her thin glossed lips, she gives them both her winning smile. Holding out her hand she says, 'Penelope Forsythe – it's so nice to meet you both.'

I see John's penetrating look at us both, and I say, 'Penny has just arrived to stay for a few days but the attic room isn't ready which is where she'll be staying.'

The DS takes her hand and shakes it firmly. I see a flicker of surprise in Penny's eyes as though she wasn't expecting such a firm grip.

The DS turns on her heel and asks Penny, 'Could you come along to the breakfast room, please?'

'I'd love to,' she drawls. 'I'll just get my jacket.'

Alfie proceeds to follow her, but I ease him back holding his collar. I'd thought it would have been my turn next and sigh, knowing I'll not be able to walk Alfie until much later.

John looks me up and down with a smirk on his face now and, with a tease playing around his lips, he says, 'I'll talk to you last because you've a lot to say for yourself.'

When John and the DS have strode off down the corridor, Penny pulls on her jacket and passes by me whispering, 'He fancies you!'

'Don't be ridiculous – that's utter rubbish,' I declare, but all the same I can't help wondering.

Chapter Sixteen

While Penny is in the breakfast room, I'm deep in thought. Maybe the memories of our schooldays have made me pensive. I think of all my years with Allan and how Olivia was born with so much love and adoration from us both. I'd strived to give her the best childhood ever and she had been our main focus right up until she married. Well, until now really, because she still is.

I remember my daily routine and love of writing when working with editors, cover designers, the endless book signings and talks. It had been non stop. As soon as my first novel had been successful, they wanted me to write another and I'd jumped onto the merry-go-round of publishing good quality crime novels.

As our daughter grew older, I scheduled my writing in between Olivia's school activities. I'd drop her off and write straight through until collecting her again and preparing tea. The older she got, the more activities progressed into athletics, dance classes and sleep overs. I would often snatch two hours in-between these sessions, writing here and there to meet deadlines, chapter after chapter, until I could write the blessed words "The End".

I feel exhausted now just thinking about it and pause to take in a deep breath. But, I wonder, how much of her growing up did I miss with this tight timetable year after year and should I have given more of my time to her and Allan's needs? My stomach knots and I shake my head knowing it's too late for regrets about the mismanagement of my time.

I sigh, between my book career, my daughter and husband, where had I been? I struggle to remember now and ask myself the question - did I forget about the woman who I was?

I decide our so called "tricky marriage" started around the time Olivia got married and moved out of the house. I know this is often called "empty nest syndrome", but although I missed her at first, I was glad to see her move on and be happy. Afterwards, there was only us two. Me and Allan navigating a new path around the rooms and each other.

I remember telling Olivia on her wedding day that love can be fun but it can also cause pain and heartache along the way. Fortunately, this hasn't happened to her as yet and when she announced our granddaughter twins were expected, I couldn't have been more delighted.

When they were babies, I used to go to see her in Sunderland twice a week and help with the never-ending stream of feeds and nappies. However, now they're at school they tend to come to us at weekends for meals and family gatherings. So, once again, I feel a little redundant.

My dream had always been to become a published author, which I achieved in my thirties, so what do I dream about doing now? Do I aspire to becoming a well known dog-walking-and-sitter expert, if there is such a thing? Or, at the tender age of fifty-five, look for another academic career. Do I travel and visit the places I've always wanted to see rather than exclusive beach holidays that Allan loved? I suppose, to use the phrase "the world is now my oyster", I sigh, knowing I've an awful lot of thinking to do.

When I left university my father told me to get a proper job in law or medicine because as he put it, I had the brains to do this rather than working in a bookstore.

'But I want to be an author!' I'd cried.

'Ha!' he'd laughed. 'You're living in a dream world.'

I'd been annoyed at his lack of confidence in me and thought this was ludicrous coming from a man who'd been a Sub-Postmaster all his life and never moved a step out of our village.

However, Mam encouraged me all of the way through my career by saying, 'If it's what you want to do, then do it! Don't live your life with regrets.'

I'd wondered what regrets she'd had married to my father but never asked. However, when my first crime novel had been published and I presented my father with a copy, his eyes had filled with tears. He'd asked, 'And you wrote all of this?'

I'd nodded, seeing the pride in his puffed-up chest. 'Yes, it's all my own work and has sold four hundred copies so far.'

He'd shaken his head in wonderment and I knew I had achieved my goal. At last I'd done something to make him proud.

My reverie is broken when Penny bursts back into the room and Alfie jumps up to her. She heads straight for her suitcase, opens it out flat on the floor and pulls out her running gear.

Heading into the bathroom, she says, 'I'm going to run on the beach – shall I take Alfie?'

His ears prick up and I smile. 'Yes, he'd love that, but don't take him off his lead – it's a new place and he won't have his bearings.'

The bathroom door is ajar and I can hear Penny stripping off clothes and see her standing in skimpy blue shorts. I call through, 'So, what did the Inspector ask you?'

She pops her head around the door. 'Well, he said, I know you didn't arrive until after the dead man was found but does the name Lloyd Adams mean anything to you?'

I smile knowing John has been straight to the point with his questioning. There's obviously no messing about with his grilling techniques and he would want to rule out the possibility that Penny had been involved with Lloyd's death. Maybe he thinks she could have been sent here by the perpetrator under a disguise to make sure Lloyd was dead and the mission had been successful. I shake my head in disbelief, knowing my mind has flown into overdrive and strayed into the James Bond area in London and not here in South Shields.

While pulling a blue athletic vest over her head, she continues, 'I told him no, and then he asked, where I was last night from 11pm until 3am this morning?'

'And you said?'

'I told him the truth that I was at home with a man friend,' she says. 'And then he asked for his name and if he would be willing to collaborate this as an alibi, but I couldn't remember because I'd had rather a lot of champagne!'

I giggle, imagining the look on John's face as he wondered if Lloyd could have been one of Penny's lovers. With this answer, John would be under the same disillusionment that Allan and her ex-husband had about Penny Forsythe, the party girl.

She steps back into the room, tugs on whiter than white trainers and pulls out her water bottle from the case. I look at the layers and layers of clothes in the suitcase and ask, 'So, how long do you intend staying with all of that lot in there?'

She shrugs and fills up her bottle at the sink. 'Dunno, it depends how long it's going to take to sort you and your marriage problems out!'

I shake my head and murmur, 'Later, Penny, when I've had time to think it through myself.'

Alfie is jumping between the two of us as we ping pong answers back and forth, obviously excited because he knows he is going out.

'Well,' she says, heading towards the door. 'It's like I said to the Inspector when he asked why I was here. I told him you'd had an upset with your husband and my immediate response was to come to your aid.'

I drop my shoulders and feel my cheeks flush. I hadn't told John this and now he'll have formed an opinion about me and why I am here. Will he think I knew Lloyd and he is the reason I've left Allan? He might have the absurd notion that Lloyd and I were part of a love triangle and he was murdered in a spate of jealous rivalry. I know how suspicious John's mind is, and I wouldn't blame him if he thought this because I'd probably think the same myself.

'What?' She asks, 'Should I not have told him that?'

'No, it's okay – it's the truth whichever way it looks,' I say, and shrug. 'And, if I'm let out after the interview, I'll text you to meet up on the seafront.'

She smiles, opening the door wide with Alfie straining on his lead. 'Don't worry Faye, it'll soon be all sorted out and you'll be skipping off home back to Allan.'

I nod and can't help thinking, I'm not too sure of that. As I step outside the room into the corridor and then wave them off at the open front door, a longing for fresh air sweeps through me especially as the sun is shining. Alfie looks up at me as if to say "aren't you coming?" and I nod at him. 'I'll see you later,' I whisper and he trots off next to Penny down Ocean Road.

The DS bounds up to me from behind and I swing around to face her. She looks far more relaxed than first thing this morning and I hope their investigation is going well. I know they will be overjoyed if they get a positive lead into what happened to Lloyd.

'So, Faye, the Inspector has spoken to everyone that was here last night and is happy to let them leave with an instruction not to talk about what's happened to the press and general public, as it may hamper his investigation,' she says. 'If you could come along to the breakfast room, we'll talk with you now.'

'I'll just pop to the loo first,' I say.

Hurrying into the bathroom, I tut, and scoop up Penny's clothes from the bathroom floor. Folding them onto the towel rail, I mutter, 'Some things never change, it's like being back at college.'

My hair is messy and I slide two combs into my curls more securely, and sigh. Now that Penny has told John about the upset with Allan, I bite my lip. How much do I tell him and is it relevant to his enquiries? Do I keep it basic and just say it was a simple domestic argument or will he want exact details?

Another scenario suggests itself to me. I've already reassured Allan that I wouldn't say anything about his divorce papers - well only to Penny - which he knows will be a given as we are so close. But I suppose the whiff of a bigamy case - albeit thirty five years ago - will set off John's antennae onto red alert although it has no bearing upon Lloyd's murder.

I swallow down the humiliation connected to the word "bigamy", especially attached to my husband and against me - his wife. Once more the resentment towards Allan flares up inside my chest. So far, within forty eight hours, I've managed to curb these feelings by hanging him up onto the worry tree, but now the branches are definitely shaking as he's about to plop down onto the grass in front of me like the proverbial bad apple.

I take three long deep breaths in and out, pull back my shoulders and determine not to let it overtake me. With leaden feet, I trail along the corridor to the breakfast room, although, I reassure myself, I've nothing to fear or feel guilty about.

Chapter Seventeen

John stands up when I enter the room and pulls out a chair opposite to him for me to sit down. Hmm, nice manners, I think. There's no sign of the DS and I feel pleased that it's just me and John, unless of course, she's coming in later. I slide onto the chair at the table. I know Mark and Brigit have been questioned and I would have loved to be the fly on the proverbial wall, but I'm the last of the guests and I smile at him.

John looks behind me and raises his eyebrow. I turn thinking someone else has entered the room, but see no one.

'Where's Alfie?'

I smile at the look of slight disappointment in his eyes as though he'd been looking forward to seeing him.

'Ah, Penny has taken him down to the beach for a run,' I say, and give him my biggest smile tilting my head to one side. 'I didn't think you'd want to question him?'

He smiles at my joke and I notice his thinning hair which is cut behind his small ears. It's nice to see him smile because he usually has a serious almost melancholy look on his face which I suppose doing the job he does is more than understandable.

He says, 'No, but Alfie has been the star of this mayhem so far and, once again, I thank you.'

John is upright even when sitting on the chair with tense shoulders and I've noticed he even walks in a straight line with arms by his sides. I wonder if he's been in the army or other services. I want to say "hey, it's okay, I'm not going to bite" but sit quietly with my hands in my lap.

'I've left you to last because out of all the guests and staff in this house, you're probably the only person with a modicum of intelligence and insight into what has happened or how it occurred,' he says. 'And I won't bother with the routine questions because you've already told me when you arrived, and your few words with Lloyd the night before.'

My cheeks flush at his roundabout compliment. I reckon this man has a gentle strength which from his appearance is unexpected – he's certainly not half-hearted.

'Oh, right,' I say. 'Well, lets just say it's not uncommon for my suspicious mind to work in the same way as yours does because I've written many incidents like this in my novels.'

John leans forward now as though he doesn't want anyone to hear our conversation, which is unnecessary as we are alone. I follow his lead and sit further forward on my chair. He smells good with a sandalwood earthy aftershave.

'I'm thinking this is a not a random killing because if it had been then you and Alfie would have been every bit susceptible to being attacked in the opposite room.'

I gulp and wish Alfie was here so I could pull him close into me like I used to do with Olivia when she was little. My knees tremble under the table and I swallow hard. I'd felt quite safe in the guest house last night, but now I'm not so sure, although I console myself that Penny will be sleeping in my room tonight.

He must have seen my face pale and stumbles over his words now. 'I...I mean, it's not been a burglary gone wrong,' he says, and softly looks into my eyes. 'Who ever did this knows Lloyd and that he was staying here.'

I take in a deep breath and nod feeling reassured. These had been my original thoughts so I'm pleased to have this confirmed. My phone is lying on the table top and it tinkles with a photo image of Alfie and Penny down on the seafront. I tell John and show him the photo.

'Oh yes, Penny is quite a character, but she's nothing like you – she seems quite giddy.'

I can't help smiling at his word "giddy" and know over the years Penny has been called much worse than this. I can also tell he's wondering how we gel together as good friends which people have always done. And I can't answer that question. I never have been able to since the day we met at school. But I'm just grateful that we do and I know she feels the same.

'Probably not,' I say. 'But as the saying goes – total opposites attract.'

He smiles, ruffling his sheet of papers together. I bite my lip wondering if he thought my comment was directed at us. Visually we are total opposites and I'm not quite sure if I would describe what is between us as attraction, but there's definitely something.

He clears his throat and looks down at his hands lying on top of the papers. This action reminds me of yesterday and how I'd lain my hands over Allan's divorce papers and realise John hasn't asked me why I'm here.

'So, we are doing forensics, taking routine statements and searching all of the outside areas now we know the perpetrator came in through the back yard and door, which is routine. Although, so far, the statements haven't shown up anything to note and none of the guests seem to have anything to hide regarding Lloyd.'

I decide to tell him what I found out about the other guests, and Shirley and Luba. You never know, I think, any little detail may just help his investigation.

'Well, Luba the Polish cleaner and I both think Ken looks a little creepy wearing the sunglasses indoors, but Shirley tells us that he's harmless and how the couple have got a little bizarre over the years. And, his rucksack holds small notebooks which he seems to scribble in with a pencil.'

John nods and writes this down on his papers. I'm pleased he isn't scoffing at my observations now as he'd done earlier and relax my shoulders.

'Yes, I'd noticed the rucksack when I interviewed them. I could tell Ken was lying to me because he was too quick to say he'd slept all night with waking once and heard nothing. Lily raised her eyebrow and shook her head behind his back as if to say "pull the other one it's got bells on it!"'

I gasp and fold my hands together on top of the table. 'And?'

He nods. 'I reckon Ken had seen this gesture out of the corner of his eye and rounded on her with anger blazing in his eyes. She shrank down into the chair as if expecting a blow and I could tell she was scared of him, or had been in the past.'

Phew, I think, John is very sharp-eyed. I'm mega impressed he can pick up people's characterisations just by watching them, which is what I've always done. I'm not sure if the others have told John the gossip about Mark and how he's an old has-been actor, but I do now.

John smiles. 'Yes, we had quite an altercation about him visiting the theatre later to see his play. But I've decided to let him and the others go out now, including yourself.'

I imagine the altercation with John's off-hand sarcastic mannerisms. I know who I would bet my money on coming out as the winner, and it wouldn't have been Mark. 'And, I reckon if the killer had been a woman it couldn't be Shirley because of her disability; she hasn't the movement or strength in her left hand after the stroke. And, although Luba could be quite strong, I figure she'd never risk anything of this kind because of her son, Borys. Lily is too old and feeble and Brigit, who I haven't spoken with yet, seems to be like a quiet little mouse in awe of her husband.'

John stares directly into my eyes now. 'Ahh,' he says, and raises an eyebrow. 'But often the quiet ones are the worst.'

I hold his gaze as he keeps staring at me and shuffle on my chair. Is Penny right? Is he attracted to me? I'm not using the word "fancy" which is childish, but he does seem to be flirting with me at every opportunity now. I look away from him deciding I'm not exactly sure what flirting is anymore - it's such a long time since Allan and I have done anything remotely like this.

John is clever as well as observant. There's a quiet stillness about him where only his head seems to move with his eyes transversing the room and nodding at me as I speak.

He continues, 'You know, all parts of policing rely on intelligence. We work on factual, honest information and stick by the rules. And if we don't know the facts, we launch an investigation.'

His authoritative voice is strong and powerful in these few sentences and he now reminds me of Adam Dalgliesh in the PD James novels.

I quite like him, but caution myself. This is not the best time in my life to begin a new relationship with my marriage in such a mess, although I can't help but join in with his secret smiles and expectant looks. It's too tempting not to and I know it will be very easy to succumb to his advances - if he makes any, of course.

His eyes are downcast now, and with his finger, he traces down comments on his papers. I figure he's bringing the interview to an end and I want to sigh in disappointment. It's a shame because I've enjoyed talking with him and know I'd like to carry on the conversation, although not in this formal manner. I'd like to get to know him better in a more relaxed atmosphere over a drink perhaps.

'So Faye, thanks for your input and can I ask you to be a second pair of ears and eyes for me? If you see anything more suspicious, please come and find me or ring.'

He slides a white business card across the table and I pick it up. Is this his roundabout way of offering more contact between us? Or has he given all of the guests his card and asked the same of them? I scrape my chair back and smile. Just as I turn to leave, the DS bounds into the room.

I hurry along the corridor to my room and collect my handbag, sunglasses and Penny's bag. My mind is in a whirl as I head out of the front door, relishing in the fresh air and freedom from lock down.

***

Walking briskly down Ocean Road, I recap over the last fifteen minutes with John and how I'd felt. A tinkle on my phone alerts me to a text and I glance at the screen to see my husband's name again. I ignore it.

I know it's wrong and I shouldn't be doing this, but I can't help comparing him to John. Allan has always been intelligent and quick-witted, especially in his business dealings when he first started and his drive was relentless to make money. He was confident and as my mam had once said, 'Allan's full of himself and very cocky.' And now, I wonder, was this why I'd been drawn to him in my inexperienced youth?

When we fist met, I let him take charge of us, our lives and plans for the future. It seemed easier than arguments and now I can see how I took a backseat in our lives, with the exception of my novels. I was in charge of them and he had nothing to do with my narrative. I'd always loved this, because they were mine. Not his. It was my own career.

When I think of John's strength and confidence mixed with his experience and intelligence, I can tell his values come from a decent inner core. However, after years of marriage, I realise Allan's cocky attitude is not a façade for his hidden depths because he doesn't have any. He is shallow without an inner core of substance. I am the one in our relationship who has this strength – not him. And as I reach the seafront, I'm thankful our daughter takes after me.

Chapter Eighteen

I wander along to the car park at the beginning of the stone pier and pass the blue hut where two caricature models in seafaring uniforms are positioned. The signage tells me this is the South Shields Volunteer Life Brigade.

Half way down the pier, I can see Alfie up ahead running around gleefully on his long lead while Penny is sitting on a bench wiping sweat from her forehead with a tissue.

'Hey!' I call out and Penny lets Alfie off his lead. He races down the pier and practically throws himself at my legs. I bend down and cuddle his head and neck in my arms. 'Oh Alfie, I've missed you!'

I know it's only been a short while, but I don't think I've left him for any great length of time since we got him. I saunter up to Penny and plonk myself down next to her. I've brought her handbag down from the guest house as requested, and give it to her.

Rummaging inside her bag, she pulls out a small hand mirror. Her face is red and sweat is standing on her upper lip as she wipes it again and applies a new coat of lip gloss. She asks, 'How did it go?'

'Oh, it was okay,' I say, and stretch out my legs. Alfie jumps up onto the seat and sits between us as we both look out to sea. I know he's registered my melancholy mood and, of course, so has Penny.

'Tell me,' she says quietly.

I don't have to ask which bit she wants to know about. We know each other better than this, so I start at the beginning of yesterday morning and how I'd found the divorce papers in the bureau, the argument with Allan and what happened thirty years ago.

Penny listens intently without commenting. I know this is her HR experience coming into practise, which is one of her biggest assets. Of course, I've talked to her over the years about petty squabbles and the more important issue about having more children. At the time, she'd urged me not to give up because I'd regret it in the future. And, there's that word "regret" again.

Now, I sigh, maybe she was right and back then I should have been more assertive with Allan. She had suggested I go ahead and stop taking the contraceptive pill but I'd refused, knowing another child had to be by mutual consent from us both.

I sit back on the bench looking across the expanse of sea to the lighthouse in North Shields. There are a few people swimming far out in the sea and I can see the need for the life boat station and the relevant history of Grace Darling. To the other side is the wide golden sand with many families grouped together enjoying the warm weather and intermittent sunshine at the end of the day.

I turn to look at her. 'I mean, bigamy is such an ugly word, isn't it?'

I'd expected shouting and foul language calling Allan all the names under the sun, but she faces me now with eyes awash with tears. 'Dear God, I'd sort of figured it had to be something big for you to walk away from Allan and home, but this?'

I shrug my shoulders. 'It was the shock that made me want too run away because I couldn't get my head around it all,' I say. 'And I still can't even now.'

She nods and clasps my hands in hers. 'Of course, you can't, Faye. This is major and just because it happened over thirty years ago, it doesn't make it any less shocking.'

'Well, he's rang a couple of times and sent messages, but I still can't bring myself to speak to him. So, I've hung him onto my worry tree for the moment.'

Penny knows and had helped me through my episode of poor mental health, so I figure no explanation of the worry tree is necessary.

She smiles and nods. 'Good reasoning and leave him there clinging onto his branch until you're ready to shake him on down, eh?'

I know this is her way of making light of the situation. Still holding hands, I grip and shake hers firmly in an effort to hold back the tears which are collecting in the back of my throat. 'Yes, you're right, there's no hurry to settle this with a decision of what to do next.'

'And Olivia?' She probes gently.

Penny is Olivia's Godmother and loves her to bits. She's been there for my daughter as much as I have over the years. And I know Penny's first thought would be how this has affected her.

'Well, I've spoken to Olivia and played the situation down saying I just wanted a seaside break. I haven't bad-mouthed Allan or explained what he's done because after all he's her dad and she worships him. But I figure it's up to him to explain the situation to her and what he did.'

Penny nods. 'Exactly! And it'll be better for her if it comes from him and not you.'

I sigh heavily and look down at the small flat rocks on the edge of the sand covered with green seaweed. I inhale the smell of the wet slinky links of seaweed symbolising my early memories of being on Tynemouth beach with Olivia when she was little and loved the beach. Allan had been good at making sandcastles for her, I'll give him that.

'I know I can't dismiss all of his good points just because of this one mistake, but it's making me question everything about him now. In fact I even said to him, I don't know who you are anymore.'

Penny raises her eyebrow. 'And?'

I shrug. 'He said he was the same man who'd left for work this morning and came home to me as he'd always done.'

'Ahh,' she tuts. 'That man has always had an answer for everything!'

Without asking I reach across, grab her bottle, wipe the top with my sleeve and take a gulp of the water. I feel exhausted talking about everything on top of questioning from John and feel as though I need to lift our spirits. 'So, our friendly inspector, John, was very nice. He wasn't flashy or showy and didn't ask me the usual questions, but we chatted and I told him my thoughts and gossip of the other guests,' I say, and wink at her. 'In between a few secret smiles and gazing into each others eyes!'

Penny leaps up from the bench and screeches. 'Ha! I just knew it!'

This startles Alfie, who thinks she's up for games and jumps down to trot and dance around her.

She claps her hands together in glee. 'Oh perfect, this is simply perfect, and just what you need to spread your wings and have a little dalliance behind Allan's back,' she says, nudging me in the ribs. 'And, with a randy police Inspector!'

We burst into laughter with Alfie looking between us and his tail wagging sixty-to-the-dozen. He can tell the mood has lifted and we are happy once more.

'Aww, Penny, I'm confused enough about Allan without a flirtation with John.'

She giggles. 'Exactly! John will help to put your feelings in order about Allan and whether you decide too forgive and forget, or walk away altogether into John's open arms – he'll show you what you're missing out on, eh?'

I laugh and shake my head. 'Just because you go from one man to another in succession it doesn't mean to say this is right for everyone.'

'Aww, come on, let's eat. I'm starving now!' Penny says. 'I'll treat us to a good Indian meal on Ocean Road. It's always had a good reputation, so lets put it to the test.'

I grin and we walk down the pier towards the sand and then wander along the seafront which has new LITTLEHAVEN stone artworks. There are boats sails, a stone windbreak and a little stage. We stand still at a small memorial with three poppy wreaths in front and two smooth round blocks, which Penny reckons are for people to sit on.

Walking up Ocean Road, I wonder which to choose as we pass one Indian restaurant after another. It used to be called "the curry mile" although I reckon there are fewer nowadays. 'Any ideas?' I ask Penny. 'It's been years since we came down here and I don't recognise or remember which one we ate in?'

She shakes her head and stops outside a newish looking restaurant called, Tandoori International, which looks posher than the rest and is only a few doors down from the guest house.

'This will do,' she says opening the large glass swing door.

I step in behind her as a young waiter hurries up to us. 'Hello, we are just opening up now,' he says.

I look down at Alfie and ask, 'Are you dog-friendly?'

He looks behind and then hurries off to consult with an older man behind a long counter. 'We might be eating fish & chips on the seafront if Alfie can't come in here,' I say.

The older man in a good quality black suit and white shirt saunters towards us and I watch Penny pull back her shoulders and stride towards him, working her long legs into the situation. Her hand is outstretched and although I can't hear what she's saying, I can tell her charm offensive is up at top gear.

She dops her head slightly to talk quietly in his ear while stroking down her leg with her long fingers. I reckon she's apologising for being in shorts and I can see his eyes glued to her legs and visibly melting in front of her. They both walk towards me and Alfie and he outstretches his arm guiding us to the table in the window.

'As the restaurant is empty and it's early, you can have this table set aside from the main dining area, Madam,' he says.

I smile and thank him. Shooing Alfie under the table, we sit down and Penny dazzles the man with her biggest smile whilst gushing her thanks.

We are treat to a slap up meal in the upmarket restaurant. There's no old flock wallpaper here, I think looking around the plush décor on seats and tables. White linen napkins and beautiful crockery with copper bowls of delicious Indian delicacies cover the table. I smile in pleasure and feed pieces of chicken to Alfie under the table, who behaves as usual, with his impeccable manners.

I know the bill will be huge with the good bottle of Chablis white wine Penny ordered, but I gave up years ago protesting about paying for myself. Her usual reply is that she has no one else to spend her lottery money on but her family. And I know she classes me and my family as her own. I smile, looking at her bent head as she tucks into her food with relish and wonder - maybe for the hundredth time - how she can eat so much and stay so slim.

Her mobile is lying next to her knife and fork as we chat and I see her eyes glance down as it vibrates with messages. She has the good manners not to reply while we are eating as I know this irritates her, as it does me, but nods and smiles occasionally as she reads the headline on her texts. It's a secretive smile as she licks her lips and I'm not sure if this gesture is with the spicy food or passionate thoughts from whoever is sending the messages.

I'm longing to know but decide to leave the probing until we get back to the guest house. Penny settles the bill with black suited man and squeezes a £10 note into his hand. As we get up to leave, he looks as though his world has crashed down around his ears and I giggle, waiting outside at the kerb with Alfie.

In our pyjamas we are lying head to toe on top of my bed like we did at college, talking about everything in more depth. Alfie is in his basket tucked up in the blue throw and snoring ever so slightly. I reckon the fresh sea air has worn him out, as it has done me, and I yawn.

I get up and potter through to the bathroom and remove my make up in front of the mirror. In the silence of the room and even though the sash window is open, I can hear her phone pinging repeatedly. I clean my teeth and meander back to see her lying on her side facing away from me texting someone.

Is she putting her usual photos onto Instagram? Or is she replying to the messages she got in the restaurant? There's a furtive look in her eyes which I know well and I wonder what she's doing.

'Hey,' I ask. 'Who are you texting at this time of night?'

She jerks when she hears my voice and shakes her head. 'Oh, I'm just on Instagram liking everyone's photographs and they're liking mine that I took on the beach.'

My heart sinks because I know she's not exactly lying, but to use Allan's phrase "she's being economical with the truth". But why and who is she texting? I could tell by her facial expressions in the restaurant the messages are from a man and, as I slide under the duvet cover, I shiver.

Although she's never mentioned a new steady relationship, and if it was all innocent and above board, I know Penny would be boasting about a new man in her life, but she's not. Therefore, it has to be a somewhat clandestine affair, so much so, she won't even tell me about him. Which, as well as being a little hurtful, is equally just as puzzling. I wonder if we've grown apart a little over the last few years because of the pandemic and our regular meet ups have decreased.

In the second wave of lock-downs, Penny had contracted the virus and sounded rough on the phone. It had been my immediate response to go down to her because she was alone and I was worried - she's never been the best at looking after herself. She's great at giving advice to other people but rarely takes it on board when it come to her own health.

However, Allan had stopped me. 'I know you want to nurse her, and that's understandable, but what if you get the virus and bring it back here to the family?'

I'd sighed but known he was right and didn't go to see her until she was fully recovered and tested negative for a few weeks. Had this upset Penny and caused a wedge between us? I shake my head knowing it wouldn't have affected me, so it should be vice versa. But although she'd told me this was logical and didn't want me with her, I hope she meant it.

Now, I wonder about this new man. Could there be a connection between him and what's happened to Lloyd? She'd already joked that she couldn't remember his name because she was full of champagne, but was this nameless man connected to the murder case? I shake my head knowing it didn't ring true because Penny didn't even know I was here in the guest house until yesterday. I don't believe in unhappy coincidences, so know I'm definitely thinking down the wrong side of the track with this.

I chastise myself at such feelings about my dear and loyal friend. Penny isn't capable of such mysterious wrongdoings. Or at least she never has been before, but is she being used as a pawn by this nameless man? I sigh and yawn, deciding I'll make her reveal everything tomorrow and then drift off to sleep.

Chapter Nineteen

I'd tossed and turned during the night and woke up twice with Penny's feet in my face which made me cringe. As far as I could tell she hadn't woken once during the night, or if she did, I hadn't heard her.

Without opening my eyes under the duvet cover I listen intently now and can hear whispering. I know it's not one of Alfie's noises. Pulling the duvet cover down from my head, I spy Penny sitting in the bay window whispering to someone on her mobile. She's in her pyjamas with her legs bent up under her chin. The nameless man, I wonder and hear Alfie stir in his basket.

I throw the duvet aside and swing my legs out of bed. Penny hears this movement and jerks around suddenly closing her mobile. I can see her cheeks blush as she rearranges her legs and stares down at the carpet.

Gulty as charged, I think heading for the bathroom and mutter, 'Morning.'

After using the toilet, brushing my teeth and splashing my face, I drag on my tracksuit bottoms and a T-shirt.

Heading back into the room, I see Penny's normal smiling face in place.

'I slept like a top and what a lovely window this is to let in the early sun,' she says.

I nod while Alfie drinks out of his bowl. 'I'm just taking him out for a whoopsie,' I say and explain about Shirley calling it this.

She laughs a little too loudly at the joke and I can tell she feels out of kilter with what I'd seen. I head out of the room door with Alfie on his lead as she scarpers into the bathroom.

Alfie lifts his leg at the first lamppost and I stand, still frowning in puzzlement. We've never been like this before with each other and have never ever kept secrets - well, not that I know about. Maybe she's had more secrets over the years and simply not told me? But when you've known a person for over forty years you get used to their faces and, like Allan, I can read her every expression, as she will be able to do with mine. I set my jaw; what is she up to? And more to the point, who with?

Back in our room Penny is showered and dressed with even more of her clothes strewn over the floor.

She says, 'I didn't think I'd be hungry again after last night's big curry, but I am.'

I smile and nod, 'Me, too. I'll just feed Alfie and we'll head along to the breakfast room.'

Penny takes the dog food and bowl from me. 'I'll do that while you get dressed.'

I thank her and take a pink flowery dress from the wardrobe to wear.

The aroma of bacon is just as strong as yesterday as we make out way along the corridor, but I don't feel as hungry. My stomach is in knots as I walk slowly behind Penny into the room and pray my friend hasn't got herself into trouble.

Luba greets us loudly and pulls out two chairs at the table in the opposite corner to where I sat yesterday. Alfie dives under the table, and we sit down to eat. Penny goes into raptures at the selection of cereal and chooses grapefruit followed by poached eggs on toast. I ask Luba for scrambled eggs on toast while wondering why Shirley isn't in the room.

Luba pours coffee from the pot and says, 'Shirley is having a lie in this morning – she's worn out with all the upset yesterday.'

'Aww, I hope she rests up,' I say. 'It's a lot of upset for an old lady.'

Luba nods. 'I'll make her do just that. And Penny, your room will be ready by late morning as soon as I finish up here.'

I smile and take a small sigh of relief that Penny will be in her own room tonight and the carpet in our room will be devoid of clothes. After we've eaten breakfast, we pass Lily and Ken leaving by the front door. I introduce them to Penny and, although I can't see Ken's eyes behind his dark sunglasses, I'm sure he's ogling my friend's legs.

Penny packs her small bag with a towel, bikini, sun lotion and sunglasses. 'I'm heading down to the beach to top up my tan in the sun and swim in the sea - if it's not too cold.'

I nod. 'Okay, well it's a little holiday for you too, so why not?' I say, shaking up the duvet on the bed and punching the pillows. 'I'll just hang around here because I've a bit of a headache starting, but might join you later.'

She blows me an air kiss and hurries outside. Alfie looks after her longingly, but I whisper to him, 'It's okay, we'll see her later.'

The headache is simply a ruse because I want to hover around in the guest house to see if I can find out anything more about the guests. And, I admit to myself that if I bumped into John again it wouldn't totally ruin my day.

My mobile buzzes with a text from Olivia asking if I'm okay and how Allan has told her what's happened. This breaks my train of thoughts about John and makes my cheeks blush, even though I haven't actually done anything. Well, not yet. I repeat my last two words and grin. I tell my daughter how Penny is here with me and she replies with three big laughing emoji's.

Smiling, I know it'll put my daughters mind at rest. First, that I'm not wallowing in self-pity on my own and second that her madcap Aunty Penny is my companion. Olivia has loved her unconditionally from being big enough to talk and walk, and this goes both ways because Penny spoils her and the twins with far too much.

After I've picked up Penny's clothes and toiletries and stacked them into her case, I hear the soft low hum of a hoover. With Alfie at my heels, I saunter out into the corridor. Glancing up the old Victorian staircase I can see the back of Luba's tabard and know she's vacuuming the carpet. I've never ventured up the staircase so far and decide this is my ideal opportunity with the pretext to see if the room is ready.

The red and blue patterned carpet covers the whole staircase with brass stair rods holding it in place. Gosh, I think, these have to be ancient but are highly polished all the same, by Luba presumably. I can tell she takes great pride in her work and look up at the high ceilings and white deep coving. I sigh in awe at the beauty of the old architecture.

When we'd bought out house in Gosforth, it had been a fairly recent newbuild and of course I'd agreed to living there, even though I much prefer and love older properties. I sigh knowing it had been Allan's wish and he'd talked me around to the fact that newer properties were easier to clean and cheaper to maintain. He would never grasp the fact that if you love the look of old brass stair rods and a beautifully carved wooden banister then cleaning them isn't an issue. It's what is called "a labour of love".

I've reached the landing and Alfie has his nose to the carpet doing his snifarri of the landing. Two doors are opposite each other with the same black numbers three and four. Lily and Ken's room is on my left and Mark and Brigit's on my right. I know I have my post-it notes in the correct positions and smile with satisfaction.

I muse at how quickly I've come to familiarise myself with everyone and learnt the layout of the old guest house. I want to know everyone's background and figure so far, I know about Lily and Ken and Luba & Shirley, but there's only Mark and Brigit I know nothing about.

Another narrower and shorter staircase is in front of me covered in the same carpet but with a lower ceiling, which is obviously in the eves of the roof. Before I have time to check him, Alfie is bounding up to say hello to Luba.

She has the door with a black number five wedged open by her grey compartment tray of cleaning materials and the hoover.

'Sorry, Luba,' I say, mounting the last step. 'Alfie is much quicker than me and was off before I could grab him.'

She bends down to ruffle his ear. 'Ah, it's not a problem,' she says. 'My Borys wants a dog but I've refused because as much as they're lovable, they are also hard work to look after.'

I smile at her fussing Alfie who, of course, is prancing around making a game of the circular movements and she giggles demurely. This is unexpected. I'd anticipated a loud raucous laugh but the giggle softens her eyes, lowers her cheek bones and completely changes her face and demeanour. I can imagine her with Borys and how she showers him with love and attention. Mothers and children are the same the world over, or so my own mother used to say.

I peer inside the room and see it has the double bed on the furthest wall and bunk beds adjacent. The bathroom is behind a glass screen with a big walk in shower.

'Oh, Penny will love this because she's much taller than me,' I say. 'And she's had to bend her neck under the little shower over my bath.'

Luba nods. 'Well, it'll be nice to have a quieter guest up here because the Indian family who left yesterday morning were very noisy!'

I raise an eyebrow and puzzle because I've never seen a family in the guest house since I arrived, and I tell her this.

Luba explains. 'They went early at seven with a bag of continental breakfast left outside the room, which was long before we found the man that was dead,' she says. 'And, thankfully they took their two noisy kids with them who screamed and raced around every night, although they were on the beach during the day.'

I nod. 'Oh right, I bet Shirley wasn't happy, was she?'

'You're right. Shirley was glad they'd left earlier than the pre-booked week,' she says. 'But it was the parents who were noisy throughout the last day – shouting and arguing all of the time. It hurt my ears!'

She holds her hands over her ears and whispers, 'I shouldn't gossip, as you say, but I'd heard the wife screaming and accusing him of spending the night with a prostitute in Manchester and how she'd found out!'

I know my mouth has dropped open with surprise and I close it quickly. 'And what did he say?'

Luba takes out a cloth from the pocket of her jeans and wipes it over the spotless dado rail then shrugs. 'He seemed terrified of his wife and tried to explain how he'd gotten a text from the prostitute demanding money or her pimp would come and beat him up,' she says. 'And he shouted back, but I don't want to lose you all just because of one crazy night!'

Phew, I think, this is amazing and my suspicious mind whirls into action. Did this have anything to do with the killing? Mistaken identity in Lloyd? Had the killer been the pimp sent by a prostitute to get money out of the Indian father and it had gone too far?

Although it would have been obvious by their skin colour, because Lloyd had been typically English pale faced and they would have looked like two very different men, but in the dark? I shrug, was it possible the killer have made a mistake? Or maybe this family were connected to the Indian families on Ocean Road who own and run the restaurants?

My breath quickens and, excusing myself I hurry back down the stairs. In my room, I grab Penny's case and carpet bag and then lug them both up the staircases and stand them in her attic room. 'Thanks so much, Luba,' I say, and squeeze her arm.

She begins to vacuum along the small landing and I set off to find John.

Chapter Twenty

Alfie charges down the stairs in front of me loving the freedom to run about. I jump down the last two stairs, twirl my hand around the old knob on the polished banister and practically walk into John.

'Oh, hello,' I say. 'I was just coming to look for you.'

'You were?'

'Yes, I've more news to tell you about a family that left early yesterday morning before we found Lloyd.'

'Really,' he says, and takes my arm, guiding me further down the corridor. The touch of his hand on my arm makes my bare skin tingle underneath the short sleeve of my dress. I take in a deep breath. His hand feels warm, steady and comforting somehow. He drops his hand and my arm suddenly feels bereft. He looks into my eyes and I wonder if he felt the same reaction. I swallow hard and determine to concentrate as I relate the story from Luba about the Indian man and his family.

'So,' he asks, 'You reckon they could have done a moonlight flit?'

I shake my head. 'Well no, because they'd paid for the whole week but only stayed three nights, therefore Shirley isn't out of pocket, but obviously the man didn't want to hang around once the wife had discovered his wrongdoings.'

Today, John is wearing a double-breasted navy blazer with brass buttons, which seem to have lost their shine. He pulls at the cuffs on his white shirt - a little like King Charles does - and somehow I know the shirt will be expertly ironed. While I'm talking, he opens the blazer and hitches up the waistband of grey baggy trousers which look too big for him and I wonder if he has lost weight?

I smile at him. 'I mean, is it possible that the killer was the pimp and mistook the Indian man for Lloyd?' I say, tilting my head to the side. 'But that doesn't make sense, does it?'

He shakes his head slowly and I can almost see the clogs of his brain working over my words and suggestion. 'No, but it's suspicious all the same and I can see where you are coming from,' he says.

'Also, I wondered if the family were connected to the Indian businesses on Ocean Road who own the restaurants? But this would throw another spanner into the works and is probably not connected at all.'

A wide grin spreads across his face and his eyes gleam with obvious excitement. John turns on his heel, rushes along the corridor towards the hall table and I hurry along behind him. He flips open the guest book, and I watch him jot down the mobile number for the Indian man.

His excitement is contagious and my pulse begins to race. The fact that the Indian man's details would be in this book had escaped me, and not for the first time, I'm amazed at how quick John's mind works.

I chip in saying, 'Luba reckons they live in Manchester.'

He rubs his hands together in glee. 'That's a great lead, I can send the DS down to talk with him,' he says. 'Especially now we have a established time of death between 12 midnight and 2 a.m.'

Another piece of information confirmed I think and feel pleased he has shared this information.

However, it doesn't make much difference as all the guests swear to not hearing anything during the entire night. But it'll be more documented data for his spreadsheet, I decide and smile.

'Oh, right,' I say. 'So that means the Indian family would have still been here.'

He smiles and whips out his mobile, presses a number and shouts down the telephone, 'Come straight back to the guest house now!' And then mutters to himself, 'She'll love a drive down to Manchester.'

I can tell the call had been to his DS because his voice had changed from ease and friendliness with me and then back into professional mode and shouting orders. He begins to pace the corridor and I wander towards the front door with Alfie at my heels.

He calls out, 'You're not going, are you?'

I swing around to face him and see disappointment in the droop of his shoulders and hear it in the heavy sigh he gives. Or maybe, I think, that's just wishful thinking.

'Well, yes,' I say. 'We aren't locked down anymore, are we?'

He shakes his head, looks down at the carpet and mutters, 'No, more's the pity.'

Does he mean, he doesn't want any of us to go out? Or is it just me that he would like to be kept in lockdown? I bite my lip not knowing whether to hang around or leave.

It's on the tip of my tongue to mention Penny and her nameless man but decide to investigate this further with her today. I'm 95% certain there'll be a perfectly reasonable explanation, and sigh, but why am I not 100% sure?

Alfie gives a tug on his lead and I know it's not fair to keep him hemmed inside all day. Plus, I grin thinking of the saying "absence makes the heart grow fonder" and saunter to the front door.

He follows me and gushes his thanks with that same gleam in his eyes. 'I knew meeting you could only be a good thing,' he says.

'Oh right, thanks, see you later,' I say, and sail out of the front door as though I'm floating on a cloud in the bright blue sky.

Chapter Twenty One

As soon as we are outside, Alfie hurries to his favourite lamp post and I turn to see Mark sitting on a garden bench under the bay window amongst the pot plants. The police tape has been removed and he is holding his face up to the sun. They are the only couple I haven't spoken with much and decide to play up to his ego.

I wander to the bench and gesture to sit down next to him. He nods and moves along the bench a little. Alfie has a sniff around his feet but I can tell Mark is not one of the nation's dog lovers, and I extend his lead. Automatically, Alfie hops up and down the three stone steps away from us so as not to distract Mark.

Dogs seem to have an inbuilt antennae for people who don't like them, although this can alter as in the case of John. At first, Allfie had been wary of him but now after they've made friends, he is happy to approach him. Somehow, I don't think this will be the case with Mark.

I smile and say, 'Now, I'm sure I know you from somewhere? Don't tell me because I know I'll figure it out. Are you on the TV? Or maybe in a film?'

Mark grins. 'Yeah, I'm an actor and was in a soap opera set in Yorkshire.'

I never watch soaps on TV but muddle through. 'That's it!' I say, and clap my hands together. 'Me and my hubby loved that show!'

I watch him jut out his chin and smirk. 'Well, I've just read for a part in a new play called Double Jeopardy and it's right up my street,' he says. 'And I'm sure the part is going to be brilliant.'

So, he seems to think he's got the part already and oozes self-confidence. This irritates me and I want to smirk back, but don't. I remember how Luba told us that he'd been in one soap opera over ten years ago and had nothing since, but he does TV adverts which he thinks are beneath him. I think of the quote which Agatha Christie had once said "everyone loves a good liar" and decide Mark was certainly that.

I push these thoughts aside and carry on with my charade. 'Wow!' I cry. 'You'll be fantastic in it I'm sure and you must let me know when and where it'll be staged. I'll definitely come along.'

I try to flutter my eye lashes at him, which I'm more than capable of doing to John who I admire and respect, but not this upstart. However, I can tell he is almost swooning in my false adoration and attention.

'Yeah,' he says. 'Well, famous people aren't always useful I'm afraid, and know I'll have to make life changes when this does happen.'

Mark is medium build and I look down at his legs clad in knee length shorts. Along with the startling turquoise vest he is wearing, I figure the clothes would look much better on a thirty year old. Which he is certainly not. There are grey streaks in his brown sideburns and the large knobbly varicose veins on his calves tell me he must be mid-forties at least. And, from a female point of view, these veins aren't attractive and should be covered up at all costs.

As an opener to my questions about Lloyd's death, I say, 'I've just been chatting to our friendly Inspector and he asked me about the night Lloyd died and if I'd heard any disturbance, but unfortunately I didn't. Did you and Brigit because your room was right above his?'

I motion to look around for her and raise my eyebrow because there's no sign of his wife.

Mark says, 'She's upstairs getting ready. We're going up to the new library called The Word.'

Mark waves his hand nonchalantly and avoids my previous question by talking about himself. 'I'm just relaxing here in the sun and, to be honest, I'm not particularly interested in the dead man or the Inspector, but we did get to see the play last night which was amazing!'

I'd noticed the small building painted grey with a green and yellow sign on the end of Ocean Road and wonder if the play is still running tonight because Penny might enjoy the show. 'Oh, is that on at the Westovian Theatre which they call the Peir Pavilion?'

There's an air of contempt around him as he snorts. 'Nooo, the play is on at the Custom's House which is the main theatre here in South Shields.'

He sets a pet lip and moans, 'I'm not sure why I get knocked back from things since I studied film and cultural studies and got a first because I was so good. And producers don't even want me for reality TV shows where I could make a little money,' he says, pinching his thin lips together. 'After university, I worked in a cinema for a few years writing a couple of critiques about films for a trade magazine which were bloody great!'

I latch onto this statement as a commonality and tell him about my crime and thriller books.

Mark says, 'Okay, I enjoy a good mystery and might look for one of your books while we are in the library, Faye.'

'Hey, that'd be good,' I say, and smile. 'I'd appreciate your opinion being who you are.'

He puts his hands behind his head, stretches out his legs and to use an old saying "opens up to me like a flower in bloom" by telling me his life story.

'My old governess called me a devilishly handsome extravert, even though I'd been home-schooled and wasn't used to mixing with other children. I always thought of her as a replacement for my frequently absent mother. I've had money from my father all my life as a backup but last year it dried up because he stupidly invested in a crap scheme and his broker lost most of the money,' he says, and looks to me for more empathy.

I squeeze his chubby hand and fingers which are lying on the bench. 'But that's dreadful – poor old you!'

He nods. 'No Faye, don't feel sorry for me or I might lose control altogether. My father still lives in a seven bedroom manor house in Yorkshire which will eventually be mine to sell because I hate the old run down ruin of a place. So, although we can't afford holidays now, he did send a little money which of course wouldn't stretch to our usual fortnight in Biarritz,' he says. 'Originally I'd wanted to stay in the new apartments with large balconies overlooking the sea in Scarborough, but then I heard about the play here and changed my mind.'

I'm struggling to keep the derision from my voice, but know to keep him talking I need to relay sympathy even though I want to call him a contemptable idiot. I exclaim, 'Oh, Mark,' I soothe, 'What an awful thing to happen!'

He makes the noise of a short sob in the back of his throat and nods. 'I know, but life deals us these blows, Faye, and we just have to cope with it all. Father once told me that I wanted champagne with only beer money to pay for it!'

I retort, 'Aww, now that's simply not fair!'

I cannot believe the audacity of this pathetic excuse for a man and his crocodile tears. If I thought for one moment there was an ounce of genuine upset in him, I wouldn't be making fun, but I know he's playing this part for an Oscar winning role.

He looks down at his leather open sandals and wipes sweat from his top lip with his finger. 'And on top of all this, my marriage is nearly over, but Brigit won't accept it and clings on to me,' he says.

The sun is beating down on the back of my neck and I wish I'd brought a sunhat or suncream. I wiggle further around on the bench to move my position, which means I'm facing him now. 'I'm so sorry to hear that Mark, but you seem the perfect couple?'

'Well, appearances can be deceptive I'm afraid, but I had been having a tiny little affair with a young massage therapist who thought the world of me. I met her one day in the gym and had been equally as taken with her as she was with me. She had an amazing figure, even though she had a half-shaved head and a ring through her nose.'

I want to hoot, I really do, but swallow it down in the back of my throat. You sad pathetic creep, I think, hounding younger girls because you can't accept your own fate of getting old like we all have to do. But, I say, 'Mark, you don't have to tell me all this if it's too upsetting?'

He shrugs his shoulders. 'No, Faye, I need to get all this out because you're such a good listener and I need to talk to someone,' he says, and waves his arm around theatrically. 'She worked in the sauna and had tried to get me onto an exercise bike, but I ended up all sweaty, plus I hated the Lycra. Everyone kept shouting "you've got this!" But I hadn't known what that meant - got what? She'd given me a water flask to carry around with a straw in it which irritated me. I mean, I'd rather sip from the carton but apparently this wasn't the done thing. Anyway, she finished our affair and told me that although I didn't look my age, I certainly acted it and was boring to say the least. She found a new boyfriend who was a body builder!'

Now he drops his head down to his chest and I think he is ready for tears. I make soothing noises of comfort, but bite my lip trying not collapse into fits of laughter and imagine telling Penny later. I know she'll be in hysterics at this sleazebag as will I.

Tired of running around the same area, Alfie bounces up to me and I stand up ready to leave Mark to his own devices. I see Brigit through the open front door coming down the stairs wearing blue striped linen trousers, a white blouse and a string of fine delicate pearls around her neck. Deciding I've exhausted myself with questioning for one day, I bid Mark goodbye and head up Ocean Road in the opposite direction to the seafront.

***

Alfie trots along beside me and I whisper, 'No beach today, lets have a look around the town centre and we'll catch up with Penny later.'

As I walk, I wonder if Mark is short of money because his guaranteed family income is depleted, how desperate would it make him? I consider the fact that he might have had something to do with the death of Lloyd, but shake my head. He's such a tired old has been, I can't see him with enough strength or energy to attack and stab a man, unless of course, there was money to be gained. And could this couple be involved in some way?

My mind creates more scenarios and I wonder, if he treat the massage therapist badly, could the body builder have come looking for him? I think of Lloyd's room and know John found £300 stashed in his sock drawer. Had Mark known it was there and been caught out while searching for it? John seemed to think this murder was a random act and not well thought out, so I suppose anything was possible on the spur of the moment.

Chapter Twenty Two

I drop down onto a bench in the middle of the main shopping street and look online at, The Word. I gasp in awe at the amazing photographs of the new building – it's stunning. Mark is right, it'll be well worth a visit whether my books are in there or not.

After a little window shopping and a sandwich, I head up the road from the metro station and walk into the old market place. I read on Google how South Shields Marketplace lies to the east of the site and has been home to a market for almost 250 years. The centre of the Marketplace is occupied by the Grade I listed Old Town Hall. The Old Town Hall is a landmark at the end of King Street which continues directly onto the Tyne via Dean Street. To the east, King Street leads on to Ocean Road and together, they form a direct route linking the River Tyne to the coast.

Impressive, I think, although there's no market in progress today, just empty metal poles where the canopies are usually erected. I look up at the Old Town Hall and the imposing stone work with steps either side leading onto a balcony with black iron railings. I suppose the major of the town stood here to talk with the people of South Shields many years ago.

The square is almost empty, but I read how there is still a flea market on a Friday and the general market runs every Saturday. I suppose everyone will be down on the beach as it's a lovely sunny day and I walk up to Ferry Approach from market place.

The ferry is in front of me now with a white and blue walkway and white tunnel chimney-like structures. I know this is the quickest and easiest way to cross the sea over to North Shields. I turn left and walk along the road at the back of The Word which takes me to an old sandstone building with big windows, arches and pediments, namely The Custom's House. I collect a brochure which tells me all about the theatre, cinema, gallery, restaurant and venue space.

Turning the corner, I see the strange looking guy with dreadlocks who had been in Sea Hotel on the day I arrived. He's wearing the same clothes and I recognise the beautiful pink shawl. He is sitting on a bench with a blonde haired woman who looks to be around the same age. She has his hands grasped in hers and, although I'm too far away to hear what she's saying, I can tell she is giving him a hard time about something. He must be in the play which Mark and Brigit saw and I congratulate myself for guessing he looked theatrical.

Walking back across the road and over to the new circular building, The Word, I'm amazed at the mixture of old and new – it works very well. I whip out my mobile and take photographs of the stunning building and zip one off to Penny. She doesn't answer straight away but I figure she could be swimming in the sea or whispering with her nameless man.

I look ahead and gasp in awe at the ten blocks of glass surrounding the main doors reaching from the roof down to the ground. The rest of the round structure is built with strips of light panelled wood. The structure reminds me of The Royal Albert Hall in London although not as big of course, but equally as majestic in it's own right.

The signage reads, THIS STATE-OF-THE-ART ATTRACTION CELEBRATES THE WRITTEN WORD IN ALL ITS FORMS. It boasts a rolling programme of events and experiences. Just on these words alone, I lick my lips and can't wait to get inside.

Walking up to the front doors, I look down at Alfie and wonder if it'll be dog-friendly. Skim reading the notices of opening times, café and rules there is nothing about dogs. Using the side door and not the rotating swing doors, I meander through the entrance. I figure if anyone stops me with Alfie, I'll be ready to tell a white lie and call him a seizure assistance dog.

If I thought the outside was impressive, inside is equally as breathtaking. The round dome is huge and has an inner circle of fat white spotlights creating a fabulous lighting display. Underneath are three wide sweeping staircases which take people up to the galleries for each level of activity and many white bookcases. Staring up at them, I'm mesmerised by the stark beauty the architect has designed. This, I know, is a far cry from old musty smelling libraries with wooden bookcases. I think of the oldest library we have in Oxford - The Bodleian - made famous by the Harry Potter films.

Looking around on the ground floor, I see three tables set up with chess sets where two groups of men and women are playing the game. Another hit for the library as a cultural venue, I think and smile. It's a great way to get the general public inside the building if there are free activities.

Along with these is a big playroom for children with a huge sign BRICK AND MIX STATION. The room is full - and I mean full - of Lego. There must be thousands of pieces with a smaller room next door displaying Souter Lighthouse and Marsden Rock, which have already been made.

Next to the café is a table with a big jigsaw set out of dinosaurs and creatures of the natural world. The outer edges have been fitted in with a sign saying IF YOU HAVE A SPARE MINUTE, PLEASE HELP US WITH OUR JIGSAW.

Another brainwave, I muse and immediately think of Lily and wonder if she has finished the jigsaw in the guest house. Or, in fact, seen and spoken to any more spirits since I left this morning. She's certainly an eccentric old lady. I make a mental note to tell her about this activity here and watch an old man saunter past. He stops, reads the sign and sits down to look for pieces to fit while two schoolgirls sit opposite to help him.

To my right are facilities next to an open café where people are enjoying coffees and snacks, but I don't go in because I have Alfie. However, the side wall of the café is all glass and the outlook is over the sea where a large DFDS ship is moored. It's a beautiful location and the architect has this section just right.

I backtrack to my left and the gift shop. Browsing the shelves of miniature glass ornaments which are probably made in Sunderland, I linger over choosing two brightly decorated coasters of the famous landmarks to South Shields - Grace Darling and Marsden Rock. I know they'll look lovely at home on our coffee table.

Out of the blue, a rush of home-sickness sweeps over me, and I sigh. I'm missing our house, all my belongings and family pieces. I've always loved living in Gosforth and know it's the place that made us into the family we are and Allan played a large part in this. Especially with his business in the town and his honest, reliable reputation for handling people's money.

He's well thought of by all our neighbours who create a huge sense of community. I know Olivia still misses our little town whilst living in Sunderland.

I'd said, 'But you'll make a new community for your own family. And yes, it won't be Gosforth, but with good neighbours it could be even better.'

Allan's image comes into my mind, but I shake my head abruptly. I know with certainty that I'm still not missing him. I suppose I should by now and squeeze my eyes shut, knocking him back up onto that worry tree.

I take in a deep breath, let it out slowly and wander to the back of the ground floor to look at the IT work stations where all the books are catalogued. Nodding in satisfaction, I find that two of my books are on the library shelves and the other two being out on loan.

As I'm standing along from a glass exhibition case with a model of Vera inside, my eye catches the bright turquoise colour of Mark's vest. He is behind a large white bookshelf chatting to a beautiful, slim twenty year old in teeny white shorts showing the cheeks of her bottom. From their body language I can tell this meeting is clandestine. He's casually leaning towards her with his hand flat on the bookshelf. His knees in the denim shorts are soft and his head is bent down nearly into her blonde hair listening to her whisper.

Scenario's flood my mind. Is this the massage therapist he'd had an affair with? However, I remember his comment about the shaved head and nose ring. Shaking my head, I know this can't be the same girl. So, is this another affair or just a one-off date? Does this girl live here in South Shields or has she followed him up to the coast?

I pull further back behind the glass case in an effort not to be seen. I'd hate Mark to see me and think I'm stalking him. Although, I shrug, knowing his arrogance he would probably think I'm as besotted with him and as all the other women he seems to have hanging around him.

Alfie is looking up at me with his head to one side wondering why we are hiding. I put my finger to my lips and whisper, 'Sssh, please keep quiet.'

I can see more of the girl from this angle and reckon she's pretty enough to be an actress on the stage or maybe in the chorus line of dancers judging by her legs. Is she in the play at the Custom's House and that was why Mark was desperate not to miss it? I tut, no wonder he wasn't keen on being locked down if it was keeping him from meeting this girl.

He lifts his head up from her now, cups her sweet little face in his chunky fingers and kisses the tip of her nose. This action makes me cringe as she looks young enough to be his daughter. Is she being taken-in by him and his charming lies, I wonder?

I head back towards the café and main exit. It's only as I pass the gift shop again, that I spy Brigit. She is pretending to look at seaside memorabilia in a white display case but I can see she's staring at the back of Mark with daggers in her eyes.

Chapter Twenty Three
Brigit Reynolds

OMG, it's not Faye, Brigit thought and swallowed hard. She looked at the back of her husband and glared at his bright turquoise vest. She really thought it had been Faye he was hankering after and had arranged to meet here. But this was worse, so much worse, she raged. She could have consoled herself that she was much nicer in looks than frumpy housewife-looking Faye, and would have coped better. But not with this young girl. Brigit knew somewhere deep inside that they were getting even younger now.

She looked at the young blonde showing off her bum cheeks and groaned. Every aspect of this girl screamed sex appeal. It was in her brightly painted red luscious lips, her full pert breasts, her slim shapely legs, and that bottom? Well, Brigit knew this was the epitome of all men's dreams, at least it was for her husband. It made her flesh crawl to see him lust over this girl and Brigit rubbed her arms feeling comfort in the silky material of her blouse.

Mark hadn't wanted her to join him on his visit here. 'Oh, you'll be bored silly while I'm delving into all the books and screen plays,' he'd said. 'In fact you look quite peaky, why not take a lie down and I'll be back before you know it!'

But Brigit had seen him talking to the chubby woman, Faye, and her dog while sitting in the sun and decided he was probably chatting her up. Mark was relentless where other women were concerned now, but even this would be a first for him.

Usually, he went to great lengths to hide his discretions, so would he really chance an affair in the guest house with another woman right under his wife's nose? She'd shrugged, knowing she wouldn't put it past him - he certainly had the egotism for it, and decided to follow him. It wouldn't be the first time she'd walked in his footsteps to catch him out.

She had worked as a cleaning supervisor in a York hospital and loved the job, but took early retirement because of slight arthritis in her back, which the GP had said would only get worse.

Of course, she sighed, it had been easier for Mark to meet other women during the daytime when she was at work but then his antics had been curtailed when she was at home all day. Following him to the gym had been how she'd caught him out with the massage therapist and all the hullabaloo that occurred afterwards.

Brigit kept one eye focused on him while also looking around the library. It was a beautiful structure but there was far too much glass for her liking. She hated mirrors. She even hated to see her reflection in shop windows, that's how bad her phobia had become now. Or should she say, that's how far Mark had battered her down over the years.

Her heart sank - there was no comparison with herself to this young girl, she was the exact opposite. All Brigit saw in the glass was her older, flat chested figure like a bean pole. A very pale face with almost translucent skin which she did try to hype up with makeup, but as her husband had so delicately put it, made her look like a clown. The most she ever wore was a distinctive pink lipstick.

His head was nearly in the blonde girl's chest now and hatred bubbled up in Brigit's stomach, which knotted in anger. Any remorse or hesitation about leaving him and taking his money was well and truly quashed now.

She gritted her teeth and folded her arms across her chest, which was her usual defensive stance. Some would even say it was an aggressive posture, and she knew the response was related to a person who had someone or something to hide. Perhaps this had happened after years of living in his shadow, she thought and sighed. And, a result of always being on edge while she waited for the next woman to come along.

She'd been convinced all of their married life that he was unfaithful and had one affair after another, but she had stayed with him because she loved him. And lately, because she'd thought there would be nowhere else to go when she retired.

Sickened by the sight of him, Brigit tutted, turned on her heel and made her way smartly back through the swing doors and outside into the sunshine. She breathed in and out deeply in the hope of dispelling the foul images from her mind and walked down through the market place towards the main shopping street. Brigit watched people milling around - this was their home, their place in life and, as citizens of Tyneside, they had their own cultural backgrounds and stability.

Brigit had never had this. As an only child of parents in the army, her childhood had been sporadic moving from place to place, on no occasion staying more than two years. Brigit never felt as though she belonged anywhere, not even in York where she'd lived after meeting Mark aged eighteen. She'd followed him around like a sheep dog.

She headed down to Ocean Road and pulled back her shoulders knowing it was time. It was time to put her plans into place and pack. She reached the guest house and hurried up the stairs to their room. Unlike her snobby husband, she'd enjoyed staying in the guest house because it had been friendly and comfortable, until of course they'd found the man dead downstairs. But that scenario, she sniggered, could only benefit her plans.

Brigit pulled out the suitcase from under the bed and remembered how Mark had wanted to go to Scarborough in the swanky seafront apartments and in the same sentence had sworn the massage therapist was long gone. As ever, Brigit had believed him.

She folded clothes neatly into the bottom of her case and did mathematical calculations in her mind. The money she had now would be enough. Their ground floor flat in York was in his name only, but when she'd received her pension from the hospital, Brigit had stashed it away with her other monthly salaries into a building society account that, as far as she knew, Mark didn't know existed. She'd called it her "escape pot" and had dreamt over the years of running away to a remote Jamaican island to start anew. Now this dream had changed thanks to her father-in-law.

When she retired and with time on her hands, she travelled once a week to see her father-in-law. Never having a good word to say about him, Mark refused to join her, but she liked his father. He was the opposite to Mark and quietly spoken, like herself. He was honest, reliable and the type of old man she would have loved as a grandfather.

They spent hours in his extensive gardens where he taught her about his plants and shrubs. Under his instructions, she pottered around with a trowel in her hand and loved the peace in the gardens even if the weather wasn't good. Their flat in York didn't have a garden, so this quickly became her happy place where there was no cheating husband, no lies, no need to adopt her defensive stance and she felt free of him and, light of burdens.

On her last visit to the manor house, her father-in-law had asked, 'Why have you never had any children, Brigit?'

She'd answered truthfully. 'Well, Mark has always said he never wanted kids because he didn't want to share me with anyone else.'

The old man had raised his eyebrows and tutted at her response. 'Ha! That's typical of him – you'd think he was on the stage!'

And then he had shown Brigit his will where he'd written out Mark and left her the manor house upon his death. She'd gasped and protested all afternoon to no avail - he wouldn't change his mind.

Therefore, Brigit knew her future was secure and eventually she would live in the manor house because she loved the place and gardens, but until he left this mortal coil, she would need somewhere else to live.

She pulled along the zip to her suitcase and gazed out of the window down onto Ocean Road. On the night Lloyd died, she'd woken at 12.30 am and realised Mark wasn't next to her in bed. She'd scrambled out of bed and looked out of the window to see him down on the path next to one of the restaurants. Brigit had known it was him because she recognised his cream jacket, even though he had his back to the guest house under the street light.

Brigit hadn't been able to see which woman he had his arms around because she'd been in the dark shadow, but her arms had been draped around his neck as they kissed. There'd been two young women in the play at the Customs House, so she'd figured it could have been either of them. Brigit had slid back into bed and feigned sleep when, ten minutes later, he'd climbed back into their bed with cold feet. Disgusted by what she'd seen, Brigit had lain awake for hours and made her plans to leave him.

While Mark had been chatting to Faye earlier that morning, she'd written a small note to the Inspector telling him exactly what she'd seen that night and how Mark had lied to him and the DS. They hadn't both slept soundly all night without waking, and Mark had been hanging around outside with a woman on Ocean Road. And, although she hadn't seen anything suspicious other than her husband kissing another woman and didn't know what time Lloyd had been killed, her husband had definitely lied to the police for some reason.

Her husband was now obsessed with money or the lack of it and Brigit had heard Lilly say the police found £300 in Lloyd's room. If Mark knew this money was there - had he been in his room that night looking for it? She shuddered and left her mobile number on the note in case the Inspector wanted to talk further with her.

As Brigit bumped her suitcase down the stairs, she wondered if telling lies to the police was an offence? Was this what was called "perverting the course of justice"? She could only hope so and her husband would get some type of punishment for his behaviour and deceit.

Chapter Twenty Four

On my way back down the shopping street, I stop at what had been the old library with beautiful arched doorways and a lion sitting on top of a pillar at the bottom of the stone steps. The pink brickwork and window arches in white stone have obviously been cleaned and the wording on one side reads THE LIBRARY, and the opposite side READING ROOM. I shake my head in awe at the difference from this old structure to the new building of The Word.

Move with the times, I hear my father say, although I love the message in the old reading room and imagine people sitting there enjoying books and newspapers. The small board outside tells me it is now a museum and art gallery exploring the fascinating history of South Shields through interactive displays and exhibitions with a Victorian pantry. I memorise this for another outing tomorrow, hoping Penny might keep Alfie while I browse.

Needing to spend a penny, I walk down and cross over to Ocean Road. As I approach our guest house, I see Brigit pulling a big suitcase down the last step onto the path. She turns to me and smiles.

I can't help noticing how different she looks to the last time I saw her glaring at Mark's back in the gift shop. I look up the steps and behind the open front door for Mark, but there's no sign of him. I decide he's still probably up in The Word with his white shortie lass.

Brigit's eyes are shining when she smiles at me. I think it's the first time I've ever seen her smile and know it's a huge improvement upon her looks. However, are these signs of relief? She certainly looks much happier as I look down at the suitcase. I wonder if she is leaving him? Or has she packed for them both and meeting him later? I remember Mark saying they'd booked in for the week, so that doesn't figure.

'Oh, hello,' she says. 'I've been looking for the Inspector but couldn't find him, so would you give him this, please?'

She parks up her suitcase and hands me an envelope. I ask, 'Are you and Mark leaving?'

Brigit nods and pulls her shoulders back. 'Just me,' she says. 'I don't know what he's doing, but I've had enough!'

I hope she doesn't think I'm prying, which I suppose I am, but would love to know her version of events. 'Oh dear, I'm sorry we haven't had much time to talk to one another during our stay,' I say. 'Although Mark told me earlier about his employment and money situation.'

She hoots. 'Ha! I wouldn't believe a word he says, Faye. I've listened to his sob story for years now and believe me, it's all an act.'

I nod. 'I did get that impression, but his father does seem like a tyrant, especially about his inheritance?'

Brigit picks up the handle of her case. 'His father is a lovely old man who I see regularly. He lives in a manor house with the most amazing gardens, which is where I'm off to right now. I know he'll let me stay a while until I can find somewhere else to live,' she says. 'And quite frankly, I don't mind where I end up as long as it's nowhere near my philandering bloody husband! All I want now is some peace and quiet in my life.'

She turns on her heel and, before I have time to ask anything more, Brigit scurries off down towards the seafront, pulling the case behind her.

I tuck the envelope into my satchel and hurry through to our room and into the bathroom. Alfie sniffs around the room and looks up at me as if to say "oh not in here again". I feel sorry that I've not done much with him for a while, although I didn't have much choice in the lockdown, and whisper, 'Don't worry, I'll take you into the park next.'

As we leave the room, John calls out a greeting and I swing around to face him.

'Hey, there,' I say. 'I've news for you about Mark and Brigit.'

He smiles. 'And I'm in desperate need of fresh air – will you walk with me?'

I nod and he holds open the front door. We leave together down the steps and, with his hand on the small of my back, he guides me past the postman.

'Excuse us,' he mumbles to the postie, who smiles.

***

With Alfie trotting along between us, we walk down and I look up the side streets with big terraced houses going uphill from Ocean Road, namely, Salmon Street and Roman Road.

I say, 'They're big houses around here, aren't they?'

John nods. 'Yeah, and the guest house has an old brown wooden gate that's seen better days in the back lane. The wood has rotted in places although the brickwork around it is still solid, but we've scoured all the lanes to this side of Ocean Road and there's no new leads,' he says, and throws up his arms in a sign of defeat. 'And because I still have no ID on Lloyd - only a set of house keys which are useless when we don't know where he's from - I've no motive to work with, Faye. So anything that is the slightest bit suspicious to you is worth noting and investigating.'

We've reached the opening to North Marine Park and I see Alfie lift his ears hopefully, but John continues walking a little further down to the Grace Darling boat and monument. There are three short viewing benches around the boat and he walks us to the middle bench facing the long side of the boat and sits down. He pats the bench next to him as if to say "please sit" and I do as he bids.

His shoulders are slumped and I can tell he's floundering with the case. I wish there was something I could do to help him and lift his spirits. The sun is shining on the pale blue and white boat and I smile in pleasure.

'It's a beautiful boat, isn't it?'

He nods. 'It sure is and I've no idea how those people operated such a lifeboat in the olden days, they must have been very brave.'

I wonder if this is something that interests him and ask, 'Do you like the sea?'

He turns to me and smiles. 'Yes, I love the coast and live near The Leas, overlooking the beach and Souter Lighthouse,' he says. 'I have a skiff, a wetsuit and paddle board.'

I nod as if I knew what a skiff boat was, but I can imagine him in a wetsuit on his paddle board. I've seen people using these on the waves and have been impressed. I also imagine him in a waterproof tramping the beach and collecting shells from the sand. I can't help wondering if he is married with children, but don't want to appear nosey, so I don't ask.

Opposite to us is the side entrance into the South Marine park. Alfie's ears prick up when he hears the old sounding "toot toot" noise from the miniature steam train going around the edges of the park. We watch little billows of steam rise up into the sky behind the trees.

Deciding to keep the conversation on track, I tell him about Mark in The Word and the young girl he was canoodling with. How Brigit had been spying on him and then has walked away dragging her suitcase. I reach into my satchel and pull out the envelope from her.

'Ahh, hell hath no fury like a woman scorned,' he says.

I grin at the old saying while he tells me about their interview and his observations of them as a couple which basically meets my own.

'I knew Mark was being shifty and lying about something and, as you detected Brigit hardly spoke a word, although I thought she had a cunning look on her face. It was as if she had a plan in mind and now with this, I was right and she's gone,' he says, waving the note. 'Brigit wore a vivid pink lipstick so I asked my DS to look at the evidence items we bagged in the crime scene. Namely, the cup from the tea tray, toothbrush mug in bathroom and the whiskey glass for traces of the lipstick. It was a long shot but I knew there was something suspicious between them.'

I'd also noticed her lipstick mainly because her skin was almost translucent and it stood out, but it never entered my head to check for traces on the room items which would have linked Brigit to the case.

This man is good, I think once more with a satisfied smile on my lips.

I tell him about Mark's redundant career and the fact that he's worried about money now he has exhausted his father's contributions. 'I wondered if the money you found in Lloyd's room had anything to do with Mark? I mean, did he know it was there and was ready to steal in his desperation?'

Carefully, he opens the envelope and skim reads the contents. I lean towards him, hoping to look over his shoulder as I'm desperate to know what Brigit has written. I breathe in that faint aftershave again. Heat is radiating from his shoulders in the blazer and I want to remove it from him so he can relax. I bite my lip and take a deep breath, not knowing how to deal with this closeness between us. He must be able to feel it too and it can't be only in my imagination, can it?

John has a slight receding hairline and when he speaks, he looks up to the sky as if thinking and choosing his words carefully or even pondering upon the words he's just spoken. My father would have called this studious. I figure he's older than I first thought, but maybe this is just his old-fashioned habits and mannerisms.

He turns, smiles and hands me the note. Reading through Brigit's words, I gasp. By the look of hatred on her face in The Word while staring at Mark's back, I could well imagine her with a knife in her hand and using it on him.

I cry, 'But the killer came in through the back door, so Mark wouldn't have seen anything that night at the front – would he?'

John nods. 'The only thing I'm sure about is that the culprit did get in through the back. The Post Mortem results tell us that Lloyd had a temporary filling, which looks like it's been done professionally and is around two weeks old. There's a large circular indent near Lloyd's collarbone, which is suggestive of a ring being pressed into the skin whilst holding him down in the chair. The one and only print we found which Alfie sniffed out, doesn't match any records we have in police files. So, I reckon the killer has to be a man because as I've said before, I doubt a woman would have the strength to use the knife in that way and hold him down.'

The bristles stand up on the back of my neck and hope he's not going to down the misogynistic route again, but now I know him better, I'm sure his comment isn't derogatory.

I pull back my shoulders and tease. 'Oh well, I'm not sure about that because I'm quite strong and could probably stab him!'

He chortles. 'Yep, I reckon you could.'

I bunch up my biceps and squeeze the flabbiness. 'Or maybe not!'

John smiles and asks, 'Did you play mind games as a child? I bet you were a nightmare on the opposite team because you'd get the answers right all of the time!'

I burst out laughing at his compliment. 'Well, yes, I did and I was always the winner at Monopoly!'

He actually laughs now. 'Yep, you're quick-witted and a woman who can think ahead of everyone else,' he says. 'I wish you could teach my DS to do this, I often have to take her by the hand.'

I bring the image of his sidekick into my mind and say, 'Oh really, she gives me the impression of being very ambitious.'

'Yes, she's very efficient, conscientious and makes a great effort.'

'But that's good, isn't it?'

He nods and leans forward, resting his elbows on his knees. Alfie slinks up to him and John plays with his ears. 'Of course, but thinking for herself is something she hasn't quite mastered yet.'

I can see his comments are said with crinkly eyes and a fondness for her. I think of the first day we'd met and how the DS and PCs were talking about him with awe and respect.

His calm manner with all of the hullabaloo going on around him and I know he must carry a lot of responsibility on those slight shoulders.

Wanting to know more about him, I'm unable to stop myself asking, 'So, what does the J stands for in your middle name because I'd heard the others call you, JJ?'

He glances up at me. 'It's Jasper,' he says, and tuts. 'God knows what my mother was thinking at the time, but it is an old family name apparently which I got tortured over at school!'

I roll his name around in my mind, John Jasper Jackson. It is a bit of a mouthful, but now I've got to know him a little more, it suits him. I reckon his mother knew he would cut a figure in this world whichever career he chose and wanted him to have an aristocratic name to live up to the reputation.

Now we are on a more personal level I push on, saying, 'Do you think Lloyd was married? I suppose you've looked at all of the missing persons in the area. I mean, there was no wedding ring on his finger but not everyman wears a ring, do they?'

I look down at his finger which is bare. He sits up and we look into each others eyes.

'Yes, you're right, there was no ring but if you looked closer you would have seen a faint band mark on his finger with paler skin where he had worn one.'

His observational skills are second to none and, as Mam would say, he never misses a trick. This is where his good reputation comes from and I know the DS wouldn't have scrutinised Lloyd's appearance as John has done. And neither had I.

He stares at my left hand now and my rings. Is he wondering about Allan? Penny has already told him we'd had an argument, so is he longing to ask about it? I know if I was in his place, I would.

He lays his hand over mine resting on the bench and, automatically, Alfie raises his head in protection mode at this new found familiarity. I nod at him to say it's fine and he lays back down under the bench out of the sun.

I gaze down at John's hand but don't remove it. His hand feels nice as his fingers rub the top of my rings. And then I look up into his eyes.

For one split second he lets his guard down and whispers, 'You know, my first boss called me socially awkward and even now, sometimes I think he's right,' he says. 'But it's a lonely job or can be and, when I first started out like many other detectives, I let it take over my life moving from one case to another, but now I'm beginning to regret this with no partner or family.'

I tilt my head to one side and nod at him. 'I guess it's not an easy profession to fit in with family life.'

I feel like my heart has stopped because I'm getting closer to finding out more about him and wonder why he's on his own now. I catch my breath holding out for his next words.

He shuffles on the bench. 'I relive my past more than I should,' he says. 'I'm always wondering where I went wrong. But now I've decided, it was because my mother brought me up to believe I was the best thing since sliced bread. I was smothered and mollycoddled by her, so when I married, I made the mistake of thinking I was so bloody marvellous my wife would wait around for me alone night after night, but of course she didn't. And then I realised I wasn't so bloody marvellous after all.'

'Perils of the job - a bit like Taggart?'

'Yes,' he says, with a playful twitch to his mouth. 'But without the whiskey.'

I grin at his sense of humour. I decide people will probably confuse his strong, uncommunicative manner as being grumpy, but he's not. He has flaws the same as we all do and, now he's sharing his vulnerable underbelly, I'm even more attracted to him.

I breathe properly again knowing he's divorced and not with anyone. I know I'll probably regret this later, but I lean in closer to his face and stare at his lips. His eyes cloud over and suddenly he pulls back from me and abruptly removes his hand from mine.

He springs up from the bench and in a gruff, overly emotional voice, says, 'Well, I'd better get back and see where the king of soap operas is hiding? I think I'll threaten to slap him with a perverting the course of justice offence, which is the least Brigit deserves.'

'Aww, right,' I manage to mumble and watch him stride back up to the guest house.

Chapter Twenty Five

What just happened there, I wonder feeling sad and mystified. Alfie barks and I lead him into North Marine Park with trembling legs. Perching on the end of a wooden seat, I push my knees together until they settle. I take a deep breath thinking about John and know he feels the same attraction as I do. I shake my head, but what am I doing? I'm a married woman and shouldn't even be relishing in these feelings about John, but all I know is that when I'm close to him it feels so good.

Looking around, I see it's a lovely restored park with well cut grass around the winding paths and clumps of trees. On a normal day, I would look down and appreciate the sea views, but my mind is full after the last twenty minutes of turmoil. I let Alfie off the lead and he runs off galloping around in circles.

I call to him so he knows the sound of my voice in a strange place.

'Alfie, don't go too far!'

He turns and races back to me, circling the seat and then shoots off again, having the time of his life. This will make up for being couped up in the guest house and I love watching him enjoy his freedom.

I pull out my mobile and text Penny to say I'm on my way down to beach, hoping that later we can have a fish and chip supper. It's been unusually hot for the last week in the North East, and as ever, when the weather is good, everyone heads for our beaches, which are the best in the country. Like all other seaside areas, I see the English out in force, frying themselves in the sun.

In other European countries when temperatures rise, people stay indoors, close shutters and adjust air con to keep themselves cool and safe - but not in England. We are determined to make the most of the sun, do or die. Maybe this will alter with more climate changes when we get used to hot summers on a regular basis.

The beach area is busy and I scour Littlehaven sands looking for Penny, who is usually not easy to miss. I wander through the golden sand in bare feet, carrying my sandals amongst people with red faces, shoulders and bald heads.

There is every colour of towel on the sand and many shapes of fold-up chairs and even old deckchairs. Families are well prepared for the day with tubs of sandwiches, crisp packets and big bottles of soft drinks, while children eat candy floss from The Cabin on the promenade. Older people sit in front of colourful windbreakers, although there is hardly a breeze today, but it's traditional to erect these with the wooden poles stuck down into the sand.

Eventually, I see Penny lying on a white towel with a blue stripe from the guest house and spy the back of a tall slim man walking away from her. From his stride and appearance, I reckon he's around our age with light chinos and a white T-shirt. Who was that? Just a stranger asking her for the time? Or someone who had he been with her on the beach – was it nameless man? Had he followed her here or been invited? Maybe he's dangerous, I think and hurry over to her.

'Who was that?' I ask.

Penny sits up in her yellow spotty bikini and holds a hand over her eyebrows, shading the sun. I stand with my hands on hips watching the man stride off into the distance towards the funfair.

She grins. 'Oh, it was just a guy asking for directions,' she says, and cuddles Alfie who has plonked himself onto the towel and is now lying in her lap. I don't believe her and drop down on my knees in the sand.

'Where did he want to go?'

I know if I ask outright who nameless man is, she will clam up and I'll not get any answers. I decide to try and box clever with her later. I plop down next to her on the edge of the towel.

Penny shrugs her shoulders. 'Oh, he wants to go to Marsden Rock,' she says, and changes the subject. 'Didn't you bring a swimsuit with you? It's been boiling hot today although the sea is still cold.'

I nod. 'Yeah, the North sea always is. I don't think it's ever warm, not like down south.'

I think of John on his boat and our personal conversation and bite my lip.

'What?' She asks, 'What's happened now?'

I shake my head and feel my cheeks flush red. The sun is still strong on the back of my neck even at five in the afternoon and wish I'd packed a sun hat. Sweat stands on my top lip and without asking, Penny unfolds a cap from her beach bag and gives it to me. I pull my hair up into it and turn the peak the other way to shield my neck.

'Thanks,' I mumble, and sigh.

'Tell me,' she says, and rubs my arm. 'Hey, it's me, Penny! What's going through that mixed-up mind of yours?'

My chin trembles as I look at her and take in a deep breath. I want to tell her all about John but remember how she's holding back about nameless man. The thought that, in her innocence, Penny could be mixed up with someone connected to Lloyd's murder gnaws at my stomach.

And then, I remember at school how we used to play guessing games. I say, 'I'll tell you mine, if you tell me yours?'

She knows I've hit home and pushes her toes into the sand. Now it's her turn to look embarrassed. She presses her hands against her flushed cheeks. 'Okay, so you know my neighbour, Ria, who I play golf with – she lives in the house opposite to me?'

'Yes,' I say, and scrunch up my eyebrows. 'What's this got to do with the man you're obviously seeing?'

She shrugs and looks down to the seashore. 'Well, it's Ria's hubby, Leo, that I've fallen for!'

Phew, I think and breathe out loudly. My shoulders sag and blessed relief floods my whole body, knowing this hasn't anything to do with Lloyd and the murder. My dear friend is safe.

Penny must think I've sighed at her in disappointment and she juts out her chin in defiance. 'Oh, I know I shouldn't Faye, but Leo is my guilty secret and I simply love being with him,' she says, and pouts. 'And he feels the same, in fact, he drove all the way up just to see me on the beach today. It was a great opportunity to be together, and well, I know I came up to support you, but it is my holiday, too!'

I want to laugh out loud, even though I'm a little disappointed in her for messing around with a neighbour's husband. However, it's not my place to criticise and, knowing Penny her own conscience will do just that.

I nod. 'Well, I'm pleased you've told me the truth. My mind was conjuring up all kinds of scenarios with everything that's been going on at the guest house.'

Her face brightens, and she drapes an arm along my shoulders. 'So, what's the randy Inspector been up to now?'

We both laugh and I take a deep breath and tell her about the conversation we've just had sitting opposite Grace Darling monument. 'You see, I haven't felt like being intimate with Allan for months and I can't remember the last time we had a long toe-curling kiss,' I say, trailing my finger in the sand to make a pattern. 'Other than pecks on the lips, cheeks or my forehead when he's going off to work. I mean, how sad is that? And, why am I thinking about it now? I didn't think of this last week before everything happened and he was roasting chicken while I prepared salad in he kitchen.'

Penny smiles. 'We don't think of intimate stuff when we are doing ordinary daily jobs' she says. 'And probably because you're away from him, you can look into your relationship from afar?'

I shrug. 'So why do I feel this sudden rush to be close to John? I mean, I'd wanted to kiss his lips so badly when we were staring into each others eyes, but all this has done is make me even more confused!'

I tell Penny every sentence we'd spoken and how he had rubbed the rings on my left hand but then suddenly jumped up and hurried off back to the guest house.

She whistles through her teeth. 'And he didn't ask about Allan and why he wasn't with you?'

'Nope,' I say. 'I was dying to know his marital status and more about him, but he didn't seem that interested in my circumstances.'

'Oh, he's interested all right. That's obvious in the way he looks at you and has reached out by touching your hand,' she says. 'I reckon he's like you and is out of practice and doesn't know how to react to the way he's feeling.'

'But why run off like that?'

Penny grins. 'I think you've shocked him with your open response and he isn't sure how to take the next step.'

She giggles, and I do too. 'God, I was shocked at how quickly I felt turned on by him. I mean, he's practically a stranger and it hit me right between the eyes.'

Penny nudges me and says, 'Oh, those delicious rampaging hormones!'

A woman with a nearby family arrives with cartons of fish and chips and we look at each other. I grin, 'They smell amazing – do you fancy some?'

'Yeah, we can't come to the seaside and not have them.'

Penny stands up and folds her towel while I clip on Alfie's lead. We head back along the beach and pass the funfair to reach the nearest takeaway. I insist on paying for them and we soak the fish with salt and vinegar. Sitting at an outside table, we tuck in as if we'd never been fed for weeks. The fish is fresh and battered to perfection with hot crispy chips.

Alfie looks up forlornly and I give him a few chicken treats. 'I'll get your proper dinner soon,' I say, and he wags his tail.

The noise from the big rides and rollercoasters in the fun fair behind us seems to crank up another level with children screaming and laughing.

'Come, on,' Penny says. 'I stink! I need a shower - there's sand in places where it should never be!'

I laugh at her and we stroll back up Ocean Road arm in arm.

***

We arrive back in the guest house and Penny heads upstairs with Alfie jumping up each stair in front of us. She thanks me for bringing her case upstairs and yawns. 'It's an early night for me - I'm bushed with all the sea air.'

I make sure she is comfortable and happy with the room, and then leave her to unpack. Smiling, I know she'll be free to text Leo, the named man, to her hearts content.

As I descend the top few stairs and stand on the landing outside Ken and Lily's room, I hear Mark in the corridor downstairs shouting. However, then I hear John's restrained and firm voice answering him. Looking over the top of the banister I can see they are in the doorway to the breakfast room.

'But where's she gone? I've rang her and there's no answer,' Mark wails. 'I have to find my Brigit!'

Mark will know from John that his wife saw him kissing the other woman under the streetlight on the night Lloyd died. And I know Brigit saw him with the white shortie lass in the library. I've often studied human nature in people to develop my characters when writing, and I sigh. It had been obvious when talking to Brigit that this poor woman has had as much of her husbands deceit as she could take, especially coming straight after the massage therapist.

It's with these thoughts that I don't believe Mark could have anything to do with Lloyd's death - it's just not in his pathetic nature. Although, he has proven himself to be a grade A liar, which I reckon John will think suspicious if nothing else.

I wonder if he has charged him with perverting the course of justice yet, or maybe John has had second thoughts. I reckon the threat to Mark would be enough to scare him out of his wits, if indeed he has any. I know from past research this can command a custodial sentence of one to six months, but often the judge will suggest community unpaid work. And that, I reckon, would send Mark into even more of a tizzy. If he thinks TV adverts are beneath him, the image of him sweeping up litter in a park makes me want to hoot.

Mark asks, 'Did you speak to Brigit when she gave you the note?'

I hear John answer. 'No, she didn't give it to me but left it in the guest house.'

Grumpily, Mark shouts, 'So where did she leave it or did she give it to someone?'

'I'm not at liberty to answer that question, Mr Reynolds,' John retorts. 'And would you kindly keep your voice down.'

I breathe a sigh of relief when John doesn't disclose how Brigit had given me the note and I won't be dragged into Mark's wrath and hounded by him with questions. My hero, I think dreamily, creep down the stairs quietly and hurry straight into our room.

I open the wardrobe door and chew the top of the pen, looking at my suspect post-it notes. On Penny's note, I write X, It's not her nameless man – he's called Leo and is her neighbour.

I write another post-it note with the words, It has to be a man!

I imagine John doing this in his office with a big suspect board as they do in CID with all his team around him. And then I write on Mark's post-it, X, he was at the wrong door!

My list of suspects is decreasing and I sense John's frustration. Apart from Lily and Ken, everyone else staying in the guest house has been crossed off.

I nod. So, is it the creepy old man with the dark sunglasses after all? Or of course, someone not related to the guest house in any way.

Chapter Twenty Six

The following morning over a late leisurely breakfast, I tell Penny, 'I'm thinking of walking along to Marsden Rock today, if you fancy it?'

Penny scoops up the last of her full English breakfast and smiles. 'Yeah, that'll be great, Faye. I'll just collect my things and meet you back down stairs in fifteen.'

Another warm day is forecast, although with more cloud than yesterday. Alfie and I potter along to my room but I stop still outside our door. The opposite door to Lloyd's room is open and propped ajar with a rubber door stop. I hear low voices from inside and wonder what is happening. Knowing all the investigation are finished by John and the DS, I cross the corridor and peak inside the room.

Luba is there with Shirley. They are cleaning out the room with the sash window wide open.

Luba is startled, and swings around when I call out a greeting.

'Ah, Faye, you gave me a fright,' she says. 'I don't want to be shut in the room on my own – it's so creepy!'

'Oh, sorry,' I say. 'I didn't mean to, but wasn't sure who was in here?'

Shirley is standing by the bathroom with a sponge in her good hand. She whispers, 'I'll never be able to look in this room again without seeing that poor man dead in the chair, so it's going out in the rubbish right now!'

Luba begins to drag the chair out of the room. With Alfie running in between us, I help her heave it along the corridor. We bump it down the stairs one at a time into Shirley's private rooms and out through the back door into the yard. Luba says, 'Its for council collection and Shirley has ordered a new chair.'

Walking back up the stairs, she comments, 'We've a really busy day ahead as Mark and Brigit left this morning, so I've their room to clean out as well.'

I nod. 'Oh, I knew Brigit left yesterday, but has he gone too?'

'Yep, he paid up at seven this morning and scuttled out in a hurry to reach home.'

I know they came in a car, so he couldn't have been in too much of a hurry to get home to York or he would have left last night. Perhaps, he was having his last fling with white shortie lass, before facing Brigit. However, he's in for an even bigger shock because Brigit won't be at home but safely ensconced with her father-in-law in the manor house, which she will inherit, and not him. I smirk, maybe there is some justice in the world after all.

***

Penny is downstairs waiting and we set off to walk along the seafront. There's more of a breeze this morning, but I don the cap Penny loaned me yesterday to keep the sun off my face and smooth down my curls. I've been trying to do this with my hair all my life but to no avail. Women with straight hair long for curls but I'm the opposite. Olivia bought me a mannish tweed deerstalker hat one year as a joke to cheer me up when I was writing my last crime novel. I was never good company in the middle of writing a book - it seemed to drain everything from my brain. But joking aside, now I've taken to wearing it in the winter, it tames my hair somewhat.

She'd said, 'Mam, you make this mannish style look feminine all at the same time.'

And I'd taken this as a compliment.

We walk past the amusement arcade with bowling and a soft play area which is quiet now as it doesn't open until later. We carry on alongside the fun fair and I glance at the sign telling everyone how the fair is free admission with thrilling rides, toddler friendly attractions, laser force, crazy golf and arcades. Further along, we pass a model of an old costumed pirate standing on a trellis with binoculars surrounded by palm trees looking over the park area. I point this out to Penny.

'Yeah,' she says. 'The place is all geared up for kiddies entertainment, but the noise from those dodgem cars was a nightmare last night!'

I raise my eyebrow. 'Oh, but the seaside isn't just for kids, it's for all ages. It gives us a chance to relive memories. And the younger lads and lasses get to show off their figures in bikinis and shorts,' I say. 'Plus, elderly people still believe in benefits of the salty sea for old joints.'

Penny strides ahead and, because of her height she's always been able to walk faster than I ever could. I notice she is wearing jeans today as I have done with trainers.

'You suit that orange top,' she says, changing the subject. 'It's a colour that I don't wear much because of my red hair – lucky you!'

I smile. 'But that wouldn't matter – you look good in any colour.'

As I walk with Penny, I talk about my feelings and confused state of mind. 'Well, I'm certainly not leaving here until John solves this case,' I say. 'I can't, and don't want to focus on my marriage until my head is clear.'

She asks, 'So, is that an excuse to put off the inevitable?'

'Perhaps, but if this hadn't happened with Allan would I even be looking at John in this way?'

'Debatable I suppose,' she says. 'When we meet men it can be a hit or miss affair, but with me it's always been an instant attraction thingy. If there's nothing between us from the word go, then I don't waste my time.'

I take a sideways glance at her as we walk, knowing she has much more experience in affairs of the heart than I have. Allan has been the only man in my life for so long, I know I'm floundering and these new thoughts are having a knock-on effect to every aspect of my life.

I mumble, 'So, after giving up my writing career – what do I do now? Do I stay with doggy sitting because it's something I enjoy and find more relaxing which keeps the palpitations and stress at bay, but is this really me? Or is it just a cop out?'

Penny turns to look at me and gestures to stop and sit on a seat overlooking the cliffs. I do as she bids. Alfie jumps up on the bench between us, looking from my face to Penny's, as if to say "hey what are we stopping for".

She says, 'Well, not that I'm running down dog sitting down in any shape or form, but I know my mother would have said, you're worth so much more than this, Faye. And for the record, I would agree with her. Or you could become a female amateur sleuth like Jessica Fletcher!'

I laugh, but take her words on board and know these thoughts have niggled away in the back of my mind for a while now. Not that I want to be an amateur sleuth, but I'd like to do something worthwhile.

I nod. 'Yes, you could be right. I haven't any more dreams of what I can achieve in life, and maybe I should, because I'm not just a wife and mother,' I say. 'But is this the best time to find a new path for me, and me alone, which doesn't include Allan?'

Penny smiles. 'Look, you're a savvy, intelligent and independent woman, Faye, so don't run yourself down.'

I smile. 'Yeah, I might be independent but I still want to be loved, and in love with someone,' I mutter, and then shiver. 'It's a scary thought of a new life without Allan.'

Penny strokes my shoulder. 'It's bound to be intimidating because you've been with him forever, but you can't stay with him just because it's easy. And I know you better than that,' she says. 'When I left my husband, the main feeling for months afterwards was blessed relief, which confirmed that I had done the right thing for me.'

'Hmm,' I mutter. 'I asked myself yesterday, what do I believe in and stand for in my life now? When I was an author I knew my beliefs and who I was - they were there in the written word on paper. But I don't know what mine are anymore? I feel so confused more with myself than anything else!'

'Look, just take your time making life changing decisions, Faye, because as far as I can see, this upset with Allan has opened up the proverbial can of worms in your mind, but try to look on this as a good thing.'

I giggle, thank her and stand up to walk once more. We continue in silence, both of us in deep thought, until we reach the first small craggy rock and beach area below. The entrance to the restaurant is up ahead.

Penny points further along the coast to Souter Lighthouse. 'So, I'm mega impressed with the randy Inspector being nautical and having a place overlooking the lighthouse,' she says, nudging my side. 'I bet he can't be short of a bob or two?'

I laugh. 'Oh, stop calling him that!'

The tall grey-brick tower looks as imposing as the last time I was here with Allan where the Grotto pub and restaurant are built into the rock. 'I'm trying to remember the last time I was here and reckon Olivia was about ten.'

Penny nods. 'It would have been even longer for me because I came with my hubby.'

The connecting long structure is like a passageway with a huge outdoor sign, saying BEACH FOOD, which looks a little tired now. We head into the passage and I stop to read the posters along the walkway to the lift doors, while Penny holds Alfie's lead.

I read: Blaster Jack, a retired miner in 1782 set up home in one of the caves and became a smuggler and poacher. This drew carriages of people to see the cave dwellers and his wife began serving refreshments. Followed in 1828 by Peter Allan who enlarged the cave into eight rooms and was given an ale licence. His children continued to excavate the cave until a cliff fall almost destroyed the Grotto in 1865 and the family left in 1874.

Hmm, I sigh, the name, Allan seems to be prominent at the moment. Another poster reads: The setting is wild, rugged and picturesque with the cave bar set into the 112 foot cliff. The Grotto was bought by the breweries in 1938 and adjoining passageway was rebuilt with the installation of the lift. The big rock was 109 feet in perpendicular height, 230 feet long and 120 feet wide. It had grass on the top with side steps but these have been washed away by the tides over the years.

Just as well, I reckon and smile, thinking of our health and safety procedures nowadays. At high tide, the big rock where Blaster Jack began is only accessible by boat, and is a landmark for shipping. Apparently, in the 1930s it was known as Camel Island, and I grin wondering if John has been around there in his skiff.

I hurry to Penny and Alfie as the lift doors open and we step inside travelling slowly to the bottom. The doors open up into a restaurant with many people sitting at tables eating. Penny strides ahead, weaving through the tables up to bifold glass doors. We step out onto beach level on a wide path with smatterings of sand from people's footwear. There are six tables with small chairs and Penny grabs the middle table, laying her bag down.

'I'll get us a drink,' she says, and heads back inside.

I look at the sight of dramatic rock formation in front of me, and up to the north inlet with its narrower stretch of sand and pebbles. I shake my head in awe - it is simply breathtaking. I'm appreciating this scene so much more now than I would have done when younger and value our coast line in all its natural glory.

At low tide, which is now, people can walk on the sand between the huge apertures forming the archway of the biggest rock where the family had previously made rooms. It's such a shame that most of it has been swept out to sea. However, the front of the beach is mainly covered in grey flat stones and smaller pebbles.

Looking around for Alfie, I see - much to the delight of a family at the corner table - he has his nose to the ground on his snifarri around the new territory. They fuss him while I sit down and when Penny joins me, we sit and sip our diet cokes.

Out of the blue, Penny says, 'The last time I golfed with Ria was before I'd started seeing Leo, and she'd said their marriage was over and how she was going to leave him.'

This still doesn't make it right, I want to say, but don't. I can almost hear the reasoning in her mind as though she's trying to justify the affair to herself. And to me.

I pat her hand. 'I'll use one of my fathers sayings: if it's meant to be, it'll be,' I say, and look back over to the biggest rock. The sea is all shades of blue and grey as clouds move across the sky and the smaller flatter rocks in front of the archway are covered in green seaweed.

A few couple are wandering around, and then I gasp. Down near the sand leading into the archway, I see Ken.

'Penny! Look, it's the old man from the guest house called Ken.'

She turns and squints her eyes slightly. 'Yeah, it certainly looks like him – so what?'

He's now bending down and collecting what look like different sized pebbles. I get up and walk to the end of the path where it meets the sand looking around for Lilly, but there's no sign of her.

With my back to the beach, in front of me is a small grey pebbled-dashed house adjoining the side of the restaurant. I remember reading how it was available for holiday rental and there's a pale blue picket fence around the white door and windows which looks pretty.

On the side of the house is the start of hundreds of old steps leading up the cliff side with rusty yellow railings. I reckon Blaster Jack and the other family must have had strong thighs to make it up and down before the lift was installed.

I shake my head and wander back towards Penny. As I pass by the first table, I notice what I'm sure is Ken's rucksack on top. The flap is open and my fingers twitch in desperation to know what he keeps in there.

I look around to see no one is watching and beckon to Penny who gets up and then I call Alfie.

There's a dog bowl with water underneath the table and he immediately canters towards me. I point to the bowl and he gulps at the water while I step up to the rucksack.

Penny peers over my shoulder. 'What's the matter? Has someone left their bag – we should tell the restaurant staff,' she says.

I grab her arm. 'Noooo, I'm sure it's Ken's rucksack, and I need to know what he keeps inside.'

Penny giggles. 'Go on, Jessica Fletcher, and I'll keep watch while you nosey inside.'

I mutter to myself, 'It might help the inquiry if we can see what's in there.'

Penny puts her hand over her eyebrows as a shade because the sun has reappeared and says, 'Ken is still over there by the archway – so go for it!'

My shoulders shiver and know I shouldn't be snooping but the temptation gets too much and I check around at other people sitting further away. They're not taking any notice of us at all. My mouth dries as I inhale deeply.

Penny whispers, 'He's now striding to the large rock archway to go inside and has pulled out his binoculars.'

I nod and reassure myself there's time for a peek while Penny is doing a great job of keeping tout for me. I remember John's words about a motive, and am determined to see what's inside.

I pull the sleeve of my orange top over my hand and part the booklets and a hip flask aside in the rucksack amongst pens and pencils. My heart begins to race and I bite my lip.

Underneath is an empty brown leather sheaf, which looks suspiciously like it could have held a knife. The hairs stand up on my arms and I gasp. If this scene was in a film, the music would change now to the steady beat of a drum - dum, dum, dum or a weird screeching noise like the psycho scene in Hitchcock's shower setting.

'Ken is heading back out of the archway now,' Penny hisses. 'Close the bag, quick!'

With my other hand, I pull out my mobile and take a quick photograph of the sheath then remove my hand and fold over the flap once more.

We both hurry over to our table and sit down, gulping at our cokes.

'Wow!' Penny says, and sniggers. 'That was fun! I loved being part of the investigation even if I was just the look-out.'

I giggle and feel my heart rate slow down again. 'There's a murderer in our midst,' I whisper to Penny in a creepy voice.

'Oh, it's good to see our Jessica Fletcher is back on the case,' she says. 'And being melodramatic!'

Penny takes Alfie onto the beach, carrying him like a baby across the pebbles in case he hurts his paws. I smile. He would have been fine running on them but I love her concern for him, as though he was her own.

With time to myself, I think over what I've just seen. Was that rucksack big enough to hold a knife larger than the sheaf? I think back to the scene in Lloyd's room that morning and what I'd observed. The knife had been thrust deep into Lloyd's chest and there was only the handle visible. So, I don't know how long or short the blade was. If it was short, it may well fit into this sheaf. But I don't know the answer to this and take a deep breath. I can't make accusations without fact and truth. I can almost hear John saying "conjecture and baseless speculation doesn't work".

I watch Ken wandering in and out through the huge rock and wonder, if he had done it – what would his motive be? Did he know Lloyd? Lilly had said that he didn't, but maybe Ken was doing things behind her back. Always a possibility and suspicious enough to report to John.

I take out my mobile, enter his mobile number from the business card he gave me, and text a message, attaching the photograph.

'I'm at Marsden Roack with Penny and Alfie. Ken is here although there's no sign of Lilly. He's inside the rock now but had left his rucksack on the table so I've had a snoop and found this.'

Reading his instant reply, I grin. 'Stay where you are – I'm on my way!'

Chapter Twenty Seven

Oh, he's coming, I think and to use one of his expressions, I feel giddy with excitement. However, I'm not sure how long John will be and look over at Ken. I know we mustn't lose him. We have to keep him here until John arrives.

I text Penny. 'John is coming – keep Ken there – go talk to him!'

I know she will look at the text straight away because she'll think it's from Leo. I watch her pull out her mobile from her handbag and read it. She looks across at me and gives me a thumbs up sign. With Alfie running around her legs, she strolls over to Ken.

I keep one eye on the lift waiting for John to arrive and watch Penny's body language while talking to Ken. He has one of his notebooks in his hand, and I can tell she's feigning interest in what he's saying. If anyone can play this role, it's Penny.

A sense of sadness fills me knowing we have to find a motive for this murder because if we don't, the killer will get away with the crime. And that, I know, mustn't happen. He has to pay for doing this and not only for the loss of Lloyd's life but for the upheaval in Shirley's guest house.

And then I see the lift doors open with John and the DS hurrying towards me. His face is flushed and his eyes are gleaming as he pulls on blue gloves. I point to the rucksack and then to Ken and Penny. He nods at the DS who hurries across the sand to the rock, taking Ken by the arm as if he was going to run away. I doubt at his age he'd have the energy to do this, but I can see she has a firm grip on him.

'This is great, Faye,' he says, picking up the rucksack. 'Now if you could all go back to the guest house and wait for me there, please?'

I wait for Penny and Alfie to return. John passes them on the sand and ruffles Alfie's head.

Penny hurries to me. 'So, we're going to miss all the action, Jessica,' she says.

I nod and clip on Alfie's lead. My shoulders sag as we make our way back up in the lift, and I have to admit I'm disappointed. First, that I'll not see what happens to Ken, and second, that I won't spend more time with John, which is a blow.

As we leave the passageway and up the incline onto the roadside, I spot a bus coming. We run over the road and jump onto it back along the seafront. 'It'll be quicker because I want to see Lilly and let her know what's happened.'

***

We reach the guest house and enter the front door.

Penny smiles. 'I might go to the beach as the sun is coming back out again,' she says. 'Leo is going to drive up again and we'll have a late supper together – I need to talk with him.'

'Oh, that sounds ominous?'

She nods and heads up the stairs to her attic room. 'Yeah, it is,' she says, over her shoulder. 'And if I was you, I'd let John know you're interested and see what happens.'

I see the frown on her face and know of old that there's trouble brewing. No doubt I'll hear about it later, I muse and head along the corridor to the breakfast room, looking for Lilly. There's no sign of her so I backtrack and up the stairs to their room above mine.

I tap on the door and call out softly, 'Lilly are you in there?'

There's shuffling movements and I can hear coming to the door. She opens the door and the first thing I notice is how pale she looks. She's in a white dressing gown with a blue hairnet over her shampoo and set.

'Lilly,' I ask. 'Are you okay?'

She nods, opening the door wider. 'It's just one of my migraines but I've taken some pills and have been resting on the bed - it's easing off a little now.'

She lays back up against her pillows and I perch on the end of the armchair in the bay window. It's a bigger room than mine accommodating the twin beds. The décor is the same though and I notice the same colour and shape of chair that was in Lloyd's room.

I tell her how we saw Ken actually inside Marsden Rock, and I rave about the beach and natural surroundings. I don't want to tell her about the rucksack and sheath in case it compromises John's enquiries. He might want to do this himself with Lilly to find out what she actually knows about Ken's shenanigans.

I shuffle uneasily on the chair. 'Well, the Inspector and DS were just turning up at the Grotto as we left to get into the lift, but they'd headed over the sand to talk to him. And then we got the bus back along the seafront, so I'm not sure what's happened. '

She tuts loudly and touches her eyebrows. 'Dear God, what's the silly old fool been up to now!'

I read from this how being in trouble is nothing new to Ken and wonder if John has checked with the police in Glasgow to see if he has a criminal record.

She puts her head back fully onto the pillow and closes her eyes. 'You know, I did have a cold shiver run up my spine as though I was in the cemetery and somebody had trodden on a grave,' she says. 'Was it around thirty minutes ago? I knew there would be bad news on it's way!'

I confirm the time and swallow hard, hoping she's not going into one of her trances which unsettles me for some reason as I know full well it's a load of clap trap. However, it was the correct timing and I stroke Alfie's back, drawing comfort from his familiarity. I notice he hasn't attempted to jump on the bed to be close to her, but looks up at me and I nod at him in reassurance.

'That bloody Grotto! I only went with him once and heard the spirits calling. Their voices bounced off the rock speaking so quickly I couldn't keep track of them all,' she says.

With her eyes still closed she turns her head to the window behind me. Stupidly, I twist and look behind me at the window to see if there's anything on the glass.

Her voice has a weird whisper to it now when she says, 'It was as if the spirits were all in different rooms begging to be let out. There was a woman calling for Jack,' she says, and raises her voice. 'Children's voices were shouting "Dad, Dad, where are you"? And then another woman called loudly for Mr Allan!'

I leap up off the seat and cry out at the name Allan. 'No, it couldn't have been!'

Alfie jolts and clings to my legs which are trembling. I bend down and ruffle his ears as if to say "I'm okay, it was just a shock". Maybe he'd heard the name Allan too and thought he was returning.

With her eyes still shut, Lilly nods. 'Oh yes, my dear it was, and my head was buzzing when I got back in the lift to leave, but not in a good way, if you know what I mean.'

She opens her eyes now, burps loudly and rubs her midriff. 'Ooops, excuse me,' she says. 'Those tablets are good for the pain but they play havoc with my stomach.'

I take in a deep breath but my knees are still knocking together and reach out to hold onto the chair back to steady myself. 'Er, shall I make you a cup of tea? Would that help your stomach?'

She shakes her head. 'No thanks, I'd prefer a glass of milk, but we've used all of the little pots from the tea tray.'

'Not a problem, Lilly, I'll pop down to Shirley and get some milk for you – they're bound to be somewhere downstairs.'

Pulling on Alfie's lead, I hurry us out of the room, leaving the door open. I stand with my back against the wall at the top of the stairs and feel my palpitations start. I take in deep breaths, wondering how she knew about Blaster Jack and Peter Allan in the Grotto.

After three big breaths, my legs steady and stop trembling. My heart stops thumping and I think logically. Lilly had probably read the posters like I did about the Grotto and how it had all begun. And the fact that the surname Allan was the same as my husband's, which I'd thought rationally when I read the details.

However, she had certainly rattled my head when she called out his name – my heart had nearly missed a beat with the shock.

I meander down the stairs towards Shirley's rooms remembering a girl that Penny and I knew at college who always reckoned she was telepathic. She often told us how she was capable of transmitting thoughts to other people and knowing their own thoughts. Penny had said it was a load of rubbish, but I had researched the subject of twins for one of my books and know they have a special connection between them.

So, maybe Lilly had known Ken was in trouble in a telepathic way half an hour ago? This is also how I often feel about Alfie, although animals can't talk, but there are authors of pet psychics. The term "psychic" refers to the claimed ability to perceive information unavailable to the normal senses by what is claimed to be extrasensory perception.

I shake my head and see Luba coming towards me. I ask for milk and she hurries through the breakfast room and into the small kitchen. She pours milk into a china jug and hands me a clean glass tumbler. I thank her and climb the stairs again slowly. I let my mind wander through the theories of the spirit world and wonder, is Allan trying to reach me through Lilly? Arriving in Lilly's room, I hand over the jug and glass then make a hasty retreat.

As I hurry into our room and Alfie settles in his basket, I slump down onto the end of the bed. But if Allan was trying to reach me through Lilly, this would mean that he'd passed over. I gulp and whip out my mobile to message Olivia. This is the problem with not keeping in touch since storming out of our house, I chastise myself.

My mouth dries as I stare down at my mobile on the quilt, willing it to light up with Olivia's reply. I sigh. Although I'm not thinking about our marriage problems at the moment, I couldn't bear anything awful happening to him. All the same, whether I'm still in love with him or not, he's part of my family and years of us being together flash through my mind in images. Renovating the house, birthday and anniversary celebrations, Olivia's childhood and family gatherings. They'd been good times and I rub my fingers together praying, that he's okay.

The screen lights up and she answers. 'Every one is fine, Mam. Hope you'll be home soon – we all miss you. Xxxx'

My shoulders drop and I exclaim into the empty room. 'Thank God!'

Heading into the bathroom, I run the shower and stand underneath the warm water, ridiculing myself for letting my mind fly off into silly thoughts. The name Allan was nothing more than a trivial coincidence which I've blown up from a molehill into the proverbial mountain.

Climbing out of the shower, I leave it running and call for Alfie. He jumps under the water and I lather his back, head and legs then scrub the sand and muck off his paws.

Just as I'm changed into a multi-coloured stripey dress to go out and eat, there's a rap on the door. Wondering if it's Penny, I open the door to see John standing. I can tell by the look of dejection on his face and how he shakes his head slowly, Ken is no longer a suspect.

'Have you eaten?' He asks. 'I'm heading over the road to a nice Italian bistro if you fancy joining me?'

Oooh, I think with excitement pumping through my veins. Would I fancy it? And decide, hell yes, I'd love to but, as casual as possible, I reply, 'That would be lovely, John. Give me five minutes to feed Alfie and I'll meet you at the font door, that's if it's dog-friendly of course?'

He plants his feet apart and nods. 'Well, if it isn't - I'll make it so.'

Applying lipstick and fluffing up my curls, I think of John's quiet but rock-solid authority and know from a woman's point of view, it's quite a turn on.

I watch Allfie eat his bowl of food and hope he doesn't linger. I chat to him as he turns to his water bowl and laps up the cold water. He looks at me, as if to say "right that's me ready for our big date", and I giggle. Running my fingers through his drying silky ears, I'm pleased that he too is showered and smells nice.

Chapter Twenty Eight

John guides me across Ocean Road to the small bistro and opens the door.

'May, I?' he asks, and takes Alfie's lead from my hand.

I follow them inside and wait by the door. Alfie trots along next to him perfectly at ease in his company now. I muse, Alfie feels like me - safe and protected by John. Which, I shrug, he never had been with Allan. I bite my lip, trying once more not to compare the two men, but have often seen Alfie run away from Allan, given the chance.

It's a small square room with ten tables, of which three are taken by people eating and obviously enjoying their food. I watch John talking with two waiters, see him flash his warrant card and point down to Alfie who looks up at them beseechingly. Nice touch, I think, knowing they'll never refuse his docile good dog looks.

We are taken to a table at the back near the flap doors into the kitchen. This is good because we'll not be seen from the windows at the front. I'm not sure why I am thinking this way because it's not a dinner date, but simply a meeting to discuss the happenings at Marsden this afternoon. And I'm sure John will think this way, too. Yeah right, who am I kidding? I sit down opposite him while Alfie lies over his shoes under the table.

'I told them he was our surveillance dog,' John says.

I grin and tilt my head to the side. 'Ah, so this is how CID really works?'

We order red wine and I'm glad he is partial to a Rioja, as I am. Bubbles of excitement are churning their way through my stomach and I'm not sure I'll be able to eat anything unless I calm myself down.

I tease, 'So, Inspector, what can you recommend to eat?'

'Well, the lasagne and garlic bread are always good,' he says. 'But there again, that will only work if we are both going to eat garlic, if not it may be a little awkward.'

Why, I wonder? Is he thinking of kissing me and doesn't want his breath to smell of garlic? I tut and shake the crazy thought from my mind as John picks up the tall menu card in front of his face.

'Okay,' I say, reading my menu and peeking over the top. 'I'll go with your recommendation and have the garlic bread with lasagne.'

The waiter arrives with our wine, John orders food for us both, and I take a large gulp of wine to steady myself. I can't remember, if at all, when I was last out for dinner with a man other my husband. As soon as I think this, I push it from my mind, not wanting to spoil a minute of this night thinking of Allan.

As the waiter leaves us, John lowers his voice and says, 'So, you'll be dying to know what happened with Ken at the Grotto and the knife?'

Realising he's speaking quietly because of the subject matter - namely a knife - and he wouldn't want anyone to hear this, I nod and lean further over the table towards him. 'Okay, well my knowledge of knives is zilch, but I reckon the sheath was about six inches long and three inches wide. I thought of my knives in the kitchen at home knowing most of them are slimmer than this, so maybe this wider shape was for a dagger?'

I see the look of gloom fill his eyes. 'Yeah, you're right about the dimensions and it was a dagger shape, which I figured could be from a car boot sale years ago,' he says.

'And once again the lead got us nowhere because Ken had the knife in the pocket of his mack with a small plastic bag and was innocently scraping off different coloured bits of rock.'

I sigh with disappointment. 'Oh no, not another dead end. I really thought we were on to something this time.'

'Me, too, but thanks for the call and photograph. I feel as though this case is one step forward, thanks to you, and then three steps back when it doesn't show up anything useful to lead me onto a motive.'

I raise an eyebrow. 'Is there a law against tampering with historic landmarks?'

'I'm not sure, I could look into it, but quite honestly, I felt more sorry for him than anything else especially while my DS had him by the arm. Not like Mark, who got what was coming to him,' he says. 'Poor old Ken is just that, an elderly guy with an obsessive interest in the rock.'

I brighten and smile at John while he sips his wine.

'Well, if nothing else, Lilly will be pleased,' I say, and tell him about the spirits in the Grotto.

He laughs. 'I'm beginning to think this murder has nothing to do with any of the guests in the house and it's time I thought outside of the box.'

I smile. 'I'm coming to that conclusion myself because everyone I think could be suspicious proves to be as innocent as me and Alfie. They're simply there to have a good holiday.'

He nods as the waiter brings our food to the table. I see Alfie poke his head up from under the table. I'm absolutely gobsmacked when John pulls out a small bag of doggy treats from his trouser pocket and asks, 'May, I?'

'Oh yes, of course,' I say. 'Wow - that's so thoughtful!'

My insides give a little squeeze at the gesture of generosity towards Alfie and I know, to use an old saying, this goes above and beyond the call of duty. Alfie gobbles up the treats which John holds in the palm of his hand and receives a ruffle on his head.

'Well, Alfie is responsible for my only little bit of good luck so far in this case, so he deserves a little indulgence, like we all do at times.'

I begin to eat and decide to change the subject. 'In the last few days, I've learnt the perils of having an inquisitive mind,' I say. 'At one stage I was even quizzing my oldest and dearest friend, Panny!'

I tell him about Penny and the nameless man, who is now called, Leo.

He nods. 'So, it looks like you are both coming to some type of crossroads in life?'

And I know he is referring to my own marriage with Allan. He crunches into a slice of garlic bread and shares the other half with me. It's a natural gesture as though we've been sharing garlic bread with each other for years. But I know he needs to hear my predicament from me, and no one else.

I chew the garlic bread and swallow a mouthful of red wine. 'Yes, well, you could say I'm having a break from my husband and our marriage.'

'Tell me,' he mutters, and sits back in his chair sipping his wine.

I tell him briefly that we've been together forever, and about Olivia and the grandchildren. I swallow hard and then tell him about the argument over the divorce papers, and everything that happened following this.

I wonder what he is thinking when I see the studious look descend onto his face. It's the look I've quickly become used to seeing and know he is carefully thinking through my tale of woe.

My mind spins. Perhaps he thinks I'm somehow connected to Lloyd? Maybe a love triangle gone wrong between me, Allan and Lloyd? If I was him, I'd wonder if Allan had stormed into the guest house looking for me and caught me in Lloyd's room. I take a deep breath and hope he has more sense than I obviously have and then chastise myself.

I will myself to calm down and simply enjoy his company and the food. 'So, do you think we need to do something with old the divorce papers that weren't sent? And, would Allan be classed as a bigamist?'

He shakes his head. 'You could check with a lawyer, but l think the details and accusation of bigamy would have died with his first wife,' he says. 'So I don't think your husband or you have anything to worry about and are in the clear.'

I finish the last forkful of lasagne and push away the plate. 'Thanks, John,' I say. 'I'd been dreading telling you about it because it's embarrassing, but actually, I feel quite relieved now.'

He smiles. 'You can talk to me about anything, but all the same, it must have been a shock? Did you ever meet his ex?'

I shake my head. 'No, but now I wonder what she'd felt when she heard how Allan had married me knowing he was still wed to her?'

He shrugs. 'Probably, if she'd gone off with someone else abroad she might not have even known or cared? I wouldn't torture yourself about that, Faye.'

I love the way he says my name and right at this moment I feel close to him. Not because we are working together trying to solve puzzles around Lloyd, but personally close as a good friend, or dare I even think this, as an admirer on a date.

The waiter appears and whisks off the empty plates, leaving the menus once more.

'Dessert or coffee,' John asks.

I resist the offer of dessert. 'Just a coffee please.'

He says, 'I've noticed a lot of novels in the bookstores recently are all centred around the home – have you?'

This is a complete change of conversation and I'm glad it's about something I know well. Our coffee arrives and I sip it slowly, wanting tonight to last as long as possible.

I nod. 'Yeah, I think most of these books were written during lockdowns from authors isolated and working from home. Maybe they'd been staring out of their windows as they wrote.' I say. 'And I've always thought, even though all doors on a street of houses look the same, it's the different families behind these locked doors that are so interesting. Of course, many authors have used the famous old film by Hitchcock called Rear Window as their bench mark.'

I'm thrilled that we are talking about something other than the case. 'Do you read many crime novels?' I ask. 'And if so, who is your favourite author?'

'Well, you are at the moment,' he says, and grins.

He reaches into his blazer pocket and pulls out his mobile. He scrolls down and turns the screen to face me.

I gulp, and feel my cheeks flush. I'm staring at the front cover of my last book. which he has obviously downloaded. My stomach knots with the knowledge that a professional crime officer is reading my work, but as well as being nervous, I'm thrilled at his interest in my book. 'Oh, so you're reading one of mine?'

He smiles. 'Yep, I'm a slow reader but am loving the first ten chapters so far. Your characters are so likable that they could easily get away with any crime. It makes me feel sorry for them and be on their side no matter what they've done,' he says. 'Although your murderer in the book is good looking, upper class living in a detached lovely house and speaks very well, so I reckon he's less likely to commit such a crime.'

'Ahh,' I say, and tease. 'That's what everyone thinks, but this isn't true – they're just as capable of killing as an ugly man on the street with no qualifications who can hardly string a sentence together!'

He laughs and I love to see the fun and pleasure in his eyes. He says, 'And, your detective is nothing like the usual CID brigade of men I've met!'

I giggle. 'Probably not, but mine are all fictional and not based upon anyone I've known.'

His eyes tease now. 'In fact, I've started repeating some of your catch phrases to my parrot who is loving them.'

I throw back my head now and laugh at the image of him and his parrot at home. He reaches his arm along the table towards me. I remember Penny's words of advice to let him know I'm interested, and I place my hand over his this time. His hand is cool and he looks into my eyes.

The waiter appears and discreetly place a plate with the bill onto the table.

John shakes his head slightly and then slides his hand out from under mine. 'Well, Faye, I've really enjoyed our meal, and hopefully I'll read a few more of your chapters tonight.'

He gets up and walks to the waiter to pay for the meal while my offer to pay half falls on deaf ears.

I stand up knowing he wants to leave and Alfie jumps up from under the table. I follow John out of the restaurant and, as he waves goodbye and hurries off down to the seafront, I feel crushed all over again.

Chapter Twenty Nine

Last night when we'd got back to our room, I'd opened the wardrobe door and marked the post-it note for Ken with a big X, it's not him – archaeological buff.

I'd felt really flat after John had scarpered again, but Penny turned up at my door and I knew she would help lift my spirits. I had been so pleased to see her, as was Alfie. She'd thrown herself up onto my bed in a slinky lilac jumpsuit, and punched up the pillows behind her head. No wonder Leo is besotted with her, I'd thought.

By the sadness in her eyes, I had known straight away that something important had happened with Leo, but decided to wait until she was ready to talk. With cups of hot chocolate from the sachets on the tea tray, we'd sat together and sipped the hot drink.

'I forgot how good hot chocolate is?' she'd said.

I agreed and launched into my night with John and how disappointed I'd felt.

'Okay,' she'd said. 'I reckon you've scared him out of his wits and although he wants to be with you, he's being very cautious, just as a randy Inspector should be!'

I'd known it was her way of trying to lighten my mood and nodded. 'Do you really think so?'

'Of course,' she'd said and smiled. 'It's obvious that he's interested by bringing Alfie treats and downloading your book – this shows he wants to get to know you better.'

I had smiled, grateful for her words of wisdom. 'So, what about Leo?'

Penny had sighed heavily, and then said, 'I've told Leo to go home, end his marriage and when he's officially separated to come back and find me. I figure I'm worth that at least.'

Alfie whined to be up on the bed with us, so I'd lifted the blue throw onto the bed and let him cuddle in between us. 'I agree, Penny, and the last thing you need is to get tangled up in a messy love triangle.'

She'd sloped off upstairs to bed, and I'd taken Alfie outside for his last whoopsie and then fallen into a dreamless sleep.

However, this morning, we've had breakfast together and I'm back in my room ringing my doggy-sitting clients to say I'm taking an impromptu break for a week. There's a mist rolling in from the sea this morning and Penny has gone off for a run, which she hopes will lighten her sulky mood. I hear Luba out in the corridor and open the door.

She's in knee-length shorts this morning and wearing a blue vest. The main front door is propped open as she hoovers the carpet. 'It's so hot and stuffy this morning,' she says.

I agree with her and see a small boy playing on the top stair. I wave to him and call out, 'Hello, Borys.'

He waves back, as she says, 'I'm going to change your bed and towels now if that's okay?'

'Yes, that'll be lovely. I'll just take Alfie out for an hour's run in the park.'

When we return sweating and tired, I can see that Luba has replenished the tea tray and I make myself a coffee. Alfie laps at his fresh water after his run and my mobile tinkles with a message from Allan.

'Please, let's talk - I know we can get through this — I love you! XXX'

My legs tremble as I sit on the end of the bed, breathing in the smell of freshly aired bed linen. The branch on my worry tree is quivering and I know at some time, I'll have to face up to my feelings for him. The embarrassment last night when telling John that my husband was a bigamist hangs heavily on my shoulders. However, I can't wish I'd never met him all those years ago because then I wouldn't have my beautiful family.

In those days, I felt as though I was walking on solid ground with Allan, but now his lies have created a huge crater in the road. I pull my shoulders back knowing I'm determined not to fall face down into that crater, no matter how hard he tries to fill it with new concrete.

Our solid framework is compromised and my trust in him has gone. As I read his message again, I'm not sure if I'll ever trust another word he says. And who's to say this is the only secret he's kept from me over the years? Had there been more that I don't know about and, has he had a nameless woman in his life?

Allan is a good-looking man and has an easy charm about him, although I can't remember him ever being in the wrong place at the wrong time, which would have made me suspicious. I've never had cause to search his pockets for hotel receipts or felt the need to check his messages and call log on his mobile phone. My trust in him has always been beyond question - well, up until now.

I take a deep breath, steady the branch on the tree, and type, 'I know we have to talk, Allan, but I'm just not ready yet. I will be in touch when I am.'

My finger hovers over the X letter as I would usually put kisses on his message, but don't feel as though I can. I press send and throw the mobile onto the quilt.

I open the door to thank Luba for cleaning my room and see Borys is sitting in the corridor outside the breakfast room. His eyes light up when he sees Alfie and runs along the corridor to my dog. He drops to his knees, hugging him around the neck and Alfie joins in the fun by rolling on his back with his paws up. Borys has the same striking brown eyes and black hair as Luba, and looks as cute as a button.

Luba says, 'He wants a dog, but I can't cope with one doing all the hours in here – it wouldn't be fair because I couldn't walk him as often as he needs.'

However, I see her eyes glisten over watching Borys play with Alfie and I reckon it won't be long before the little lad gets his wish.

Borys has a memory stick in the shape of a green monster clutched in his hand and Luba asks, 'Where did you get that from?'

His pet lip trembles. 'The Indian boy gave it to me because they found it on the carpet by the front door. It wasn't his, but he'd been playing with it so I thought that was okay.'

Luba sets off in a tirade of scolding him for taking something that wasn't his, and then says to me, 'I'll put it into the lost property box which Shirley has downstairs.

My antennae are up on full alert now. If this didn't belong to the Indian boy, someone else must have dropped it, and my mind spins again with another scenario. Could the killer have dropped this running away from the altercation in Lloyd's room?

'Luba, I'll take this in case it's something the Inspector needs to see.' I say, and Borys hands it to me. I smile at him, hoping to portray that he's not in trouble.

They walk along the corridor together, Luba holding his hand and Borys with his head dipped. I whisper to Alfie, 'I hope she doesn't scold him too much.'

Alfie gives a little whimper in agreement while I roll the memory stick around in the palm of my hand. Wishing, not for the first time, that I'd packed my laptop, but I didn't. I doubt Penny would have packed hers either. And can't think that Lilly or Shirley will own a iPad or laptop.

The need to ring John is mixed with the fact that after last night, I'd like it to be him who contacts me because he was the one to scurry away. I'd been prepared to stay the course and would have loved a goodnight kiss, or at least I think I would. But needs must, I suppose and ring him with the request to bring a device to use the memory stick and see what it holds.

We sit side by side with a small laptop on the corner table in the breakfast room. His greeting is friendly and he doesn't mention last night other than to say the food and my company were great.

With my hands folded calmly in my lap and a weighed-down feeling in my stomach, I agree. Keep it cordial, I think and stem the excitement at his closeness, although it feels different after last night. I decide to erect a bridge up against him and not let feelings overtake my logical and reasonable mind. I'd felt stung and hurt last night by his actions, and figure after what I'm going through with

Allan, more upset is the last thing I need. I suppress a titter with the image of sitting John next to Allan on another branch on my worry tree.

As John inserts the memory stick, photographs begin to appear alongside American stories and images of The Empire State Building, and Central Park. John keeps scrolling down and sighs with impatience.

'Well, there are no images of India,' I say. 'Which if it had belonged to that family, you'd expect to see.'

He shrugs and takes off his blazer to wrap around the back of the chair, but doesn't answer.

I push on, and ask, 'So, what did your DS find out when she went to see the Indian man and his wife?'

'Absolutely nothing,' he says. 'They hadn't heard anything up in the attic room during the night and all of them had been in their room from nine the night before, so they didn't see anything either.'

'Oh, this is useless,' he says, and sighs. 'There's zilch on here!'

'Well, at least we know it doesn't belong to the Indian children, unless of course they took a trip to New York. So, if it wasn't them who dropped it on the carpet, who does it belong to?' I say. 'It's not Luba's, and I cant see Shirley even knowing what a memory stick is. Lilly and Ken are too old, so it leaves Mark or Brigit – could you ring him?'

Joh nods. 'Yes, I'll get my DS to do that.'

And then I have a light bulb moment. With looking at images of New York, it suddenly dawns upon me.
'That's it!' I cry. 'It's Tom Ford perfume!'

'What is?'

I clap my hands together. 'It's been driving me mad trying to think what the perfume was in Lloyd's room that morning!' I shout. 'My husband has a cousin who wears it and they live in Boston now. She reckons it's the most popular American perfume.'

John sits up further in the chair and pulls back his shoulders. 'But what has an American got to do with Lloyd?'

I shrug. 'I suppose because he lives in the USA now doesn't mean to say he was born there. He could be English and knew Lloyd way back in childhood?'

I can tell John is alert now and the gleam is back in his eyes. The next photograph is of a family together which looks to be in a social club or bar with optics hanging in the background. It's in colour, but I figure by the fashions of their clothes it's about fifteen years ago.

A woman in her fifties is sitting on a chair wearing a green short skirt and flowery top, which shows her squat awkward knees rammed together. Next to her sits a young woman in her early twenties with long blonde hair and is heavily spray tanned. She's wearing black shiny leggings and a stripey top but this suits her as she's very thin and tall with skinny legs. Behind them are two young men standing with a hand each on the mother's shoulders. The shortest man has long dreadlocks and is wearing a cream jacket with drainpipe jeans. I recognise him instantly.

I shout, 'I think I've seen him outside the Customs House!'

'What!!' John yells.

I gabble, 'Z...zoom in a bit and enlarge the photo.'

John does as I bid. 'Yes, that's definitely him! He's much younger on the photo, but I'm sure it's the same guy with long dreadlocks. He was sitting with a blonde woman outside the Customs House. I thought he looked as though he was in a theatre company with his flamboyant style, but the first time I saw him was just when I arrived. He was in reception in the Sea Hotel down on the seafront when I'd gone in to ask for a room.'

'Really?' John says. 'But just because he was sitting outside the theatre doesn't mean he is an actor.'

I nod and scrutinise the photograph again. 'That's true, but I was too far away to get a good look at the blonde woman. I suppose she could be the young girl with long hair on this photo.'

John is standing up now and I do too. He puts both his hands onto my forearms as if to steady me, and says, 'Now think, Faye, tell me everything you can remember word for word about what you heard and saw.'

I take in a deep breath and try to look outwards as I used to do when writing my characters. I close my eyes and nod. 'So, I went inside the Sea Hotel and up to the reception desk. I was told they were fully booked but to try the guest houses on Ocean Road, and then I asked to use the loo. The door was locked so I sat down onto a chair to wait and that's when the man with long dreadlocks ran into reception like a whirlwind.'

John is still holding my arms and breathes out slowly, 'Yes, yes, and then what happened?'

I nod a few times. 'Well, he looked out of place in South Shields. He was around mid or late thirties, and with a definite American accent. He had long black dreadlocks, and I remember thinking he looked like the pop star Prince. He was short and skinny in a navy blue pin-stripe suit with a wide pink shawl draped over his right shoulder. He wore white leather ankle boots with brown squat heels and a zip. He ran up to the receptionist wailing in a squeaky childlike voice, 'I've lost my ring! And I'll just die without it!'

The hotel receptionist remained calm and said, 'No, you won't, Sir, we'll find it for you.' She went into a locked luggage room behind the desk and he followed her inside. Then I heard him whooping and congratulating her because they'd obviously found his ring!'

John drops his hold on me, and rubs his hands together in glee. 'And the ring?'

I take in another deep breath. 'Yes, he came out holding it and slipped it onto his forefinger, which from where I was sitting in the sun, looked like a gold thick-banded sovereign.'

My mind is spinning and I curse under my breath. 'Dear God, why didn't I remember this when you told me about the ring yesterday down at the Grace Darling boat?'

He shakes his head slowly. 'It doesn't matter – you've remembered it now which is great!'

I clip on Alfie's lead and begin to hurry after him out of the breakfast room as he rings his DS. He shouts, 'Come back to the guest house, and pick up the laptop with the memory stick and take it back to the IT guys in the office!'

My heart is racing in excitement as we hurry along the corridor. I say, 'S...so, could this sovereign ring have caused the indent in Lloyd's shoulder?'

John cries out aloud, 'Maybe, but come on, we need to be at The Sea Hotel!'

Chapter Thirty
Elijah Harrison

Lloyd hadn't been hard to find, he'd traced him up the coastline by hiding and watching. Where other men might have needed a photograph to follow and confirm identity, Elijah hadn't. Lloyd's image was imprinted in his mind from the day he'd sat opposite him – it had been a face he would never forget.

Now, he sat in his hotel room with his holdall packed ready for the off. He checked his passport and grimaced at the old photograph – it wasn't his best look. Elijah had always hated the name he'd been christened with – Billy.

As soon as he'd arrived in New York, he changed it to Elijah which he thought suited him better and fitted his new expectations. It had a Hebrew connotation even though he wasn't religious in the slightest, and wasn't born Jewish. He smiled, and thought of his past misdemeanours knowing the holy gates up above would more than likely slam the doors shut in is face.

He shrugged. All the crimes he had committed were, as he liked to think, a necessary evil, but now he was tired. Tired of covering his tracks, and being thought of as a slippery customer - it didn't suit the online business he'd created for himself. Anyone could be mistaken for thinking of him as part of the Mafia, which he wasn't. But now he'd done the family this last favour, he was going back to New York to lose himself.

Elijah had known all his life that he had the brains in the family. Much more so than his brother Steven who, not wanting to speak ill of him, was completely senseless at times. Loveable, but stupid was how Elijah often thought of him. Steven's actions had always been controlled by the feelings in his trousers, which as they'd grown older, had infuriated Elijah.

His mum Jane and sister Catherine weren't much cleverer either, therefore he'd now become head of the Harrison family. Elijah hadn't minded this lack of intelligence in the two women because they were loving and supportive, and basically they worshipped the ground he walked upon.

It had been like this since they were babies at six months old. Steven and himself had been rescued by firefighters from their cots and orphaned as their parents perished in their beds. Elijah remembered the stories told to him when he was little and how Jane had taken them into her home raising them as members of her own family.

He owed his life to his mum and her word quickly became law to him. She'd smothered them both with love and Catherine automatically became their beloved sister who could do no wrong in their eyes. Whatever they asked for, Elijah moved heaven and earth to get for them and never refused their requests. He'd never once crossed his mum and didn't intend to start now.

At eighteen, Elijah set up his own online business and began making money. Not all of his connections were kosher - a word he liked to use rather than the word scam - which he hated. Within three years, his money began to accumulate and he bought his mum a lovely new house for them all to enjoy on a select housing complex on the outskirts of Leeds. But Steven couldn't resist trips back into the city to meet his old gang friends, which was where the trouble lay.

However, Elijah felt the need to be further embedded in the action of his work contacts and after a few visits to America, he'd known it was the place for him. It had been where he felt alive and could be the person he was without ridicule over his sexuality. New York had the buzz of optimism, a hard work ethic and a reason to smile when he looked in his bank account. Quickly, he grew a standing in the community and rose to dizzying heights in his penthouse apartment.

In his eyes, it was the total opposite to miserable Old Blighty where the majority of people thought the world owed them a living. The pessimistic labour politics of union strikes and millions living on the dole with benefits rather than work at a decent job, in his opinion, had driven the country into the gutter.

His family had visited New York on many occasions and there'd been discussions of a move out to join him, until of course, Steven's arrest for grievous bodily assault. He was now in prison serving eight years and all because of this bloody interfering dentist.

Mum had asked him to sort out payback for messing with their family and he'd done just that. Although Catherine had said to just scare him silly, Elijah had gone one step further. At first, he'd tried scaremonger tactics with big threatening words on paper saying **WE ARE COMING FOR YOU** *and sending a wreath saying RIP, but this hadn't been enough. However, the knife had done the job properly. The hatred for Lloyd had wound it's way around his gut like a snake. And the moment* *he'd plunged the knife into his chest, Elijah flooded with relief. 'This one's for you, Steven,' he'd whispered.*

He was leaving South Shields later today and couldn't wait to board his flight home tomorrow from Heathrow. He had a visitor's pass to see Steven in prison and then would spend time with his mum and Catherine before jetting off once again to his beloved New York city .

His job was done. The dentist had got payback for hurting his family, which had been his main reason to fly back to England. Some would argue the dentist was a honest, upright citizen but nobody treats his family like that and gets away with it.

Chapter Thirty One

We are tearing off down Ocean Road, not actually running but walking very fast. Alfie is trotting along in between us and I know he can feel the excitement too - he probably thinks it's a game we're playing. I feel a little winded by keeping up with John's pace. I decide that when this is all over, I must shed some weight and try to get fitter.

At the same time I pray this jaunt isn't going to be another dead-end. I'm pretty confident that dreadlocks man is the same one as on the old photograph, but my last sighting of him at the Customs House was two days ago, and he could have fled South Shields by now.

John jumps up the three little steps under the blue entrance sign, SEA HOTEL, SOUTH SHIELDS with a circular logo in the corner. Alfie hops up the steps behind him with me bringing up the rear.

Thankfully, the reception area is empty and very quiet. I look around remembering our first day here and muse, it seemed like just yesterday because the days had sped over. John is at the long reception desk now with a different receptionist to the last time I came. This lady is older with black curly hair and large bright red glasses.

John flashes his warrant card and automatically I see her pull back her shoulders and sit up straighter. He has transferred the photograph from the memory stick onto his mobile and holds it up to the receptionist. 'This is an old photograph but have you seen this man in here?'

She nods. 'Oh yes, that's Mr Harrison, he's stayed here all week in a twin room.'

John asks, 'On his own?'

The receptionist shakes her head. 'No, but the woman with him wasn't his wife,' she says, and pushes her glasses further up her nose to peer further at the photograph. 'I think she was his sister - she left yesterday and he is checking out this afternoon at 4pm.'

My heart begins to race and I take a deep breath. Oh, please, don't say we've missed him, and I cast a glance at John.

His face is serious as he raises an eyebrow. 'So, is he in his room now?'

She shrugs. 'I don't think so because I saw him leave about half an hour ago. He said he was taking his last walk along the seafront before leaving at four.'

'Show me,' John snaps.

The receptionist swings her computer screen around to John and he murmurs, 'Elijah Harrison with an address in New York city. And staying in room twenty six on the first floor.'

John asks, 'Is there no mobile phone number?'

She studies the screen and shakes her head. 'There doesn't seem to be...' she mutters, and begins to open side documents on her screen.

I can see John tapping his shoes in irritation. 'It doesn't matter,' he snaps. 'I need to be inside his room right now!'

I see the receptionist's hands trembling slightly as she reaches inside a thin drawer under the desk and pulls out a door card which I reckon is a pass key.

'W...well, I'll have to ring my manager and accompany you upstairs.'

'Come along then,' he says, and hurries across to the staircase.

We all mount the staircase and I whisper to John. 'Phew, this is more than lucky and we should just catch him. But you know, John, this Elijah Harrison could have nothing to do with Lloyd and the case?'

'True, but I've a hunch we are on the right track this time, Faye.'

We all hurry along the corridor and I count the door numbers as we go until we reach room twenty six. John is on his mobile relaying all the information to his DS. The receptionist slides the pass key and opens the door. John grabs a fire extinguisher from further along the corridor and props open the door.

'Wait here please, Faye,' he says, and pulls on blue gloves and overshoes from his pocket. I note his mellower voice while speaking to me and smile.

'Don't you need a search warrant?' I ask out of interest, more than questioning his actions.

He smiles, and obviously recites the theory he knows off by heart. 'No, not if the person agrees to the search, or a delay in obtaining a warrant would be likely to defeat the ends of justice, for example that evidence will be destroyed or removed.'

John steps into the room and I peer inside from the doorway. The room is painted a light shade of grey with matching wooden bed frames and bedside tables. White linen bedding and turquoise throws and cushions adorn the room.

I bend down to Alfie and whisper. 'This would have suited us just fine, but I still prefer Shirleys guest house.'

The receptionist smirks at me. 'We don't allow dogs into our rooms.'

I plant my feet and pull my shoulders back ready to answer back but John does it for me. 'Well, you don't know what your missing!' He calls, and begins to prowl around the room.

I grin as he says. 'Faye, I can definitely smell the same Tom Ford perfume heavily in this bathroom.'

I turn at the noise of the lift doors and see the DS step out and run along to us. She pulls on blue overshoes and gloves and steps inside the room with John. I wish I could go inside too but understand the protocol of another possible crime scene and contaminating evidence. Nothing must spoil John's opportunity of catching this killer.

John places his hand on the arm of his DS, but speaks to me quietly. 'Faye, can you give the detailed description to our DS please so she can circulate it out on the radio to everyone looking for him.'

I gabble out the description to her and she taps furiously into her iPad and then makes calls to other PCs. She turns to look at me and shrugs her shoulders.

'What?' I ask.

Shaking her head, she whispers. 'It's just that I've never seen our Inspector like this with any other woman - you certainly bring out the best in him, Faye!'

I want to hoot, shout and dance a jig, but instead I simply beam at her.

John steps to the doorway and says, 'This guy, Elijah Harrison is brazen enough to hang around after he's murdered Lloyd thinking he won't get caught,' he says, and winks at me. 'But he hasn't met our Faye Chambers, has he?'

Blushing from the roots of my hairline at his compliment, I notice the DS raise an eyebrow as if she can't believe what he's just said either. My chest swells and all of my reserve about last night seems to melt into thin air. I simply can't, and don't want to resist this man.

I wonder about other women in his life. Has he had female friends since his divorce? The DS has worked with him for six years, so I figure she'd know if he had been this familiar with anyone else, especially in the line of duty, so to speak. I pause - perhaps not, and that's why she looks amazed at his comment too.

John and the DS look through the packed holdall by the window which appears to be full of toiletries and clothes. 'There's nothing in here?' John says. 'No passport, driving licence or wallet.'

I offer, 'Maybe he's got them on his person?'

John nods and turns back to face the beds. With his hands on his hips, he shakes his head and the studious look descends upon him. I can tell he is wondering which bed Elijah slept in.

I call to them, 'Perhaps his sister had slept in the neatly made bed, which would have been changed this morning by the chamber maids and he slept last night in the other which has been clumsily pulled together?'

The DS strips off all the bed linen, chucking it into the corner. I hear the receptionist tut behind me and smile knowing this has irritated her.

He steps to the side of the single bed and asks of his DS. 'Can you lift the other side?'

I want to giggle. The DS looks so strong I reckon she could lift the whole mattrass by herself but John is always the perfect gentleman. I feel like swooning at his care for us ladies as he would delicately say. After his count of 1...2...3, they lift and pull the mattrass off the bed altogether.

And there in the centre of the bed frame is a wrapped towel. Gingerly, John opens the towel-wrapped parcel with his gloves to reveal a knife. I gasp and can hear the DS do so too.

John looks jubilant. It's the only word I can use to describe the sheer joy on his face knowing he's cracked the case. He lifts up his hand and across the bed to his DS and they high-five each other.

He turns to me and shouts, 'Bingo! Faye, we've got him!'

I crane my neck to try and see further into the room and cry out, 'That towel is from the guest house - it's the same as the one we have in our room.'

'Great, and I can see tiny bits of dried blood on it!'

I frown. 'So, I wonder what he was going to do with the knife? Take it with him when he returns?' I say. 'He wouldn't have just left it here, would he?'

I turn slightly to see the receptionist's pale face and say, 'If you're feeling faint, I'd go and sit downstairs until your manager arrives.'

She walks off towards the staircase just as a tall thin young man in a grey suit appears in the corridor. He introduces himself as the manager and the DS talks to him while stretching out a length of the tape with POLICE DO NOT CROSS HERE. She tapes it to either side of the door, stressing how no one has to enter until she says otherwise.

Tall PC and small PC arrive now. I think, here we go again, although this time we've got our man.

We know who killed poor Lloyd and all we have to do now is find Elijah Harrison.

John instructs the DS and the PCs. 'Get SOCO here, and I want every person available at the station out on the seafront looking for him! You've all got the description and an old image of him, and lets face it, he won't be easily missed!' He shouts. 'And get a cordon around this hotel with some one outside this door at all times.'

He ducks under the tape and steps out into the corridor, talks to the manager and then takes a call on his mobile.

He grabs my hand and takes Alfie's lead. 'Come on, Faye, that was Shirley ringing to say a woman claiming to be Lloyd's sister has turned up in the guest house.'

We head back down the stairs, but at more of a slower pace now and walk back up Ocean Road.

I congratulate him. 'I can't believe we've found out who the killer is – well done, John!'

He smiles and I realise he's still holding my hand. 'No, thank you, Faye. It was you who recognised Elijah Harrison and gave us the lead I've been praying for in this case.'

I want to swing our hands together as we walk, but remind myself this is not a leisurely summers walk between two ordinary people.

Suddenly, John tuts. 'I didn't notice the hand towel was missing when we were first examined his room in the guest house that morning. I should have known a hand towel was misplaced!'

He's relentless, I think and retort, 'But you weren't to know that in a single room you only get one hand towel, whereas in double rooms you get two. I think you're being a little hard on yourself.'

John nods and yawns.

'Tired?'

'Yeah, I was up late finishing your book.'

I gulp. 'Really? Did you like it?'

He turns to me. 'Faye, I'm rarely surprised but you did this to me in the novel – it was fantastic!'

Happiness fills my whole being and my cheeks feel hot. It's like receiving top marks at school although I do know there's a difference between fact and fiction. For some reason, his opinion and recommendation means more to me than anyone else could ever say. Although I appreciate every review I get on Amazon, his words are more important because this is his world. And he has years of experience in crime which makes it extra special.

It's so important to me that he likes my work and I stutter, 'J…jeez, that's a great compliment.'

'You're a very clever lady, Faye.'

John is totally at ease in my company now as I am with him, which is a big step up from last night. It feels comfortable as we walk together, which is a good thing, right? I grin, loving our closeness.

We reach the guest house and he squeezes my hand before dropping it as we go up the steps and in through the front door.

Shirley is waiting for us and says, 'I've put the lady into the breakfast room for you with a cup of tea.'

Chapter Thirty Two

Penny is in the corridor as we hurry inside and cries, 'What on earth is going on? Where've you been?'

Alfie throws himself at her and she pick him up in her arms. I shout, 'Can't stop now, Penny, but will explain everything later.'

We hurry into the breakfast room and a tiny woman stands up to greet us. She has shiny brown hair and small grey eyes. Although I only met Lloyd for a few minutes, she reminds me of him. I can see a resemblance and tell her this as a single tear rolls down her cheek.

I sit down next to her and John sits opposite at the table.

'I'm Estelle Thompson, nee Jenkins, which is our family name. When I arrived, Shirley called my brother Lloyd Adams, but his name is definitely Lloyd Jenkins,' she says, and rolls her wedding ring around in agitation. 'I've been away on a cruise and just got back yesterday to the news about this.'

John whips out his small notebook and begins to scribble. He lies his mobile phone on the table and I know he's waiting for news of Elijah being spotted in town.

'Estelle?' I say. 'What a lovely name.'

Estelle pulls out a tissue from the sleeve of a white dress and dries her face. 'Thanks,' she mutters. 'Apparently, my mother was watching her favourite old film Great Expectations, when she went into labour. She loved Miss Haversham and her daughter, so decided if her baby was a girl then she'd call her, Estelle.'

I love stories like this and grin. 'How good is that! And yes, she was a great character in a truly classic film.'

I see John raise his eyebrow as if to say "get on with it" and he sighs. 'Look, could you identify Lloyd for us now so that we know who he was?'

I know we aren't going to get anywhere if he rushes this lady and how she'll want to talk about her dead brother. I know I would. I tap him on the shin under the table with my foot and use my serious voice. 'Inspector, Estelle is obviously upset because her brother has died.'

He mumbles an apology and sits back in his chair, obviously preparing himself to wait more patiently.

Estelle nods. 'It's okay, Faye, thank you and yes I do want to see him, Inspector,' she says. 'I don't think I'll believe he has actually gone until I do.'

I squeeze her hand which is lying on the table. 'It's okay, just take your time.'

'My brother is a dentist and we are from Leeds. Our father was a surgeon and had wanted Lloyd to follow in his footsteps into medicine, but Lloyd chose dentistry instead.'

I think of the old suitcase on the top of the wardrobe in Lloyd's room that I'd noted, and his immaculate hands and fingernails. All the clues are starting to add up into identifying our victim now and I can't help but nod in satisfaction.

There's a scraping noise at the door and John looks up. I know it's Alfie who has obviously escaped Penny and is looking for me. I jump up and open the door. 'Excuse me, Estelle, that'll be my dog, Alfie,' I say. 'I'll just sort him out.'

Alfie flies into the room and bypasses me to lunge at John who automatically bends over and ruffles his ears.

Estelle cries, 'Oh, just look at him - he's gorgeous!'

Alfie runs to her, and she pets him fondly. 'We had a collie dog at home growing up who followed Lloyd around day and night. The whole family were distraught when we lost him due to old age,' she says, and begins to cry softly. A...and now I've lost Lloyd.'

I glance over to John who shrugs as if to say "now what"?

I think of all the police procedure shows I've watched on TV and ask, 'Estelle, do you know of anyone who would want to harm your brother?'

She sniffs and wipes her nose. I see her take in a deep breath and nod. 'Oh yes, I know exactly who has done this to him! The family said they'd get him back and he would pay for what he'd done as a witness.'

I shuffle on the chair and ask, 'A witness to what? And which family?'

She sighs, 'Well, Lloyd had seen an assault on a woman from his surgery window overlooking the back lane last year, and called the police.'

John sits forward on red alert as I do too. We are hanging upon every word Estelle says.

'Lloyd was the main witness in court and the horrible man who'd beaten up the woman was sent to prison,' she says. 'Lloyd had been okay when he was under police protection and knew he'd done the right thing for the poor victim. My sister-in-law left him because she couldn't cope with the upset and publicity in court. However, once the protection ended he'd been terrified.'

John opens his mobile and lays it on the table in front of her. 'Now, I know this is an old photograph, but do you recognise any of these people?'

Estelle nods. 'Yes, that's the family. They were in the courtroom every day. Lloyd found out the two men were brought up by the mother because they'd been orphaned as little boys and she also had a daughter,' she says, and peers closer to the photograph. 'They're all obviously younger on this, but it's definitely them. The man with long black dreadlocks had flown over from New York for the court case and the mother was a hardened, embittered woman. She snarled insults at us when we left the courtroom, shouting "nobody messes with my family and gets away with it"!'

John is up from his chair and hurrying out of the door. 'I'll get the details from the prosecution report on the case,' he cries.

Alfie sets off to follow him, but I grab his collar. 'No, Alfie, stay here. John will be back soon.'

Estelle turns in her chair and looks at John hovering in the doorway. 'We heard nothing for five months and then Lloyd received horrible threatening letters saying they were coming for him and, a…a wreath with RIP on it! But I tried to make light of it because I could see he was scared,' she says, and wrings her small hands together. 'And just before I left on my cruise, he rang to say he was at the coast having a little holiday, but they've silenced him once and for all now.'

'Thank you so much,' John says. 'This has been an amazing help to us now we know it's definitely a payback killing.'

I hear him repeat the name "Lloyd Jenkins" and suppose he is talking to his DS. He hurries out of the room to get details from the station about the court case and I swear I see him lick his lips in anticipation.

Estelle continues, 'Lloyd met the victims family and had seen first-hand how the assault ruined her life and her family's. He had been horrified at her life-changing injuries and said that he knew he'd done the right thing.'

I sigh heavily. The two boys, one of which is Elijah Harrison, were bound to be loyal and protective to all the family. He obviously loves his adopted Mum and sister even though they aren't blood related, and of course, his own brother.

'I'm truly sorry for your loss, Estelle,' I say. 'And although I only spoke to him for a few minutes before he died, I knew Lloyd was one of the good guys.'

She dries her eyes, nods and tries to smile. 'Yes, you're right there. It's just a shame being a good guy cost him his life!'

Chapter Thirty Three

The DS arrives into the breakfast room to escort Estelle to the mortuary for an identification sign-off which I know John will want for his spreadsheet. When the DS arrived, I'd heard her tell John SOCO were at the Sea Hotel in Elijah's room.

Estelle leaves and thanks me, while I whisper extracts of what has happened to Penny who is standing outside our room.

She is all agog and squeezes my arm. 'Oh, how thrilling! You'll get him, Jessica Fletcher, just hold the faith.'

I know she's teasing and glance at my watch.

'We have an hour and forty minutes left before Elijah returns to the hotel to check out,' I say to John who is pacing up and down the corridor. 'Of course, when he sees the police outside there's no way he'll try to go up to his room to retrieve his holdall. But I figure by his appearance he's not short of money and will probably decide to leave it there.'

'Well,' he says. 'The receptionist tells us he hasn't a car, so we have a massive manhunt in progress. I've got the taxi ranks, metro and bus station covered,' he says. 'He won't get out of South Shields if I have anything to do with it!'

'That's good because we have to catch this guy for killing Lloyd – he can't get away with it!'

He nods. 'I know. And to think after all our enquiries, the motive has been a payback murder, which I wouldn't have guessed in a month of Sundays!'

I grin at his old terminology and shake my head in disbelief. 'I'd thought of love triangles, theft and greed, fear of Polish police, mistaken identity - but never this!' I say. 'I certainly didn't have payback killing on my post-it notes, either.'

I explain my note system and how I've crossed off every one of the suspects so figured it had to be someone outside of the guest house.

He smiles. 'By the way, you were brilliant in there with Estelle, and once again I thank you,' he says. 'I know my communicational skills could be better when talking with people, and unfortunately my DS takes after me, so we never get very far!'

There is that exposing underbelly again when he feels vulnerable and I smile. Just as I'm thinking of a response, his mobile rings.

'Yes, yes, oh great!' He yells. 'I'm on my way! Don't approach him, he could be dangerous - just keep him in sight.'

'Come on, Faye, he's in South Marine park.'

We set off again, and Penny runs out after us shouting, 'I'm not missing this!'

***

Penny runs on ahead with Alfie loving the exercise. John and I walk fast, trying to keep up as we turn the corner and along the seafront which is busy with holiday makers and lots of police striding around.

We hurry up to the huge iron gate entrance and John stops still, looking around the area. Penny, Alfie and I stop behind him as he surveys the scene in front of him. He's probably deciding which is the best way to tackle the situation with all the people inside the park and will want to make sure everyone is safe and, well away from Elijah.

While I catch my breath, I read the big sign on the gates in blue, SOUTH MARINE PARK and underneath in red, OPENED 1890. RESTORED 2008. I'd read online how the park is the crown jewel at the heart of the seafront and I nod in agreement – it certainly is that.

The miniature train is stationary with it's blue small engine at the front and the capital letters painted in gold, DLR. A big tub full of coal is attached with steam billowing out of its funnel. I wonder if the police have put everything on hold during the manhunt.

'Come on,' John says.

He strides ahead of us down the path towards the large wood-built café. We stand with our backs to the plastic tables and chairs in the outside seating area amongst crowds of people. Old people are having tea at the tables, children are running around and younger couples are walking their dogs.

I can see the playful look on Alfie's face and call behind to Penny. 'Keep Alfie on a firm lead or he'll be off like a shot!'

I look at the Island in the middle of the lake with two tall trees on each end and a lower cluster of bushy trees in the middle. Ducks, geese and a few white swans glide around on the still water in the sunshine where visitors can get up close to them. I know this would be a pleasant place to while away the hours if we weren't on a hunt for a murderer.

Five pedalo boats are moored up under the back of the trees and three of the older boats in the shape of white swans are already gliding around the lake with happy, smiling families in them. I swallow hard knowing this is going to be difficult.

Remembering John's words that Elijah could be dangerous, I can see how this situation could go awry. When someone is cornered, they often lash out and, although we have the knife he used on Lloyd, what's to say that Elijah doesn't have another? Or coming from New York where guns are more available? I shudder. If not carefully managed, this situation could turn into a disaster, although I have complete faith in John and know this will be uppermost in his mind too.

John shouts, 'Scan with your eyes, Faye! You take the left and I'll take the right and remember we are looking for long black dreadlocks.'

I do as he bids. Oh, where is he? We have to find him, I think, feeling my heart race with excitement. Sweat forms on my top lip and I wipe it off with the back of my hand. We can't come this far and loose him. I just couldn't bear it, if not for me, but for John and poor Shirley - we have to catch him.

The small boarding deck where two members of staff work taking money and helping people into the pedalo boats looks empty. They are big burly lads and all of a sudden, one of them walks away, and that's when I spot Elijah.

'There he is!' I scream. We both watch Elijah spin around and jump into one of the boats and then push it off from the side, beginning to peddle. Burly lads shout at him about not paying and we run along the boarding deck to them. With a flash of John's warrant card, they pull the sides of the nearest swan boat to the edge. All the boats are numbered in green circles and ours is number 16.

Penny calls, 'I'll keep Alfie with me – just go!'

However, John gathers up Alfie in his arms carefully and jumps into the boat. 'Come on, Faye, hop in!'

I jump in and Alfie slopes under the short bench at the front with his head popping out.

'I'm probably breaking every rule and regulation we've got, but we started this together, Faye, so we'll finish it together!'

We begin to peddle furiously and Alfie looks up at us as if to say "come on then, put your backs into it". The majestic white neck of the imitation swan with it's orange beak and black eye is in front of us on the boat as though it is leading the charge across the lake. I reckon Alfie thinks it is a real swan because he barks furiously at it.

John is looking all around the lake as we chase after Elijah and then yells at a PC further along the path to cover the other side of the lake. I watch the PC hurry to the boarding deck and accidently bump into an old man with a carton of tea, but the man shouts, 'Never mind the tea, get after him, son!'

I see two more PC's standing on the little train as it toots its way around to the back of the lake. Behind us, two more officers ease the crowds aside to jump into a boat while burley lads jump into another. Everyone is peddling furiously. The material of my dress is bunching up as I peddle, and I pull it up over my knees, wishing I'd worn jeans. But there again, I grin, I never dreamt I would be doing this today. My thighs are pulling and aching but I hardly notice in the foray of what's happening. We are starting to gain distance on Elijah and the closer we get, the harder I can see his short legs pumping. I recognise the cowboy brown and white zipped boots he was wearing the day I first saw him.

I shout to John, 'He might have a small physique but he must have strong legs because there's two of us and we can't catch up with him!'

A middle-aged couple in one of the smaller boats meander their way around from the back of the Island. I see their looks of incredulity as if they can't believe their eyes. I yell, 'Watch out, John!'

He expertly swerves our boat away from theirs so we won't collide. I close my eyes and cringe at the thought of a member of the public ending up in the lake, and know John will be thinking this too.

Elijah is nearing the other side of the lake and I see the smaller entrance with gates up ahead. I panic and shout, 'John, if he gets out of the boat before us he could run out through the other entrance towards Grace Darling!'

John shouts into his mobile, 'Get the side entrance opposite Grace Darling monument covered!'

John stands up in the boat and we rock a little. I bend down and ruffle Alfie's ears in case he's scared, but I also know he's a better swimmer than I am, and he seems to be loving the chase.

At John's command, the other boats change direction and peddle faster to manoeuvre themselves around Elijah's boat in a large circle so he can't go anywhere. We are getting nearer to him now and the edge of the lakeside. I look ahead to see the DS, tall PC and short PC race through the gates towards us from Grace Darling, and know Elijah is surrounded.

John shouts, 'GOTCHA!'

I throw my head back and laugh as Elijah stops peddling and his boat comes to a halt. Obviously, he knows the game is up and drops his head. He puts his hands over his face and wails like a child. I whoop loudly and clap my hands together as Alfie jumps up onto my knee. I rub my face into his neck and stare at Elijah's back. Well, that's you joining your brother in prison for killing poor Lloyd, I think, and I hope you rot in hell.

John manoeuvres our boat skilfully close to Elijah's and jumps over into his. The DS throws her hand cuffs to him, he catches them and places them on Elijah while reading him his rights.

Burley lads in their boat reach John and Elijah and hook a thick strong rope around the swan's head. Tall PC and short PC climb into Elijah's boat and stay with him while they begin to pull the boat back to the boarding deck.

Up ahead, I see a police van drive slowly into the park, avoiding the crowds which have gathered. DS and more PC's are running around the lakeside to meet them at the boarding deck.

John has climbed back in next to me and we begin to peddle back across the lake at a more leisurely pace. It's almost as though we don't want the shenanigans to end and I cuddle Alfie into my chest.

'I can't believe you just did that?' I say. 'Thank God we got him!'

John chortles. 'Yeah, well I've arrested people in strange situations before, but in a swan pedalo on the lake in South Marine park has to take the biscuit!'

We talk about the chase and how he manoeuvred everyone around Elijah in the boat and covered the entrances.

'And that shout was down to you,' he says. 'You're even one step ahead of me!'

My cheeks blush. 'Oh nooo, I knew you had it covered really. I was just gabbling in excitement.'

John nods. 'I never thought I'd say this but I think we make a good pair!'

I smile and look into his eyes, knowing he is right - we do make a good team. We reach the boarding deck and I stand up as burley lads tie back our number 16 pedalo. I rub my thighs which seem to have gone numb with all the peddling and sway a little.

John catches my arm and steadies me straight again as I climb out of the boat.

'Don't worry, I've got you,' he says.

And I smile, knowing he has which is more than Allan has ever done. Penny joins us and takes Alfie from my arms.

John and I turn to face the crowds which have gathered in front of the café and have been watching our antics on the lake. They all begin to clap and cheer as we walk along the boarding deck and I giggle. John gives them a small bow and, feeling on a high, I drop a little curtsy to the crowd. I can feel the appreciation and good feeling towards us after our escapade.

John is still linking my arm but I don't push it aside. I love having his arm there even though my legs have steadied now. We begin to saunter back up to the guest house.

'For some reason, you bring out the protective side in me,' he says, as we walk. 'Although I don't know why, because if anyone can look after themselves – it's you!'

I nod and feel my cheeks blush. 'It's nice to have you there, John.'

Penny follows closely behind and has Alfie by his lead, trotting alongside. Even he looks disappointed that all the excitement in the swan pedalo is over. I turn to look at Penny who is grinning at us both, as if to say "I told you so".

Chapter Thirty Four

Penny goes upstairs to pack while John and I go downstairs to see Shirley. She is sitting in her usual chair with apprehension in her small face and eyes.

'W…well?'

I hurry to the old lady and take her good hand in mine. 'It's all over, Shirley, we've got him!'

Luba is in the kitchen and hurries through, drying her hands on a tea-towel. 'You did?'

John nods. 'Yes, we've caught the murderer, and there's no way he'll be anywhere near this guest house ever again.

Luba shouts, 'Hurra!' And claps her hands.

I take this to be Polish for "whoopie" and I stroke Shirley's hand. She lays her head back on a cushion, and with a flushed face to match her pink blouse, she breathes out a huge sigh of relief.

John says, 'We're waiting for DNA results from Mr Harrison to match the ring indent on Lloyd's chest and on the knife, which should clinch it for us. We'll also get the print on the back door to match up with him, the towel from Lloyd's room, and the fact that he fled the scene of a crime will all add up to a strong case for the CPS.'

A solitary tear runs down Shirley's cheek. 'Thank the lord,' she whispers.

Luba asks, 'And what did his sister tell you?'

Not being sure if John is allowed to do this, I intervene knowing they'll be desperate to know the background to the murder. 'Well, apparently Lloyd was a witness in a court case to a woman being assaulted near his dental surgery. He testified in court and the culprit was sent to prison for eight years, who was Mr Harrison's brother.'

Luba clasps her hands over her mouth and mutters something in Polish.

Shirley shakes her head slowly. 'Dear God, that poor, poor man!'

John says, 'I'd prepare yourselves because it could be all over the newspapers and TV tomorrow.'

Shirley's face pales, but she takes my hand in hers. 'Faye, I can't thank you enough for what you've done here in my guest house,' she says. 'Oh, and you too, of course, Inspector.'

I shrug. 'But I haven't done anything in here?'

She nods and stands up. 'Yes, you have, Faye. Apart from keeping us all sane, I've felt safe having you around the house,' she says. 'I knew I could trust and rely on you from the very first day you checked into room one.'

Now, I feel my cheeks flush and wave my hand in the air. 'Aww, I just wish we could have done it sooner but now at least you know your good reputation is intact and everyone will see this has nothing to do with you and Luba.'

Shirley looks up at Luba and squeezes my hand. 'You have both been like a rock to cling onto during this week, and I don't know at my age what I would have done without you.'

She is obviously emotional as her hand trembles and feels feeble in mine. 'I hope you don't close the guest house, Shirley?' I tease. 'Because me and Alfie might want to come back again.'

She shakes my hand. 'And you'd be more than welcome, love,' she says. 'I'll give it this year and see how I feel by Christmas. I've thought of retiring, although I don't know what I'd do with myself in a retirement home.'

I say, 'Well, the closure of this great little guest house would be such a shame and a very sad day, but don't let poor Lloyd's demise waver your decision because it's all over now.'

John has gone back upstairs and is on his mobile in the corridor. I think of him and the DS questioning Elijah later and would love to be in the room. Unless of course, he uses "no comment" throughout the interview. In all stories there's another side to events and although I know our version of what happened to Lloyd, I'd love to hear Elijah's. Instead, I nod in satisfaction knowing it'll be a long time, if ever, before he sees New York city again.

After gushy farewells and cuddles with both women, I follow him upstairs and along the corridor into our room. Opening the wardrobe door, and with a pen I write on Elijah's post-it note X GOTCHA!

Sadly, I peel off the post-it notes and tuck them into the side of my case, as a keepsake. Looking around the room, I know we have been comfortable and happy for most of our stay.

The people on my post-it notes have filled my enquiring mind all week. From Shirley with her disability and bravery running the guest house at an elderly age. Luba, who I first thought had a fear of our police, but was only protecting her son from an ex-husband. Poor Lloyd who did the right thing when witnessing an assault but lost his life for being a decent law-abiding citizen. His shocked and tearful sister with the lovely name, Estelle. Bizarre Ken with his creepy dark sunglasses and rucksack who had scraped off pieces of Marsden Rock. His spiritualistic wife, Lilly who has rattled my mind on a couple of occasions. Philanderer Mark with his hareem of different young girls and browbeaten wife, Brigit who turned the tables on him - I do hope she makes a new life for herself. And, my dear friend Penny, with a nameless man who turned out to be her neighbour and a married man. The Indian family I didn't meet, but thankfully their son picked up the memory stick. And finally, the Harrison family with Elijah at the head who was the culprit. We finally got our murderer.

Phew, I think, it's been a busy week all in all, but if I'm honest with myself, I've loved every minute tracing them and trying to fit each one into a jigsaw puzzle of Lilly's .

'Time to go home, Alfie,' I say. I swear he looks as sad as I feel. His ears droop and he tilts his head to one side, as if to say "oh no, I don't want to go".

My eyelids feel sticky and I take in a deep breath, holding tears at bay as I look at the suitcase underneath the bed. I remember the day I checked-in with the stress and upset I'd felt leaving Allan. It suddenly dawns upon me that I haven't had many palpitations since then, although I've been through lots of upheaval in the guest house, and with John.

I nod, and whisper to Alfie, 'Yep, I feel as though I've coped with the stress rather well and, with very little anxiety.'

He wags his tail and I stroke his ears. Maybe my poor mental health is taking a turn towards being good again, I think, and hear a tap on our door.

I open it wide to see Ken and Lily standing in the corridor with a huge suitcase. 'Your friend Penny told us upstairs what happened in the park and how the killer has been arrested,' she says. 'Of which I'm glad.'

'Yeah, we are all very relieved, especially Shirley,' I say. 'Are you leaving now?'

Lilly nods. 'Yes, apparently a hospital appointment with the prostate specialist has arrived for Ken, so our daughter is driving down to pick us up. It's one night sooner than we were supposed to leave, but necessary all the same.'

I look at Ken and remember the incident at Marsden Rock when he was high up on my list of suspects, and how I haven't spoken to him since. He takes my hand and shakes it firmly, although I still can't see his eyes behind the dark sunglasses.

I smile. 'That's good news, Ken. And I hope everything goes well for you at the hospital.'

Lilly takes my other hand and lowers her voice. 'And, I know you don't believe in the spirit world but an hour ago I heard from an old woman who was looking for her daughter.'

Oh no, not this again, I think, but decide to pacify her as we are parting company. They are travelling back to Glasgow, never to be seen again. 'Was she?' I ask. 'And what did she have to say?'

Lily smiles. 'Well, the old lady was called Mary and said to tell her daughter "not to live her life with regrets".'

'Come on, Lilly,' Ken mutters. 'Here's our lift outside.'

Lilly still has the bag of crochet on her arm and pulls up her white lacy gloves, which makes me smile. I think of all the people I've lived with in the guest house and decide I'll miss them in a strange sort of way.

They both wave to us and hurry out of the front door while I close our room door quietly and then slump down onto the end of the bed. My knees begin to tremble and I shiver as a cold feeling runs up my back. My mam's name was Mary, and that had been her saying to me. I repeat the words again slowly "don't live your life with regrets".

I was still on the boat with John an hour ago which was when the spirit spoke to Lilly. Was it Mam trying to tell me to go for it with John? It's a comforting thought that she is looking out for me, but maybe I'm being a little crazy thinking like this. Perhaps, it's because I do want to be with John that I'm steering myself away from my husband.

The last time Lilly told me about the spirits at Marsden Grotto, I panicked over the crazy coincidence with the name Allan, but this time it's different because Mam has passed over.

Alfie makes to climb up on the bed and, knowing Luba will be changing the linen later when we've left, I let him jump up and cuddle him close.

'It's time to bring Allan back down from that worry tree and be brave,' I whisper.

He looks up at me and I know it's time. It's time to deal with my feelings and come to a decision about Allan. I still can't forgive his transgression and know it'll be impossible for me to carry on as we did before.

Of course I love him because he's all I've ever known, and we could try to change things in our marriage, but do I really want to do this?

I want to make the right decision for myself. Not for Allan or Olivia, but for me. I shrug, knowing I've made important decisions on my own before, so I will do again. I think of hurrying through the door to our house and know when I see him, I won't be falling into his arms, kissing and making up. That's not going to happen. I've still too much resentment built up against him.

So, do I stay with him day after day, week after week, month after month, trying to work these feelings through to get us back to where we were before I found the divorce papers? It sounds exhausting and I'm not sure I have the energy to do this. Or, if I even want to.

And then there is John. I think of Mam and know she is right. If I don't take it further with him, I may live to regret it. Penny reckons a dalliance with John wouldn't do me any harm at all, as long as it was short and sweet. But I'm not sure because I don't know how to have an affair. I also think there's more between us than just a dalliance. However, I can't just walk away from him without seeing what could happen between us. When I'm with John, I want to take our relationship further - it makes me feel alive.

The thought of saying goodbye to him and never seeing my lovely Inspector again makes my stomach churn. So, there's no point in trying with Allan when I feel like this, it wouldn't be fair to either of them, and certainly not me.

Chapter Thirty Five

I hear a commotion on the stairs and shake myself up from the bed. Opening the door again, I see John humping Penny's huge suitcase downstairs. It's on the tip of my tongue to tease him because I carried it upstairs on my own when she arrived.

Penny alights at the bottom of the stairs. 'This lovely Inspector has arranged a lift for me to the station,' she says.

Smiling, I'm pleased she said he was lovely, and didn't use the word "randy" because that would have been mega embarrassing.

John raises an eyebrow and I want to giggle.

'Oh right, Penny,' I say. 'You've packed quickly?'

'Yes,' she nods. 'I'm going to catch a game of golf later.'

She winks at me and I know this will involve Leo in some way. I note her glamorous travel outfit and grin.

John says, 'And the offer for a lift also extends to you, Faye. It's the least the force can do for everything you've done.'

'But I'm just starting to pack now,' I say, and bite my lip.

'That's okay, whenever you're ready – it's Gosforth, isn't it?'

The thoughtful look descends upon his face and I guess he's wondering if I'm going straight home to throw myself into Allan's arms. My feelings must be written all over my face because Penny scrunches her eyebrows in puzzlement. I know she wants to tell John that I've made a decision about my marriage.

Instead, she says, 'Look, go home, talk to Allan, and if you don't want to stay with him and need more time away then you get on a train and come straight to me. I'll pick you up from Darlington station. I've plenty of room especially for our Jessica!'

John looks confused, and asks, 'Who's Jessica?'

I explain. 'Penny is teasing me about becoming an amateur sleuth and calling me Jessica Fletcher.'

He says, 'Well, that's not a bad idea, in fact, I think you'd be very good at that, but maybe in a type of private investigator. You're great at talking to people, but most of all, you are a great listener.'

'Really,' I say. 'Do you think so?'

'I wouldn't say it if I didn't think so, Faye.'

And there's the lilt in his voice again when he says my name. I think yes to both these things as Alfie wags his tail. I'm going to miss so much about John.

Penny and I hug each other tightly and she whispers in my ear. 'Talk to him and please give it a chance.'

I nod and wave goodbye to Penny in the police car as it pulls away from the front door. We both turn, and walk into our room with Alfie between us. John sits on the chair in the bay window. We are alone together at last, and I throw my suitcase onto the bed to pack with clothes.

'Will you be safe at home?' He asks, 'I mean, is your husband violent?'

There's that protective policeman side to him again and I pat his hand resting on the arm of the chair. I realise I've painted a bad picture of Allan by telling him about the bigamy and know I have to put this straight. 'Nooo, not at all,' I say. 'He's kind, gentle and caring most days.'

He raises an eyebrow. 'And on the other days?'

I shrug. 'Big headed and dominant, arranging our lifestyle to suit his image of the perfect couple, which irritates me beyond belief now.'

'Just now?'

I nod. 'Yeah, hands up, I'm guilty of letting him do this since we married but now that I've had space and time away from him, I know I want a different type of relationship.'

He grins. 'More of a mutual bond that is gained as a team working together towards their common goal?'

I know he's teasing because we've done just that together over the last few days tracing and catching the culprit. My lips twist into a smile. 'Yes, you could say that.'

John frowns. 'This doesn't correspond to the woman I've spent time with this week? The Faye Chambers I know is very independent,' he says. 'And the definition for independence is being reliant on one's own will and judgement.'

'Ah,' I say, and shrug. 'That's because this week has been about my academic abilities in crime writing and putting clues together. I guess in the past when it came to relationships and family I wasn't independent, but now I've realised this, it's going to change.'

He gets up from the chair and stands in front of me. Alfie sniffs around both our ankles and I know he is as expectant as I am.

'Weve been through a lot together and I'm really attracted to you,' he says, shuffling his feet. 'But it's such a long time since I've been with a woman, I guess I'm a little scared and, I'm sorry for running away from you.'

I glance down at those endearing polished shoes. 'I'm equally scared, John but I've felt the same as you since we first met.'

He closes in nearer to me and his face is right in front of mine now. Oh, please kiss me, for goodness sake! I want to cry aloud. I stare into his eyes and know because it's a leap year, if he doesn't then I will.

John snakes his arms around my waist and pulls me into him. He kisses me full on the lips which seems to last forever. It's a gentle kiss but with strong undertones and I weaken against his body. And as we pull apart, I know I want more. I want to devour him as all my senses are heightened - even the roots of my hairline are tingling. Our lips fit together perfectly as everything seems to between us.

He runs his hands through my hair and grins. 'I've wanted to do that since the first time I saw you outside Lloyd's room.'

I tease, 'Oh, you mean when you accused me of reading "Vera" novels?'

He throws his head back and laughs. 'You're very special to me, Faye.'

I smile and nod. 'Same here, John but I need to go home and sort things out before we take this any further,' I say, and snuggle my face into his warm neck. 'But in the words of Arnie Schwarzenegger, I'll be back!'

Printed in Great Britain
by Amazon